THE MIDNIGHT ROOM

Praise for Ronica Black

"Ronica Black's debut novel *In Too Deep* has everything from nonstop action and intriguing well-developed characters to steamy erotic love scenes. From the opening scenes where Black plunges the reader headfirst into the story to the explosive unexpected ending, In Too Deep has what it takes to rise to the top. Black has a winner with In Too Deep, one that will keep the reader turning the pages until the very last one."—*Independent Gay Writer*

In Too Deep is "an exciting, page turning read, full of mystery, sex, and suspense."—*MegaScene*

"[A] challenging murder mystery—sections of this mixed-genre novel are hot, hot, hot. Black juggles the assorted elements of her first book with assured pacing and estimable panache."—*Q Syndicate*

"Black's characterization is skillful, and the sexual chemistry surrounding the three major characters is palpable and definitely hot-hot-hot…if you're looking for a solid read with ample amounts of eroticism and a red herring or two you're sure to find *In Too Deep* a satisfying read."—*L Word Literature*

"Black is a master at teasing the reader with her use of domination and desire. Black's first novel, *In Too Deep*, was a finalist for a 2005 Lammy…With *Wild Abandon*, the author continues her winning ways, writing like a seasoned pro. This is one romance I will not soon forget."—*Just About Write*

"The sophomore novel by Ronica Black is hot, hot, hot."—*Books to Watch Out For*

"Sleek storytelling and terrific characters are the backbone of Ronica Black's third and best novel, *Hearts Aflame*. Prepare to hop on for an emotional ride with this thrilling story of love in the outback… Wonderful storytelling and rich characterization make this a high recommendation."—*Lambda Book Report*

"This sequel to Ronica Black's debut novel, *In Too Deep*, is an electrifying thriller. The author's development as a fine storyteller shines with this tightly written story. …[The mystery] keeps the story charged—never unraveling or leading us to a predictable conclusion. More than once I gasped in surprise at the dark and twisted paths this book took."—*Curve* magazine

In *Flesh and Bone*, "Ronica Black handles a traditional range of lesbian fantasies with gusto and sincerity. The reader wants to know these women as well as they come to know each other. When Black's characters ignore their realistic fears to follow their passion, this reader admires their chutzpah and cheers them on…These stories make good bedtime reading, and could lead to sweet dreams. Read them and see."—*Erotica Revealed*

"Ronica Black's books just keep getting stronger and stronger… This is such a tightly written plot-driven novel that readers will find themselves glued to the pages and ignoring phone calls. *The Seeker* is a great read, with an exciting plot, great characters, and great sex."—*Just About Write*

"Ronica Black's writing is fluid, and lots of dialogue makes this a fast read. If you like steamy erotica with intense sexual situations, you'll like *Chasing Love*."—*Queer Magazine Online*

By the Author

In Too Deep

Deeper

Wild Abandon

Hearts Aflame

The Seeker

Chasing Love

Conquest

Wholehearted

The Midnight Room

Visit us at www.boldstrokesbooks.com

THE MIDNIGHT ROOM

by

Ronica Black

2012

THE MIDNIGHT ROOM

© 2012 By Ronica Black. All Rights Reserved.

ISBN 13: 978-1-60282-766-0

This Trade Paperback Original Is Published By
Bold Strokes Books, Inc.
P.O. Box 249
Valley Falls, NY 12185

First Edition: December 2012

CREDITS
EDITOR: CINDY CRESAP
PRODUCTION DESIGN: STACIA SEAMAN
COVER DESIGN BY SHERI (GRAPHICARTIST2020@HOTMAIL.COM)

Acknowledgments

Heartfelt thanks to my wonderful friend Connie. And to Cait, my love, for always being so patient with the process. A special thanks to everyone at Bold Strokes, especially my editor, Cindy. Thanks so much for the continued support.

For Cait

CHAPTER ONE

Lillian Gray turned into the wind and stared up at the cold rain flecking her face.

"There are some that come broken, but they're repairable," the stranger next to her said, seemingly oblivious to her presence.

The night wind blew harder, causing Lillian's already chilled skin to tighten further beneath the mist of rain. She shoved her hands into her pockets and took the unusual weather on full force, a part of her liking the way it felt, the way it punished and yet awakened her.

The cell phone conversation continued next to her with the woman huddling down into her pullover.

"No, I don't care. I want them. I can fix them," she said.

Lillian stared into the half-full parking lot, lulled by the heavy-looking cones of light breathing down upon the cars. The woman's conversation reminded Lillian of her job, her life, and her heart. By day, she did her best to mend people's relationships, and by night, she did her best to not break down completely over her own broken and shattered existence.

Some things, she mused, couldn't be repaired despite what the stranger thought. As if driving the point home, a group of laughing women shouldered and bumped their way past Lillian as they hurried toward the entrance of the club, anxious to escape the rain. She held her ground, but the contact felt cold and brutal, just like the world itself. Hard shoulders and rough bumps happened, and you had to do your best to remain standing. But how much more could she take? Her eyes stung at the threat of tears.

There are some that come broken, but they're repairable.

The woman had disappeared into the club with the others, leaving Lillian to wonder about the conclusion to her conversation. What had she been talking about? Could she fix Lillian? Her own phone beeped as if to answer. She pulled it from her pocket and read the text. Her friends were looking for her. Time to face the music. She listened to the muffled sound of the banging beats. The Griffin was hopping as usual but not full to the brim as it had been the night before. She'd bypassed it on her way to volunteer at the church, and she'd been glad to have a valid excuse as to why she couldn't stop. An excuse would be great tonight, but evening church service was long over, and her friends, who frequented the club nearly every night, knew it.

She turned to head inside, leaving the rain behind save for the press of it upon her hair and skin, which she did nothing about. Let it remain. Let it soak into her hair and run down her face. Who cared? She didn't. Not tonight or any night, for that matter. It wasn't that she didn't care how she looked or what people thought. But at The Griffin it was different. The club was all about one thing, and when she pushed through the door and breezed by the silent bouncer, she was at once visually assaulted by it.

Everywhere she looked she saw it. Bodies slithering together on the dance floor, bodies entwined in dark corners, bodies huddled together at tables watching, wishing they were as engaged as those around them.

Lust at The Griffin was like prayer at her church. It seemed to permeate the air, and suddenly, she missed the polished wood and new carpet smell of her favorite chapel. Missed the peace and tranquility, the polite gentleness of her fellow churchgoers. They were people who didn't want her, who didn't come on to her or expect her to leave her ex, Holly, in the past. At church, she could wallow safely in her grief and huddle warmly in her prayers for Holly's return. But at The Griffin, all was laid out on the table, on the dance floor, and even at the bar. The Griffin wanted to expose her insides, her sexuality, her most savage needs. It didn't play kindly to her need for healing and self-preservation. In fact, it laughed at the whole notion.

She wound her way through carefully, avoiding glances, walking quickly away from the moan of the club that seemed to be calling her name again and again. She wanted to tell it to shut up, to screw off. To scream at it and tell it she wasn't a prude. She was just…finished. Sad. Lost. Defeated.

But the neon green stripes lining the interior pressed upon her, kissing her with the lustful light, trying to penetrate her skin just like it seemed to penetrate the polished wood of the walls. Women eyed her, nodded, spoke, turned away, danced, and drank. There was laughter, thumping bass, bottles and glasses clanking, and the smell of beer, sweat, and perfume in the air. Women in top hats, bow ties, and not much else edged through the clusters of bodies balancing drink trays on long-fingered hands.

Her own fingers skimmed the dark wood of the bar as she moved, as if the bar were base and if she kept touching it, she'd be safe and shielded from the hungry libidos of others and, most importantly, her own.

Though she thought about it often, she had no need for sex, much less another woman. The mere thought of dating or even a dance made her stomach tighten with anxious knots. And the knots always led to that immediate craving for alcohol. Her mind groaned wickedly, and she had to push away from the bar.

Oh God. Oh, yes. The yearning came warmly and swiftly from seemingly nowhere. A drink. How she would love a drink. Jameson, no ice. Ice got in the way. Ice melted and ruined the whiskey. Fucking ice.

"No." She stopped mid–dance floor and pressed on her temples. "I'm not going to do this to myself." She'd quit drinking six months before and she wasn't going back. Holly or no Holly. She set her jaw and readied herself for a dozen more nos before the night was over. The Griffin brought them out in her just as it seemed to bring out the lust in others.

"No?"

Lillian nearly gasped. Audrey McCarthy was staring at her, covered in a thin sheen of sweat, looking as drop-dead gorgeous as ever. In fact, she was the one, the only one, Lillian ever allowed herself to stare at.

"I…"

Audrey raised an eyebrow. God, she had great eyebrows. They were as dark as her short, shaggy hair and they stretched wickedly over her black-as-ink eyes. Those eyes flashed at Lillian as Audrey smiled again. This time coyly as she gently pushed the woman she'd been dancing with away from her.

She's so…sexy. This is why I stare at her. And stare and stare and stare.

Yeah, me and everyone else.

Lillian tried to shake her off, not bothering to return the smile or to dwell any longer in her attractiveness. Audrey was a player with a capital P and everyone knew it. She was the most-wanted woman at the club. And it seemed with the coyness and then confidence in her smile, she knew it too.

"You were saying something," Audrey said, placing a strong hand on Lillian's hip. "And I think it was going to be something very bad." The corner of her delicious-looking mouth turned up as she spoke.

Lillian flushed, and she told herself it was because she knew she looked a mess and not because of Audrey. She thought briefly about running her hands through her hair, but then she once again chided herself for even worrying about it. She didn't care any other night. So a simple touch from The Griffin's hottest woman wasn't going to change that. She'd be damned.

"I wasn't talking to you," she said as she tried to turn.

"You should be."

Lillian blinked at her forwardness. "Why is that?"

"Because I know what you want."

"Is that so?"

"Oh, yes."

"And what is it that I want?"

Audrey smiled, and Lillian fought the urge to melt. "Me."

"Ha." She glanced away, her nerves getting the better of her.

"Tell me I'm wrong."

"I'll do you one better. I'll leave." Lillian pulled away, but the knots inside twisted, tightening. *I am not interested. I am not interested.* Holly reentered her mind, and she nearly stopped and bent, hand on her stomach. When would the pain go away? When would Holly's face vanish from her mind, never to torture her again? She straightened as one of her friends hopped up from their table near the wall and came to her side.

"Are you okay?" It was Rain, and her blue eyes were big and round with frightened concern. The freckles on her nose seemed to be analyzing her as well. "Lil?"

"I'm fine." She took Rain's hand and walked slowly to the table.

"The pains again?" Carmen asked, rising to come to her side. She had obviously gone beyond concerned and right into pissed off, based on the look she was giving Lillian.

"I'm fine," Lillian said.

I lose it in front of my friends too often.

"No, you're not. You look like an alien's going to come tearing out your gut at any second," Carmen said.

Lillian scoffed. "Stop it." She sat and put on her best smile. *Please don't let me tremble; please don't let me tremble.* Her friends worrying only made the knots worse and the call for alcohol louder. "I said I'm okay."

Carmen sank back into her chair while Rain went for more drinks. Lillian almost cringed, knowing an assault from the no-nonsense Carmen was coming. It seemed that lately the verbal tirades were happening more and more frequently. Lillian wondered why.

The look Carmen was giving her was preemptive, as if Carmen were marinating her with her stare, waiting for just the right moment in which to sink her teeth.

"This bullshit's gotta stop."

"Carmen—"

"I mean it, Lil. Holly's gone. She's never coming back. She doesn't want to be with you."

Lillian felt the first tooth sink in. "You think I don't know that?" She brushed back her hair nervously, finding it damp and tangled, just as she'd feared.

Carmen's beautiful Latin skin crimsoned at her cheekbones, making Lillian feel all the more unattractive.

"Do you? Because you're still pining for her."

"I am not." But the words came out softly, with little conviction.

"She's ruining your life and she's not even here."

"She's not ruining my life."

"You were never good enough, Lil, remember? It was always something. You need to just let her go and realize that you were too good for her."

"But I wasn't, Carmen."

"Bullshit. She brainwashed you with all that criticism. Can't you see how wonderful you are?"

Lillian wanted to laugh. "Wonderful? I'm a therapist and I let my relationship fall apart right in front of my face."

"Don't blame yourself, Lil. Look around. Other people think you're wonderful. Because you are wonderful."

"I don't know." But the knots weren't easing up.

"You have to believe that and stop letting Holly ruin your life."

"Carmen, she's not ruining my life." Couldn't they just let it go? She'd screwed up, she hadn't been good enough, Holly had left.

"What about the pains? You literally just looked like you were going to pass out."

"It's—just anxiety." She should know. It was one of her specialties. What would she tell one of her clients to do? She shook her head, unwilling to think about the fact that her own problems sometimes mirrored those of her clients.

"What is?" Rain asked, placing a club soda in front of Lillian as she slid into her chair. The music kicked up again, and they had to speak louder and lean in closer. The thumping caused Lillian to roll her eyes and rub her temples.

"Lillian's stomach pains," Carmen explained. "She says they're just anxiety."

"Oh." Rain studied her as Lillian continued to massage her head. "That's good, right? I mean at least it isn't because you need a drink."

Lillian closed her eyes. *Dear God, help me get through this night, and I swear on everything holy I will never ask for another thing.*

"Lil?"

"Hmm?" She opened her eyes and downed her club soda in a single shot, praying it would burn away all her worries and memories. When it did nothing, she slouched and pushed the glass away. Walking into The Griffin was difficult enough, but having to face the lure of alcohol could sometimes be torturous. Just one more thing her friends couldn't quite understand without experiencing it firsthand. She'd tried to explain, but The Griffin was their favorite haunt. She couldn't ask them to hang with her at church, and getting coffee was, well, boring. At least here there were distractions. Here her friends could focus on women and dancing and get all excited about the rumor mill rather than focusing on her mundane existence. At least most nights they could.

She caught Carmen's stare as she chewed a piece of ice. She was still looking at her with contemplation and anger, so she decided to change the topic.

"Where's Rain?"

"I don't know. She took her beer and said she'd be right back."

Rain bounded back up to them with a smirk on her face.

"What's that about?" Carmen asked, ever the intuitive.

"Oh, nothing." She tugged on her beer with a hungry mouth. Her lips smacked as she pulled the bottle away. "Just had something to take care of."

Carmen pushed out a frustrated breath. "I'm getting too old for this shit. Anyone else feel that way?" Her gaze fell to Lillian, where it locked. She knew Lillian felt the same. They'd discussed it many times. But it always came back to Rain. And Carmen didn't exactly have anyone to go home to.

What would happen if one of them actually met someone worthwhile? Would it go back to the way it was when she was with Holly? The one who was involved staying home with her lover and 2.3 dogs?

Lillian nodded and pressed her lips together. She was tired of the single atmosphere and seeing her friends parade and often times stumble through it. What she wanted was Holly and their fireplace with Coda and Mink at their feet as they watched television. She sighed heavily. She missed Coda and Mink. Holly had even taken them.

She rested her cheek in her hand and fingered the sweat resting on the bottom of her glass. Home sure beat The Griffin. At least it used to.

"Well, you and Lillian don't have to come here," Rain said. "I mean, don't come on my behalf."

Carmen studied her nails. "Oh, knock it off. You know we come for you and we will always support you. Even though you chase your own tail like you did when you were nineteen."

"I'm not chasing my own tail," Rain said. "In fact, I've got my eye on—"

"A P.E. teacher. Yeah, we know. When are you going to ask her out, Rain? Never?" Carmen was sinking her teeth into everyone tonight. Lillian again wondered why.

"I'm biding my time," Rain said. "I still have five pounds to lose."

Lillian closed her eyes again. *Dear God—*

But Carmen wouldn't allow a silent thought. "Come off it, Rain. If she doesn't like you now, she'll never like you. Meet her, find out, and move on, for Christ's sake."

"I have a plan," Rain said. "I'm going to ask Audrey McCarthy for help."

"Audrey McCarthy?" Carmen laughed. "Yeah, right."

All eyes shifted to the dance floor where the five-foot-ten, raven-haired McCarthy moved in rhythm with another woman. Lillian felt like shrinking as her name resounded in her mind. Her heart fluttered despite itself as she recalled the heat of her touch and the press of her gaze. Eyes as black as ink had stared into her soul, flashing in the light of the strobes. She'd done her best to ignore her, but seeing her sway seductively on the dance floor brought her attraction once again to the foreground.

"She's..." Lillian started, unsure why she was speaking aloud.

"Hot," Rain finished.

The only woman I allow myself to stare at. Lillian continued to watch her, captivated. Her short dark hair seemed to melt into her tan skin, especially when the sheen of sweat glistened off her jaw and neck as it did now. Lillian rose to get another club soda, forcing herself to look away from the lithe muscular body dressed in worn jeans and a tight black tank.

"She's a personal trainer," Rain said, nodding in excitement. "I recently hired her."

Lillian walked toward the bar, leaving the conversation behind. Audrey McCarthy was a tigress, the whole world her prey. She'd chew Rain up and spit her out with her head still spinning.

She leaned on the bar, laughing, causing the bartender to saunter over.

"Enjoying yourself tonight?" she asked, wiping her hands on a towel.

"Not really." She laughed again, trying hard not to look over at Audrey as she continued to move on the dance floor. This time she had two women dancing with her, both of them moving seductively against her thighs.

"Could've fooled me." Her smile seemed broad and genuine.

"It's not a fun laugh, trust me. It's an 'Oh my God, I'm losing my mind' laugh."

"I see." She planted muscled arms on the bar and followed Lillian's line of sight. "That one drives everyone out of their mind."

Lillian jerked, unaware she'd even been staring. She felt the flush start at her feet and burn her all the way up.

"I wasn't—"

The bartender raised a palm. "Don't even."

"But I—"

"I'm used to it. She's hard to compete with."

Lillian fought to speak, but no words came.

The bartender merely chuckled and straightened her broad back. She was cute in an extremely built kind of way. "Club soda?" she asked Lillian.

"I come here that often?"

"'Fraid so."

Lillian sighed.

"Like it's a bad thing?" the bartender asked, grabbing a glass and filling it halfway with ice.

"It is for me."

She squirted in the club soda and handed it over. "You know we have other sobers here."

Lillian felt her eyebrow rise. She'd never considered that possibility.

"Me, for one," the bartender said. "Six years."

"Wow. I'm only six months." Would she be as calm and cool as this woman when she was six years in? At the moment, it sure didn't feel like it.

"Good for you."

The club soda was cold and refreshing. She tugged up some more through her tiny straw.

"Cocaine," the bartender said, opening a bottle of beer. "It about killed me."

"Oh."

"We have other recovering alcoholics here too, though. You aren't the only one."

"How did you know I was—"

"The club sodas, the panic attacks, the 'get me the hell out of here' looks."

"I guess I need to work on being less obvious." There was a brief silence as Lillian considered just how obvious she really was.

"Can I ask you something?"

Lillian nodded.

"Why do you come here if you're so uncomfortable?"

"My friends."

"Is that all?" She shifted her eyes toward Audrey on the dance floor.

"Yes, that's all."

"Well, then, how about having coffee with me sometime? Outside of here?"

Lillian was surprised, and though she should be pleased, she felt exposed and vulnerable. As if just by being asked, she'd somehow opened herself up for hurt and betrayal. Had she been too friendly? Said too much?

"I can't," she stammered. "I mean, I don't date."

The bartender glanced away and then nodded slowly.

"It's not because of you," Lillian blurted. "You're...very attractive...I just—"

"It's okay." She said it lightly, but she busied herself wiping the bar.

"No, it's not." Lillian sat very still, heart pounding. She could feel the disappointment and disbelief misting off the woman. God, she hated this, this place, this whole atmosphere. "Maybe sometime soon, okay?"

The bartender studied her for a moment and then nodded as if she didn't quite believe her. "Let me know when you need another club soda," she said just before turning to walk toward another customer.

"Great," Lillian said, swiveling on the bar stool to stand. "Just great."

She stalked back to her seat and sulked, sliding her glass away. Her friends asked questions, but she ignored them, watching the bartender instead.

"I think I'm going to go," she finally said.

Rain jerked forward. "No! You can't, not yet."

"Why not?" She was mentally drained and embarrassed. There was nothing for her here.

"What happened?" Carmen asked, obviously bored.

"I saw Brea talking to you," Rain said. "She's nice."

"Yes, she is," Lillian said.

"So what's wrong?" Carmen slugged her beer bottle back for an angry swig.

"I don't—it doesn't—this whole place doesn't feel right."

Carmen laughed. "She asked you out, didn't she?"

"Oh my God, she did?" Rain squeezed her shoulder.

"And let me guess. You said no," Carmen said.

"Sort of," Lillian countered, growing just as angry at Carmen's attitude.

"But why? She's so nice and she can probably bench-press me. That's hot," Rain said.

"Doesn't matter," Carmen said. "Doesn't matter how hot she is. Little Miss I'm Pining Away for Holly doesn't give a screw. She'd rather go home and take a cold shower."

Lillian felt her anger grow and burn just beneath her skin. "I would not."

"Would so."

"What gives you the right—"

"Because I'm your friend, Lil. That's why. Because I'm tired of seeing you act like some high-and-mighty prude when I know deep down inside, you want to date. You want to have fun and experience passion, and more than that, you want to find love again."

Lillian said nothing. Just sat and stared. She wanted to argue, to tell Carmen to get lost, but she just didn't have the strength. Especially when Carmen was bordering on the truth.

"You don't know me," she finally managed to say.

Carmen stood and slid her beer across the table. "Yeah. Right." She wound through the crowd and disappeared into the back where the restrooms were. Lillian slumped, feeling completely drained. The call of the drink was torturous now, and she needed to leave. Her hands shook with nerves, and she so badly wanted Holly to hold her and whisper in her ear, to tell her everything was going to be all right. But Holly wasn't there. Holly didn't care. Holly had fucked her over.

Lillian pushed back from the table and stood. Here she was. Doing just what Carmen said she'd do. Pining over Holly. Shit.

"You can't leave," Rain said once again, gripping her arm.

"Why—"

But the music stopped and the deejay spoke into the mic, spotlight shining brightly on her booth.

"Ladies, it's that time again," she said and the crowd went nuts. "Time for two lusciously lucky ladies to take a trip into the Midnight Room."

The crowd whooped, and several women whistled. Lillian sank back into her chair and sighed. She'd never make it out now that the dance floor was jam-packed with excited, waiting women.

"I hate this Midnight Room shit," she said to Rain. "I mean really. Who wants to go make out with a complete stranger in some sex room?"

"It's not a sex room. Well, not really. It's just a place to go to get to know someone better."

"Come off it, Rain. It's a sex room."

The deejay cut them off again as one of the cocktail waitresses slinked up to the booth with her top hat in hand. The hat was no doubt full of the names of eager young women anxious to be plucked out for a good make out session with a stranger. Lillian couldn't be paid to drop her name in for such a drawing. The whole thing was frivolous, asinine, and—

"And our first lucky lady is Lillian Gray!"

Lillian jerked in her seat. Rain went crazy, grabbing her shoulders and arms, yanking her to a stand.

"What?" She squinted into the spotlight as it found their table. "What's going on? Why was my name called?"

The deejay continued talking over the whooping crowd. "And our other lucky lady is…Audrey McCarthy!"

The crowd roared and the deejay started playing "Let's Get It On."

"Come on, you two. Time to head off into the Midnight Room."

Lillian stumbled as Rain tried to lead her from the table.

"No. I'm not going." Her heart pounded and her brain was trying desperately to catch up. What was happening? How did this happen? Audrey McCarthy? No, she couldn't. She couldn't possibly go into the Midnight Room with Audrey McCarthy. No way.

"You're going," Rain said, laughing. "Come on, move."

Lillian pulled away and took several steps toward the dance floor, intent on leaving. But Audrey McCarthy stepped into her path and smiled that coy smile.

Lillian's breath caught once again at her dark beauty.

"Lillian?"

Lillian said nothing, just fought melting under the obvious approval of Audrey's wicked gaze.

"Yes, she's Lillian," Rain offered, sounding eager.

Audrey held out her hand. "Shall we?"

Lillian remained still and silent.

Carmen walked up slowly, stopping at Lillian's side. Her eyes were huge, her face hard.

"Lil?" Carmen asked, looking into her face. "You don't have to do this."

Lillian hesitated, searching Audrey's face for purpose. She saw nothing but pure passion, passion that called to her. She was tired of hearing about how she was letting Holly do this and do that. No one thought she could live without her. She'd show them.

Lillian stiffened her jaw. Her hand nearly sizzled in Audrey's, and her heart was damn near beating out of her chest. And as her nose caught the scent of the masculine cologne coating Audrey's gorgeous body, Lillian knew what she must do. What she *wanted* to do.

Looking away from Carmen, she nodded at Audrey and said with stern determination, "Yeah, let's go."

CHAPTER TWO

Audrey McCarthy moved through the crowd easily, head held high, feeling on top of the world. Around her, The Griffin spun its web of women and beer and music. Laughter and whistles called out into the music, egging her on. She smiled broadly, having wanted this one for a while now. She'd have to thank Corey, the deejay, later for hooking her up. Usually, she didn't like it when others requested her for the Midnight Room without her knowing, but this Lillian was special. And for a twenty spot, she'd gotten Audrey.

Audrey had nearly considered paying the deejay herself in order to get her, but paying went against her pride, and mostly, the women always came to her. This one, however, had been playing hard to get, intriguing her even more. She wondered what had changed the beautiful Lillian's mind. Had it been their brief dance and discussion? And here Audrey had thought it had gone badly, with her sounding like an ass. But she often came off cocky when she was nervous, and she had to admit, this one made her a little so.

"I like you even more now," Audrey said, squeezing her hand. She was amused and impressed by Lillian's initiative, never having pegged her for the type to request the Midnight Room. She seemed too reserved, too quiet, and frankly, too good.

Lillian gave her an annoyed look and then plowed through the crowd, pulling on Audrey.

"Whoa, there, gorgeous. We've got all night," Audrey said. She seriously hoped their hookup went well into the night. She could have a lot of fun with this one. Oh sure, she had fun with almost every woman she had the pleasure to be with, but she sensed Lillian was different.

"Just come on," Lillian said, obviously irritated.

Her insistence made Audrey all the more curious. Who was this delicately beautiful woman who, just like her name, reminded her of a lily? Was she a virgin? Audrey seriously doubted it, just based on her age alone. But still, there was something about her, something off-limits, something secretive. Audrey desperately wanted to find out what that something was.

Curiosity for a woman had eluded her lately, and she was beginning to doubt she'd ever experience it again. They were all so easy to pin. Most wanted sex, a few wanted passion, and even fewer wanted an actual connection. It was just easier to get your needs met with someone you found attractive. She just happened to be the woman most found attractive. So she gave them what they wanted and kept things simple. The situation always worked out for her. She didn't want a clinger-on. She wanted her life just the way it was, with maybe a little more intrigue in her women. Enough to keep things interesting.

Interesting meant distraction. Distraction meant less time to think.

She had to focus, keep thoughts and memories away. It was what she did best. She was the master of denial, and Lillian would be another perfect distraction.

"Hey," a woman to her right said seductively as they moved past her.

"Hi." Audrey smiled but remained intent on Lillian.

Another one nodded a silent come-on, which Audrey ignored. She was with Lillian for now, and she wasn't about to let her get away. Besides, would any of these women even compare to her? She had to lean toward the negative on that thought.

Yes, Lillian would be memorable. She could almost guarantee it. She grinned again at her luck as the club spun around them. Lillian met her gaze again, and Audrey noted the challenge there. Lillian had agreed to go, but now she was scowling as if she didn't want to?

What gives?

Was she still playing hard to get?

I hope so.

Whatever it was Audrey wanted, this Lillian seemed to have it. By the bucket load.

"Move," Lillian urged her on.

"There's no hurry," Audrey said, more than a little turned on. What was the hurry? Was she that anxious to get it on? And here Audrey thought she was cranky but shy.

"Trust me, there is." Lillian tugged harder on her hand.

"I was hoping we could take our time," Audrey said slowly. "You know, go nice and slow, really enjoy each other. You telling me what you want, how good it feels, how badly you want me to give it to you."

Lillian stopped and turned. "Please shut up before I change my mind."

Audrey reared back and then laughed. "What?"

"I'm serious."

Audrey pulled her in closer. "I am too, Lillian. Deadly so."

But Lillian only moved away and demanded somebody else give them space to get through.

Maybe this one was a little more eager than Audrey had given her credit for. Maybe she really did just want to get right down to business. No talk, just play. She'd have to take control to ensure they went nice and slow.

More bodies slid outward, giving them a path.

Lillian tugged on her hand again as they neared the Midnight Room. Opaque wall panels extended from the entrance, showing the nearly nude women behind them in shadow. The hired dancers moved seductively, pressing their bodies against the glass, welcoming them in silence. The Griffin went all out for its illustrious Midnight Room, and it seemed to be paying off. Every woman who entered the club wanted a go.

A female bouncer stood waiting at the suede-tasseled door, killing any semblance of a mood at once. She was thin and sinewy with muscle, an angry look forever pinched on her face. Audrey always referred to her as Beastly due to her attitude and the large Tasmanian Devil tattooed on her forearm.

"No sex," Beastly said and then angrily pulled back the tassels.

"Right," Audrey said, having heard it time and again. There was also a sign posted over her head in case patrons somehow missed the clue.

Audrey never paid attention to the rule, and from what she heard, neither did anyone else. You just had to be quick was all. Kiss a little, fondle here and there, and then quickly and oh so deftly, a hand goes down the pants and…

"You coming?" Lillian asked.

"You first and last," Audrey said as they entered. When they stopped in the middle of the room, Audrey could tell Lillian had never been inside before. She stood very still with her mouth agape, beautiful ice blue eyes scanning every inch of the red velvet room. The walls, the sofas, even the bar in the corner, were all covered in varying shades of red velvet. A lush deep-purple carpet blanketed the floor, and two small chandelier lamps gently breathed light into the room from their carefully chosen spots on antique Victorian tables.

"This is incredible," Lillian said. Pale hands pushed her shoulder-length brown hair from her face, and her thick lips seemed to flush along with her high cheeks. She was elegantly beautiful, and Audrey had the distinct feeling she didn't even know it.

"Would you like to sit on the chaise lounge?" Audrey asked as the thought of slowly kissing those full lips coursed through her. "Or perhaps the big couch?" Either would do just fine, and had in the recent past. Even the velvet covered bar stools at the small bar in the corner worked well for what she had in mind.

But Lillian looked around and then moved toward her as if she hadn't heard her.

"How long do we get in here?" Her legs strode powerfully, the curve of her hips sashaying as she walked. Her baby blue blouse seemed to cling to her as if the front had been wet not long ago. The knees on her khakis looked damp as well.

She wasn't dressed like most others at The Griffin, not at all. And how long had she been out in the rain?

"Did you hear me?"

Audrey cleared her mind, her curiosity for Lillian growing by the second. "Uh, yes. Usually it's about fifteen minutes before Beastly pops her head in."

"That's not much time." She stopped in front of Audrey and panted. "Not much time at all."

"It can be," Audrey said, reaching out to touch her hair. "There's always my place."

Lillian shook her head defiantly. Then, with one powerful thrust, she shoved Audrey backward, nearly knocking her from her feet.

Audrey tried to laugh it off, but it was difficult.

"What the hell?"

Lillian kept coming at her, backing her up without touching her.

"What's this?" Audrey asked.

Lillian's eyes glinted and hooded with seduction. "What's what?"

Audrey swallowed, feet searching behind her. Soon she felt the wall and she laughed again. They were in the corner, the darkest corner, away from all the furniture. Her nails bit into the velvet as Lillian approached.

"This is what you had in mind?" Audrey asked.

"Not exactly, but it will have to do."

Audrey stepped forward. "Okay." She could get into this. She could definitely get into Lillian like this, all seductive and husky-sounding. "I like you like this." Audrey touched her face, and at once, she felt it heat and felt Lillian sharply inhale. It made Audrey's pulse double and a rush of noise filled her ears, almost like the sound of the ocean. She was turned on, truly, madly.

She stared into Lillian's eyes as heat came to the forefront of her own skin. Lillian wanted her; she could see it. Angling her head, Audrey dipped in for a kiss. Lillian met her eagerly with soft, supple lips. The warmth from them eased onto Audrey's like the caress from the sun on a late spring day. It spread from her dizzy head all the way down to the tips of her toes. She wanted more of that warmth, more of that tantalizing mouth, and she ducked in for another kiss, this one powerful and led by her. She felt Lillian's tongue with her own, and the sensation shot instantly to her center. She held Lillian tighter, so turned on she was on her tiptoes, but the kiss was halted as Lillian pulled away.

"Stop."

"But that was…nice," Audrey managed to say, thumb brushing Lillian's jaw. "It was really nice." The nicest she'd ever had. What was happening?

But Lillian just stared at her, eyes no longer swimming in bliss.

"You okay?"

Lillian didn't speak, didn't even blink.

"Lillian?"

A dangerously sexy look overcame her, and her pupils widened like a cat's. She flicked at her lips with her tongue and stepped into Audrey, this time pinning her to the wall.

"Shh. Don't talk."

Audrey laughed a little. "Why not?"

She tried to switch their positions, but Lillian wouldn't have it.

"You move and I walk out."

Audrey blinked. "What?"

Lillian pressed into her harder and kissed her, parting Audrey's lips with a searing hot tongue. She plunged confidently and deeply, seeking Audrey's best-kept secrets.

At first, Audrey stiffened, overcome by the sudden force of the smaller woman. Audrey was the one always in control; never had it been reversed. But the taste and scent of Lillian sent her head spinning, and the feel of her white-hot tongue sent more blood pounding between her legs. There was no way she was stopping this kiss.

Audrey groaned, felt her eyes roll back in bliss, and met Lillian's tongue with her own. Lillian made a noise of meek surrender and Audrey felt her chance. She cupped Lillian's ass and pulled her closer, needing more of her. But as she tried to turn them, Lillian pushed herself away, leaving Audrey's lips swollen and pulsating.

"What's wrong?"

Lillian backed up a little and touched her lips. "Nothing." But her eyes were liquid and seeking. She was searching for answers, but Audrey didn't even know the questions.

The club boomed around them, and Audrey felt warm and cocooned in red velvet. Cocooned with Lillian. She reached out and pulled her back to her.

"Then kiss me."

Lillian leaned away. "I can't."

Audrey cocked her head and felt a half smile drift across her lips. "You just did. And it was beyond fucking wonderful."

"I know. Which is why I can't."

"You've lost me."

Lillian turned away and whispered, "I've never even had you."

Audrey gently placed a hand on her shoulder. "Hey, what's going on?" She was so confused and her ears still thrummed with desire, as did her lips. "You want to get out of here?"

Lillian laughed. "Yes, but not with you."

"Ouch." Audrey dropped her hand. What the hell was going on?

Lillian turned and shook her head. "I'm sorry."

Audrey ran a hand through her hair and pushed out a long, confused breath. It wasn't supposed to be like this. Lillian was supposed to somewhat easily surrender, letting Audrey have her way with her, with Lillian loving every second. This was the way it always was.

But hadn't she wanted something different?

Audrey ran another hand through her hair, her classic nervous yet suave-looking move.

She had Lillian, and there was something different about her.

Wonderfully different. And yet all Audrey yearned to do was the same old thing. She wanted to take Lillian. She'd never wanted it more than she did at that second.

Lillian watched her, studied her. She spoke as Audrey stepped toward her, trying to touch her once again.

"Audrey," she said softly.

"Yes?"

"You are the most beautiful thing I've ever seen."

Audrey heated, her desire climbing once again. How she wanted this woman. She reached out and Lillian took her hand, halting her.

"Listen. If I stay, I can't kiss you. Not on the mouth."

"But I don't under—"

"It doesn't matter. It's what I have to do for me."

"Then why stay at all?"

"Because I—want to."

Audrey saw her eyes glint with desire once again.

"Then stay," Audrey said.

"You have to follow my rules."

Had it been any other woman, Audrey would've walked out, leaving her alone in the velvet room. But this was Lillian. Quiet, distant, hard to get. A woman who had just kissed her like no other, ever.

Audrey was staying and she would do anything to get Lillian to stay too.

"I want you to stay."

Lillian pressed her lips together.

"Then listen to me."

Audrey thought about arguing, but the look in Lillian's eyes told her she was serious.

"Okay."

"I can touch, but you can't," Lillian said.

"But—"

"No buts. My rules."

She backed Audrey to the wall as she spoke.

"I can kiss, but you can't."

Audrey's anxiety and excitement grew as she reached the wall. Lillian came at her hungrily, almost toying with her.

"I can do all these things, but you can't. In fact, the only thing you can do is…come."

Audrey bit her lower lip in anticipation.

"Do you agree?" Lillian's gaze was fierce, demanding an answer.

A groan escaped Audrey. One of barely harbored frustration and excitement. "I'll try."

"No." Lillian shoved up Audrey's tank to expose her bare breasts, causing Audrey to momentarily lose her breath. "You must agree." With hot hands, she traced her way up to Audrey's nipples where she pinched, tugging on them firmly.

"Agh." Audrey went up to the tips of her toes again, the ecstasy like a bolt of lightning rushing right through her. "Okay, okay."

"Gooood. Now we can play." She lowered her head and consumed Audrey's breast in one swift motion, pulling slowly and insistently on her nipples, drawing out the pleasure until Audrey was clawing at the wall with her nails and panting for sweet release.

"Please," she kept saying. "Please, oh God." What the fuck was happening? Oh God. Oh God. It felt so good. But she couldn't say, couldn't react. She had to have control.

"Nice," Lillian purred, licking the edges of the one nipple and then setting in on the other. "I like the way you feel. The way you try not to react."

Audrey moaned as Lillian licked first and then blew on her waiting breast, teasing her relentlessly.

"Tell me it feels good," she said.

"It does," Audrey managed, going back up to her tiptoes.

"You want to grab my head, don't you?" she asked, flicking her tongue along the bunched nerves.

Audrey bit her lower lip and squeezed her legs together. "Yes."

"Then do it. Knot your hands in my hair and hold my head to you."

She sucked hard then, taking nearly Audrey's entire breast into her mouth. Desperate to anchor herself, Audrey grabbed Lillian's head and sank her fingers into her hair, trying to pull her away, the mounting pleasure too much. But Lillian just groaned and laughed and sucked her all the harder.

"You going to come in your pants?" she asked when she finally unlatched her mouth to tease once again with her tongue.

Audrey couldn't speak, too caught up in struggling for her bearings as well as for a breath.

"You better not. Not yet." She laughed again and rose to yank Audrey's tank top up over her head. She cast it aside and stared into her eyes. Her warm hand rested on Audrey's cheek, and Audrey at once wanted to close her eyes from the intimate gesture.

"I—"

"Shh, no talking."

Audrey groaned. She was totally out of her element, totally out of control. Every ounce of her wanted to throw Lillian on the couch and ravish her in return.

"Oh, such the bad girl." Lillian stroked her face as she spoke. "Such the bad, beautiful girl. Whatever shall we do with you?" Her hand fell to once again stroke Audrey's breast, this time careful to avoid the nipple. "I've already tasted these," she said, leaning in to whisper in her ear. "How about your neck? Does it taste as good as it smells?"

Audrey's breath hitched as she felt Lillian's mouth tease her skin, first with lips and tongue and then with teeth.

"Mmm, yes. So good," she said as she licked and nibbled. "Almost as good as these." Her fingertips caressed and then tugged on Audrey's nipples, causing her to shudder and reach for Lillian's head.

"That's it. Hold me tightly." She laughed as she bit once again. "Hold me while I devour every last inch of you."

"Kiss me," Audrey managed to say. She tried to pull Lillian to her, but Lillian refused, laughing as she moved lower.

"Not on the mouth."

"Please," Audrey breathed, still holding fast to her head.

Lillian bit her firm nipple. "No."

Audrey jerked and felt her knees quake as another rush of hot arousal flooded her center. Lillian licked and teased, breathing hot breath upon Audrey's sensitive flesh. She moaned as she traced her abdominal muscles with her tongue.

"You're gorgeous, so absolutely gorgeous."

She moved lower, nimble fingers unbuttoning Audrey's jeans.

Audrey watched with hazy vision, her clit pounding with need.

"Fuck," she whispered, knowing she was about to lose all control. She yanked Lillian by the hair, forcing her to look up. "I've never let anyone do this," she said before Lillian could interrupt.

"Until now," Lillian said. She licked her lips and held eye contact as she tugged Audrey's jeans down over her hips.

Audrey held fast to her, quivering.

"You want me to do this, don't you?" It was a statement more than it was a question.

Audrey could feel her hot breath on her thighs. And when Lillian kissed her cunt through her panties, she all but shattered from the inside out.

"Yes?" Lillian asked.

Audrey threw her head back and clenched her eyes closed. Her hands knotted in Lillian's hair. Control was gone, completely lost. Even if she had wanted to, she didn't have the strength to fight it. This was it. Sweet, sweet surrender.

"Say it," Lillian said, licking her way up her inner thighs to once again kiss her through her panties. "Say it or I'll stop."

Audrey struggled for breath, for strength, but both were just out of reach. She looked down and saw Lillian's liquid-fire eyes staring up at her as she attached herself to Audrey's center.

"Ye-es. Yes!" Audrey finally said.

Lillian pulled away, laughed, and yanked down her panties.

She spread her quickly with gentle thumbs and then attached herself, swirling her tongue around and around her aching clit.

Audrey cried out and clung to her harder, legs threatening to buckle beneath her.

"Oh fuck." Audrey hissed, the pleasure searing right up through her. "Oh fuck."

"Mmm, so damn good," Lillian said as she wrapped her hands back around her buttocks. "Your pussy is as hot and sweet as you are."

Audrey watched as her long, agile tongue snuck out to flick her, teasing her hidden clit. Again and again, Lillian played with her, teasing her mercilessly.

"You want to come?" she asked, her voice low and husky.

Audrey swallowed as a shudder rushed through her.

"Yes," she whispered.

"Then let go of me."

Audrey hesitated, unsure if she could stand on her own.

"Let go of me and I'll make you come."

Slowly, Audrey released her. She watched breathlessly as Lillian pulled her in closer and snuggled her mouth into her flesh. Her hot tongue found her once again, this time pressing and lapping in long, slow, tantalizing circles. Audrey found herself moving with her, swaying her hips in motion with Lillian's tongue. She clawed desperately at the velvet wall behind her. She could feel the soft material slip and slide beneath her nails.

She was desperate to say something, to call out, to grab hold of Lillian's head. But she feared Lillian would stop, and she wanted nothing stopping her now.

Her groans became pants of desperation. Sweat dampened her temples and upper lip. Her legs shook and her body thrummed and moved on its own. Lillian feasted on her, eyes looking up at her sheepishly, wickedly.

What was this woman doing to her? Oh God, it was so fucking good. The best ever. The fucking best ever.

One last shudder passed through Audrey, and she let out a hoarse cry as she came, body thrusting madly, legs caving beneath her. She clung to Lillian then, desperate to keep her attached as her body continued to pulse into her. Lillian stayed with her as she sank to the floor, giving to her until the last possible spasm rushed through her.

When Audrey opened her eyes, she found herself seated, legs splayed before her, tremors passing through them. Lillian was watching her from her knees.

"Kiss me," Audrey begged. "Please." She was hoarse and weak and so damn desperate to touch her. She didn't want anything as badly as she wanted this. She needed that connection, that hot spark between them. An anxious feeling was coursing up through her. A new feeling.

Lillian didn't speak.

"Please, I—"

"Hey!" Beastly's voice came from near the entrance. Audrey did her best to stand and clumsily pulled up her pants.

"Fuck off." Lillian stalked to the door. She squared off with Beastly as Audrey slipped into her tank top. "I said fuck off."

Beastly retreated quickly and quietly.

Audrey ran her hands nervously through her hair as Lillian returned to her, moving very slowly and almost shy.

"She gone?" Audrey had never heard anyone tell Beastly to fuck off before. Had she not been in such emotional turmoil, she would've laughed.

"Yes. And I think she's afraid."

"I would be."

Audrey sank her hands into her back pockets. She approached Lillian carefully, feeling shy as well.

"Don't." Lillian stopped her.

"But I—"

"I have to go." She turned and headed for the door.

"Lillian, wait."

Lillian stopped. Then she turned and stepped into Audrey quickly, kissing her long and sweet and deep.

Audrey felt her head spin and her body heat. And then in a flash, it was gone. Lillian was gone.

❖

The noise from the club slammed into Audrey as she ran through the hanging tassels of the doorway. The crowd seemed to have swallowed Lillian whole. Audrey searched desperately, her heart racing, her mind and body yearning for more. No one had ever made her feel that way or done such things to her body and her psyche.

"Hey, your girl went that way," Beastly said, jerking her thumb toward the entrance of the club. "She was in one hell of a hurry. Mean little fucker too. I told you no sex."

"Whatever." Audrey pushed through the crowd while Beastly called out behind her.

"How about a thank-you!"

Audrey hurried beyond the glass-paneled walls and out onto the throbbing dance floor. Her ears pulsed in a static-like adrenaline, helping her to tunnel and focus. Lights flashed and swooshed through the surrounding women like thick lasers. She wished the strobes would disintegrate each body they touched so she could better spot Lillian.

"How was she?" a woman asked, stroking Audrey's arm. "I'm better." This one had been hitting on her for a while now. Audrey wasn't interested.

"Not now," Audrey said, pushing away from her. She wound her way through more sweaty women, her heart hammering as she hurriedly rushed toward the exit. When she came out the other end, she found the doorway dimly lit and devoid of dancing women. A bouncer studied her nails from her position on a stool.

"She ran out," she said. "Said for you not to follow her because she was leaving right away."

Audrey pushed open the heavy door and stared out into the gusty rain. Taillights tracked just beyond the quiet parking lot. She slammed the door.

"Shit!" Audrey pounded her leg with her fist. "Damn it!"

"Rough night?" the bouncer asked, this time biting off a hangnail.

Audrey paced and pushed out a long breath. She was gone. Just gone.

"You know, her friends are still here," the bouncer said, tonguing her finger where she'd bitten. "Back in the corner."

Audrey perked up. Of course. Her friends!

She took off back into the crowd, pushing and winding her way through. Another couple was being called into the Midnight Room, and the crowd went wild. Audrey wished like hell that she and Lillian could get another shot.

She sure as shit wouldn't let her just leave.

She reached the far back corner and took the time to smooth down her tank and jeans before she approached. For some reason, she felt like she needed to make a good impression. She swallowed hard and fought to pay no mind to the wetness that still tingled between her shaky legs. Desire still rocked her every few seconds, and even more so if she allowed herself to recall the look in Lillian's eyes when she'd made her come.

Why did she have to leave?

Lillian's friends came into view, and they seemed to be searching for her by the way they were craning their necks and eyeing the crowd. When Audrey approached, they seemed to inhale at the same time.

"Audrey McCarthy," the one Audrey recognized as Rain finally breathed.

"Where's Lillian?" the one with dark hair asked, not amused in any way whatsoever.

"I was hoping you could tell me," Audrey said. "She left."

"Oh no. Was she upset? It's all my fault," Rain said, laying her head down on her arms. "I seriously fucked up."

"It's not your fault, Rain. You were just trying to get her to live a little."

"I'm not following," Audrey said.

"Carmen, tell her," Rain said.

Carmen, the one with dark hair and attitude, leaned forward a little and locked eyes with Audrey. "Rain paid the deejay. She wanted you two to hook up."

Audrey sank into an empty chair, her legs feeling weak. "You mean Lillian didn't do it?"

Carmen belted out a laugh. "Do it? Hell no. She wouldn't dare even dream it."

Audrey felt sick to her stomach. What did this mean? Just what the hell had happened back there? If Lillian didn't want it, why did she insist on giving it to her?

"What exactly happened anyway?" Carmen asked, lifting a curious eyebrow.

"I need to know where I can find her." She seriously needed to talk to her now. She had to know why. And she had to know why she just took off.

"Why?" Rain sat up.

"I need to talk to her."

Carmen stood. "You didn't hurt her, did you?"

"No, of course not."

"Because if you did—"

Audrey stood, unnerved and horrified. "I didn't. I would never."

"Why did she leave?" Rain asked. "Is she upset?"

Audrey shook her head. "I don't know. I just know I need to find her."

"Tell us why," Carmen said.

Audrey squared off with her and knew at once by the look in her eyes that there would be no answers until Audrey 'fessed up. This woman cared deeply about Lillian, and Audrey couldn't afford to fuck things up. She needed to get past the gatekeeper.

"Because I—" Should she say it?

They waited, staring at her.

Audrey caved and relented to telling the truth.

"I like her."

Carmen blinked in what seemed like confusion and returned to her chair.

Rain smiled. "Oh my God."

Audrey felt the heat rush to her face. "Can you just tell me where to find her?"

"If you really want to find her, and if you really like her, you'll go to her church," Rain said.

"Church?" Audrey thought they were kidding for a second.

"Yeah. She's there almost every night helping out and stuff," Rain said with a smile.

Audrey studied their faces, unsure what to say.

"Cat got your tongue?" Carmen asked. "Or did we just scare you away? Because Lillian doesn't fuck around, you know. And she's very serious about her faith."

Audrey cleared her throat. "Can you give me the address?"

"It's the nondenominational on Hatley and Thirty-First Street. Can't miss it."

Carmen laughed. "She'll miss, it all right. I don't think church is exactly her thing."

Audrey ignored her and looked at Rain. "Thanks," she said and shook her hand. Audrey recognized her from the track meets she attended where she coached special-needs kids. Rain was often there helping out. She seemed like a nice person, and it felt good knowing she was Lillian's friend.

"Don't fuck with Lillian," Carmen said, biting into her thoughts.

"I wasn't planning on it."

"That church...it's all she has. So if you don't mind, don't bother her there."

Audrey wasn't sure what she meant.

"Then how can I find her? A phone number maybe?" It would be much easier if they would just give her the number.

"No chance."

"Why not?"

"Because we don't know if Lillian likes you back," Carmen said.

"Then how?"

"I suggest coming here."

"Oh come on, Carmen," Rain said.

"No, you come on, Rain. We don't know this woman and I'm not selling out Lillian."

Audrey didn't miss a beat. She'd do whatever it took to see her again. "When will she be here again?"

Carmen shrugged. "Who knows?"

Audrey slapped her hand on her thigh. "Great, thanks."

"Don't mention it."

Rain spoke up again. "I was wondering if I could make an appointment with you for some personal training?"

"I have to get going." She dug out her business card and handed it to Rain. "Call me. And please give my number to Lillian. She can call any time."

"I wouldn't bet on her calling," Carmen said.

"We'll make sure she gets it," Rain said softly. "I promise."

"Thanks."

Audrey pushed out a long breath, noticed the bartender giving her an angry eye, and headed for the door. What a night. And what was with Carmen and now the bartender? When she reached the exit, the bouncer, who now had a Band-Aid around her finger, said, "Rough night?"

Audrey shoved the door open and paused just before walking out into the steady drizzle. "No, actually it's been the best night yet."

CHAPTER THREE

L illian climbed into bed and switched off her bedside lamp. Her hand trembled as she brought in the covers, snuggling down deep. She hadn't been able to calm herself since leaving the club. Squeezing the steering wheel for dear life hadn't helped, and neither had taking a long, hot shower. Now, lying cool and damp in the bed, her body still shook and thrummed from her encounter with Audrey McCarthy.

She'd never done anything like that in her life, and she wasn't sure what to think of herself. She'd taken charge and conquered a woman completely. And the woman happened to be Audrey McCarthy, the hottest and most sought-after woman at the club.

What had she been thinking doing something crazy like that?

She wasn't some sex goddess or some confident, seductive woman like Audrey.

She'd even told a woman to fuck off!

Lillian sighed and pulled the covers over her head, remembering how wonderful the kissing had been. So wonderful she'd even had to stop doing it for fear of losing control.

Why did I do it? Any of it?

As embarrassed and confused as she was, no answers were forthcoming. Just more flushing of the skin and insane little giggles.

"I'm crazy," she said, feeling anxiety come again.

At least the tears she'd shed on the way home were gone. She rolled over, wrapping herself in the soft duvet, thinking about how she'd cried over her guilt at having made love to a near stranger. Could Holly ever forgive her should she find out? Holly had always insisted on everything being perfect, including Lillian. What if she came home tomorrow and saw her so distressed? She'd know for sure that something was wrong. Lillian would have to tell her the truth, and Holly would turn and walk right back out the door for sure then. Her whole plan for Holly's return would be ruined.

How could she have been so careless?

Holly coming back had been her only concern for what seemed like an eternity. Now she'd just gone and thrown her chances to the wind.

It was certifiable insanity. And so not like her at all.

What was worse was that everyone would know. Audrey McCarthy was as popular as they came, and anyone who was at the club now knew that they'd hooked up. And so did their friends and anyone else they might've told.

Oh God, was it possible Holly already knew? Was she friends with any of those women at the club? The possibility was there.

Shit, what would she do?

She flipped onto her back and stared upward. The previous owners had pushed glow-in-the-dark stars into the ceiling, and each night she lay very still and carefully took in each constellation. The patterns usually soothed her and helped to clear her head.

Holly had hated the stars. She'd said they were childish and that they should take them down. Lillian had ignored her, and to this day, she was convinced it was one of the reasons why Holly had left. Something so silly and meaningless and yet they'd argued over it countless times. But what else could it have been? Their lives had been ideal, with good jobs, a nice home, a calm, stable relationship. What more could anyone ask for? People begged for that sort of life every day. Client after client paid her to help them achieve just that. A calm, stable relationship. Yet it hadn't been good enough for Holly. It hadn't been perfect enough. Lillian hadn't been perfect enough.

She wiped away a wayward tear and inhaled deeply as another thought came.

What would it be like to have Audrey lying next to her staring up at the stars? Would she like them? Would she hold her hand and point out all the different constellations to her? Would they kiss and neck and—

She rolled over, forcing the thought from her mind. Just thinking about Audrey brought back memories of the Midnight Room and their heated encounter. Suddenly, she could smell her masculine cologne again, feel her hot skin, taste her sweet flesh. God, how intense it had been. She'd never wanted anyone so badly in her life. Not even Holly.

She gripped the covers as guilt once again swept over her. What had she done? And why, dear sweet Lord, why had she liked it so much? She sat upright and tried to control her breathing.

"No." She threw back the covers and stumbled in the dark for a glass of water. She'd wanted Audrey McCarthy. She had for months. So when she'd finally gotten her chance, she'd taken it. She'd given Audrey McCarthy exactly what she felt toward her. Hot, powerful lust. And she'd done it the only way she could've. By taking total and complete control.

"I liked it." She gulped down the water and placed the glass in the sink just as her hand started to tremble again. "Dear God, I loved it."

She stared down the dark hallway and considered going back to bed. But she knew all that awaited her were guilt and memories. Just more Holly. Holly. Holly. And for the first time since Holly left, Lillian avoided the thoughts. Tonight, she wanted anything but Holly. Just absolute peace would be best.

As she headed for the couch, she thought about having a drink. But to her surprise, even that thought didn't seem to calm her mind. She lay down and got comfortable under the throw blanket, staring at the vast ceiling. Her hand found her flesh just beneath her pajama bottoms. Slowly, she began to stroke herself, trapping her clit between her fingers. As she closed her eyes in pleasure, she found that only one thing seemed to calm her and excite her like no other.

Audrey McCarthy.

❖

"Just give her a call," Rain said into the phone as Lillian pulled out of the Starbucks drive-thru. Lillian sipped her iced mocha and eased back into morning traffic.

"You call me at seven in the morning to tell me to call Audrey McCarthy?" Actually, Lillian was glad she had. The call had awakened her, saving her from being late to her first appointment. She'd spent the night on the couch touching herself as she relived the encounter with Audrey. She'd finally crashed into a deep sleep sometime before three.

"Um, yeah. Why else would I call so early?"

"Well, I'd say you're ridiculous, but you saved my ass from being late. So, thanks."

"Don't mention it. So are you gonna call her?"

"Oh." Lillian laughed a little. "No."

"What?" Rain shouted it so loud Lillian automatically braked in response.

"Jesus, Rain." She made sure her mocha was spill-free as she accelerated once again. "You just about caused me to wreck."

"You have to call her. Have to."

"Well, I probably won't."

"She wants you to. She likes you. She even said so."

"So? That woman likes everyone, Rain."

"No, Lillian, I think this was different. You should've seen her."

Lillian had to admit she was curious, but not enough to call her. What happened was a one-time thing, and that would have to be good enough. She couldn't afford to get all tangled up with a woman like Audrey. She had enough troubles, thank you very much. And she had to remain focused on Holly.

"I don't want to see her." Lie. She did want to at least secretly stare at her some more. But the memory of her would have to suffice.

"How could you not want to! She wants to see you. She gave us her number, asked where to find you."

"Guess I'll have to avoid the club for a while, then." Shit, there went the secret staring.

"No, don't! Come on, Lil. Don't do this. Audrey is smoking hot and she likes you. What's the holdup?"

Lillian turned on her blinker and changed lanes as she neared her exit. "Let me count the reasons. Number one, she's a player."

"You don't know that. Not for sure."

"Rain, she never has a girlfriend, and she hooks up with someone almost nightly. Player."

"Maybe she'd change for you."

"Ha. Good one."

"Well, what's number two?"

"Number two is me. I'm happy the way things are."

"You mean being desperately alone waiting for Holly's return?"

Lillian scowled into the phone. No one understood. Not a single damn person. "What happened last night was a mistake. I lost my head. It will not happen again."

There was a brief silence. "Lil?"

"Yeah?"

"What exactly did happen last night?"

Lillian laughed. "You think I'm going to tell you? You're the one who set me up for the damn thing in the first place."

"I know. I'm really sorry. I was just trying to get you out of your funk, you know?"

"I'm not in a funk, Rain. I'm perfectly fine."

Another silence. This one longer. "Did you guys, you know?"

"What?"

"Get it on?"

Lillian laughed again. "Not telling."

"Come on. You have to tell."

"No, I don't."

"Please. Was she as good as they say?"

Lillian sipped her mocha and considered how to answer. Memories flooded her. Audrey's smell, Audrey's taste, Audrey's sighs.

"Yeah."

"I knew it! Oh my God, I knew it! Go, Lil!"

Lillian turned right at the light and then eased into the parking lot of her practice. When Rain calmed down, she finally spoke. "Easy, girl, it's not what you think. But I'm not sharing any more."

"Oh my God, I'm so proud of you."

Lillian swung into a parking space and sighed as she put her car in park. "Calm down, calm down. You sound like a sixteen-year-old. I'm already regretting telling you."

"We would've found out. Anything Audrey does usually comes out eventually."

"Great." Would Audrey really tell? Somehow, she thought not. Their encounter seemed a little too unconventional for that. Something told her Audrey was usually the one in control.

"But don't worry. We won't let the gossip get out of hand."

"No, you won't let the gossip get going at all. Understand? I will not be the topic of such ridiculousness. You owe me that much, considering what you did."

She heard Rain sigh.

"Say it, Rain. We're too old for this shit. And you know how I feel about it."

"Okay, fine."

"Good. Now go teach and pretend you're an adult for the next seven hours."

"Do I have to?"

"Yes."

Lillian ended the call and crawled from the car. She shouldered her messenger bag and headed inside. The day was promising to be bright and sunny, maybe some sporadic clouds. By the time she stepped out for lunch, she'd no longer need her cardigan.

"Hiya, Lil," Nadine said from behind the computer screen and a large half-eaten bagel with cream cheese.

"Good morning."

Nadine looked at her curiously and then removed the bagel from her mouth. "You look different."

"Tired?" She dropped her messenger bag and dug into the bag of fresh bagels.

"Noooo, something else."

"Don't even say hungover or I'll kick your ass." Lillian was a recovering alcoholic; everyone knew that.

Nadine scoffed. "I wouldn't dare. Besides, I know better."

"Good. So how's my day look?"

"Your day looks like the usual. Don't get off track here."

Lillian thought about sinking into the other desk chair but then thought better of it. Nadine was homing in on her much like Carmen always did.

"You look…fresh. Rosy-cheeked."

"Really? I hadn't noticed."

She retrieved her bag and peeked around the enclosed space to the waiting room. Her first appointment was already there. Minus one half of the couple. Great. It was always wonderful to work on a couple's relationship with just one half of the actual couple.

"We'll talk at lunch?" Nadine asked as Lillian moved toward her office.

"Busy."

"No way. I'll find you."

"No, you won't."

"Yes, I will."

Lillian laughed and closed her door. Her encounter with Audrey McCarthy just didn't seem like it was going to go away.

She busied herself retrieving her file, recorder, and pen, putting everything else out of her mind.

When she was ready, she plugged in her scented air freshener, fluffed the pillows on the couch, and opened her door. She walked briskly to the front room and called softly for Gary.

He rose like a man condemned and followed her, apelike, back to her office. When he was seated, she closed the door and took her seat in her leather chair.

"Beth's not coming," he said before she had a chance to ask. "Said she's through wasting your time."

"Oh?"

"Yeah. She said I'm a waste of time. Nothing's getting through to me. So we shouldn't come here and waste your time in return."

"You're not wasting my time, Gary."

He laughed. "That's what I said. I mean, we're paying you, right?"

"Yes, but that's not what I meant."

"It doesn't matter what she says. I know you're helping."

Lillian crossed her legs. "I think it does matter what she says. Can you tell me what else she says? How she thinks this isn't working?"

"Just the same old shit. I'm boring. I'm cold. I don't care about her feelings. I'm not romantic enough."

Lillian swallowed. Some of what he said was resonating with a part of her. Holly had always complained about something. So much so that Lillian finally had stopped listening.

"How so?"

He shrugged. "I don't know. I'm just me."

"Sounds like she's feeling alone."

"Alone? Hell, she's not alone. I go to work and come right back. We're together every night and every weekend."

"You don't have to physically be by yourself to feel alone."

He seemed to think for a moment. "I would've never thought of that. Maybe you're right."

"Let's explore that. How does it make you feel to know she may be feeling alone?"

She reached for her mocha and cleared her throat as he thought. The room felt suddenly warm and stifling. Memories from her time with Holly threatened to swarm, but she wouldn't let them. Not here, not now. Even if she had let them, she knew they wouldn't make sense. They were just hot little puzzle pieces being set free from the vault in her mind. They didn't yet have a place to settle, but she felt their heat and seeking just the same.

"I guess it makes me feel like shit."

"Try not to feel bad, Gary. Try to think of ways you can help. One of the best ways to mend relationships is to truly listen to what your partner is saying."

Why did I stop? Is that why she left?

"If she's saying you're cold, what do you think that means?"

"That I'm not affectionate."

"Okay. How do you feel about being more affectionate?"

He shrugged once again. "I guess I'm okay with it."

"Really?"

He shifted. "Well, okay, I think it sucks, but I'll do it."

"Why do you think it sucks?"

"I don't know. I hate thinking about it. I mean, why does she need so much? Why can't I just be me and it be good enough?"

"You are good enough, Gary. But she's human and just being herself. She may need more affection than you. Do you have a problem with giving affection? Does it make you uncomfortable?"

"No."

"Then try taking it slow. Give her a long hug today when you get home. Hold her hand while you're watching television. It doesn't take much."

He nodded. "Okay, I'll try that."

"And remember, the main thing is listening. Truly hear what she has to say and see how it applies to the two of you together." She gripped her pen as she started to grow a bit dizzy. Holly's face kept flashing in her mind.

Listen to me. Listen to me. She kept saying it over and over.

"And what about you? How are you feeling with your relationship, Gary?"

"Me? I'm fine as is. I think we have a good life. I don't have any problems."

"Physically, you think the relationship is fine?"

"You mean sex? Yeah, I guess."

"Emotionally, you feel fine?"

"Yeah, that's just it. I'm happy. I'm good. I don't have any complaints except that she's not happy."

Lillian fought closing her eyes as the puzzle pieces began to find places to settle in her mind. The dizziness intensified and she wanted so badly to make it all go away.

"Does that make sense?" he asked.

She nodded. "Yes. Yes, it does." It makes perfect sense.

CHAPTER FOUR

A udrey slammed her hand down on the menacing alarm and then rolled over on her back to enjoy the sweet silence. Overhead, her ceiling fan whirled, breathing cool air down upon her awakening nipples. From behind, sunlight squeezed through the wood blinds to burn her sensitive eyes. As best she could see, she was alone in her apartment, awakened yet again to deal with a new damn day.

Nights she could handle; she was the queen. But fresh new days were her kryptonite.

The unbearable silence of her surroundings always seemed to pulse in her ears, suffocating her senses. It was like having a pillow shoved over her face by a force unwilling to let go.

The morning pillow. Pressing and pressing.

The only thing that made it better was a hangover. At least then she had something else to focus on rather than the bright, shining loneliness.

She moved slowly and realized she was completely twisted in her sheets. One foot was jammed into the side of a pillow, causing her to kick several times for it to loosen. When it finally came free, she was out of breath and nauseous.

"God," she sighed as she rested again, this time shielding her eyes. It seemed the drunker she was, the wilder she slept. Sometimes, she even awoke half off the bed or completely on the floor. Other times, she wasn't even in her room at all, and she'd always wondered how she'd ended up halfway down the hall.

It must've been the women. Nothing else explained her wild sleeping positions.

Unwinding herself from the sheets, she groaned and noticed she still had on her jeans. A foul taste was in her mouth, and her trusty hangover headache was present. As she stood clumsily and walked slowly to her dresser, she felt something hanging from her back pocket.

"What the hell?"

She leaned against the drawers and pulled out a red lacy bra much like a magician pulls out a mysterious line of colorful handkerchiefs. It hung from her finger like a complete stranger, a totally foreign element. Its owner's face flashed in her mind like a drunken haze. The features were fuzzy, the laughter loud. The woman had been blond, busty. She'd had a broad smile.

A woman. Yep, that explained the mangling of the bed and the foot jammed into the pillow. What else would she find? Panties on the doorknob? A high heel in the fridge? Or maybe the woman was still there, tucked away in a passed-out coma inside the bathtub.

It had happened before, and she seriously hoped it wasn't the case this morning. She was in no mood to play nurse.

She gave the bra one last glance and then tossed it aside to amble toward the bathroom. The light inside the white tiled room was so bright she almost walked right into the toilet. A quick pull back of the shower curtain revealed an empty tub, so she peeled off her jeans, relieved herself, and then stepped into a steaming-hot shower. Nausea once again crept at her throat as the water pounded her stiff shoulders.

Memories of the night before came again, along with the continued dizziness. She'd brought home a woman whose name she either never caught or never asked for. They'd fucked in the bed for what, at the time, felt like an eternity. But thinking about it now with the water rushing over her ears and eyes, she knew it hadn't been for very long. The woman had wanted to do her, but Audrey hadn't allowed it. She'd insisted on keeping her jeans on just to be sure.

She dropped the shampoo and groaned as she retrieved it. As

she soaped her hair, she recalled the only woman in recent years who had touched her there.

Lillian.

She'd done nothing but think about her all evening long even as the drinks came one after another. And here she was doing it again, sick from the night before and barely standing upright.

I will not think about her. I will not think about her.

But the more she said it, the more she knew she'd fail. Lillian was in her mind for good. Or at least until she had a chance to taste her. Then she wondered if the memory of her too would fade, just like the woman she'd had last night. Would any woman ever gain and hold her attention? If any woman could, it would be Lillian. If only she would talk to her. Then Audrey wouldn't have to occupy her mind and time with other women. She was growing weary of the game. The same night after night. Woman after woman. No in-depth conversations, no passion, just clumsy, wet sex.

But however bad it was, it was still better than being alone.

She sighed as she rinsed her hair and soaped her body.

She hated to admit it, but Lillian was avoiding her. She'd never had a woman avoid her before and it stung, deeply. What had she done wrong? Was Lillian seriously just not interested? What about those kisses? They weren't one-sided.

Still, Lillian was avoiding her. It was clear. She hadn't been back to the club since their encounter when Audrey knew she frequented The Griffin at least four nights a week. Her friends had clammed up as well, although Rain always looked like she wanted to help. Carmen though, always seemed to crack the whip.

She only wanted to talk to the woman, for Christ's sake, and okay, obviously, have sex again. And again. And again. But it was more than that. She wanted to get to know her, make her smile, hear her laugh, inhale her scent. She stood under the water, allowing what she'd just realized to soak into her skin. She'd never cared like this before. Never thought this way about a woman. Sure, she'd dreamt of it, but here it was right in her face. What did it mean?

It hurt her head to ponder it anymore, so she tried to let it go.

The water seemed to help wash the hangover away, sloughing it gently off her skin, pounding it out of her muscles. Lillian too, for the time being, swirled down the drain with the water. Audrey felt halfway alive for the first time since she'd peeled open her eyes.

When she emerged from the shower, she pulled on her robe and padded into the kitchen. The coffee machine had gifted her with its morning brew, and she sipped some carefully as she sat at her small kitchen table and allowed her eyes to adjust to the light. She sat and stared, constantly having to push Lillian from her mind. She instead took in the little things and pretended like she was an outside observer.

Her apartment was small for two bedrooms, with her kitchenette intruding upon the small living room. A single couch, coffee table, and one end table adorned one side, while a wicker chair she'd splurged on at Pier One Imports sat in the corner. Framed photos of her longtime friends sat on the entertainment center next to the television and stereo, along with scented candles and other odds and ends.

Though small, she liked her little abode. It was cozy and warm. Safe from the storms of life, for the most part, depending upon what she sometimes brought home. The living room smelled like lavender and fresh coffee, and feeling nostalgic, she rose and studied the photos next to the silent television. Most of the pictures had been taken two or three years before. They were full of color and life, and she couldn't help but smile as she took them in. The poses varied from her and her friends partying wildly to more serious ones where they were out on adventures like hiking in Sedona or riding the rapids of the Colorado River.

Those were happy times and they seemed so long ago. She gently touched the frames, missing those times and missing her friends more. She wished she could go back in time, relive those fun times again. Back before Becky and Viv met their soul mates and settled down. Viv even had children now. Boy, how times had changed. She thought back to the last time she'd seen them. It had been at a baby shower almost two years before. They'd all sat around and talked about mortgages, kids, carpooling, and other married topics. Audrey had felt lost and hopelessly left behind.

How could she compete with that?

She'd tried to tell them about the new Midnight Room at The Griffin, but they had all scoffed and laughed, obviously having no interest. Audrey had clammed up, embarrassed at having even brought it up. She'd left quietly after a short while, kissing Viv on the forehead as the sunshine gleamed off her hair and warmed the scent of baby powder in the air. No one had really noticed, and definitely no one had protested her departure.

She'd texted them from time to time, hoping to do shots with Becky, hang out in Tempe with Viv. But her invites were always turned down, and sometimes even went unanswered, as did her invites to hike or to travel. Everyone was busy with life, and their lives no longer mirrored hers.

She was alone, and the feeling scared the hell out of her when she had the time and impartial mentality to think about it. It brought on a lung-pressing dread that she often found difficult to shake. It was that suffocating feeling again, her body threatened by the doings of her mind.

Would a relationship be just as suffocating?

At least with the lonely feelings, she could medicate with drinking, sex, and exercise. She could stand up and walk out of her apartment, forcing herself to do something else.

With a person, though, you couldn't escape that easily. Even when they weren't there, their memory was.

Audrey sank into her wicker chair and studied the room from a different vantage point.

It helped to ease the sense of dread beginning to settle on her chest. The sadness grew as she thought about her friends.

They'd moved on, outgrown her. They had, in their defense, invited her for dinner and birthday parties. But she just hadn't had the nerve to go. It seemed there was nothing there for her now. She was the odd one out.

The loner, the single lady.

When was she going to settle down?

Was she seeing anyone serious?

What about marriage?

She sipped some more coffee and scowled at the suggestion. A serious relationship was out of the question for her and they knew that. They always had. It pained her to even think about it.

Her coffee mug shook as she grew upset. She forced herself to breathe deeply and calm down. The memories could only hurt her if she let them. At the moment, she was unwilling to let them.

She didn't need friends and she didn't need a woman. All she needed was fun.

She rose, intent on starting her day. The hangover symptoms weren't quite strong enough today to cloud her thoughts. She ignored a bout of dizziness as she strode back into the kitchen, and it only upset her more. Why couldn't it have overtaken her before she'd relived the past with her friends?

She downed the rest of her coffee and set her mug on the countertop. A note sat next to the microwave along with a paper flower.

Let's do it again sometime. This time without the pants.
Love, Janis.

Her phone number was scribbled below the message, but Audrey crumpled it up and threw it away. The woman would only want more, and Audrey couldn't give it. Why did women always have to complicate things? Why did they always want more, more, more?

She finished off her coffee, popped two Advil, and dug through her fridge for the eggs. As she cooked, she realized more was exactly what she wanted when she thought about Lillian. She wanted to know everything about her. And she certainly wouldn't have minded if Lillian had been the one to leave her a note after a night of wild sex.

She stirred her eggs as she realized that when Lillian entered her thoughts, nothing else seemed to matter. Not her fears, not anything. But what did all this mean? It didn't mean she wanted a relationship. No. No way. She shook her head and tried not to think too much about it. She had the day ahead to ponder over. She was meeting with a new client, so she had to bring her A game. Maybe the late night hadn't been such a good idea.

She thought back to the night before and her average and drunken rendezvous with Janis. Blurry images of Janis laughing, moaning, and shouting assaulted her. The bra was a tease, whisked across her face and then used on her wrists as the woman had tried to tie her. The sex had been wild, fervent even.

But Janis just didn't do it for her.

She sighed as she shoveled her eggs onto a plate.

Only Lillian did.

❖

An hour and a half later, Audrey was sprinting, being verbally assaulted, and loving every minute of it.

"You're a bitch, Aud," Olivia said breathlessly as she struggled to sprint behind her. "A psychotic, mean, good-for-nothing bitch."

Audrey turned and laughed, slowing her run a bit. "Come on, woman. It's harder to run while bitching." Her voice seemed to reverberate around the empty park as their workout neared its end. She sprinted on, inhaling the fresh bloom scent of the flowers and shrubs around them, loving the high she always got from cross fit workouts.

She had to push hard today in order to clear her mind. So cross fit had been the perfect choice.

Olivia, Audrey's client for over two years, panted after her, her face contorted in pain and anguish. She'd chosen to do the running last and they were coming up on the final minute.

"Come on, Olivia, you got this," Audrey shouted. "Sprint, sprint, sprint the last few seconds."

"I can't," Olivia said. "I can't." Her short ponytail swayed as she struggled to keep running. Sweat lined her face, and the front of her T-shirt was nearly soaked through.

Audrey backtracked and ran next to her, the workout testing her limits as well. "Yes, you can. Yes, you absolutely can. Let's go. Let's go hard."

"No, I can't. Not anymore."

Audrey's legs burned and she knew Olivia was hurting as well. They'd better stop soon before they risked injury. After a quick glance to her watch, Audrey pointed.

"Dig deep, Olivia. Run to that park bench. Come on. You can do it."

Olivia caught sight of the bench and then lowered her head in determination.

"That's it. You got this, girl," Audrey said.

They ran together to the bench, and Audrey caught her before she threatened to collapse.

"Great job. Nope, not yet. Walk around slowly, arms up," Audrey said. She walked with her and handed Olivia her water bottle, which she kept on her hip. "You did awesome, champ. Fucking awesome."

Olivia smiled and squirted her with warm water. "You're still a bitch."

"A psychotic, mean—"

"Good-for-nothing," Olivia breathed.

"Ah, yes, good-for-nothing."

Olivia chuckled. "I couldn't help it. You killed me today." She placed her hands behind her head and walked in a large circle. Her breathing began to slow right away, her recovery time having improved greatly with her eighty-pound weight loss.

"Yeah, but you charged right through it," Audrey said, retrieving her own water bottle from the nearby picnic table. "Totally boss."

"You sound like my kid," Olivia said.

Audrey sipped some water and stared off into the trees. The day was slightly overcast with the warmth from the sun settling to bake between the streets and the clouds. A cool breeze would be nice, but

Audrey didn't hold out much hope. She glanced at her watch again and noted the time. Her new client was due to arrive any minute.

"It time?" Olivia asked, following her line of sight out into the parking lot.

"Yes."

"I wonder what this one will be like," Olivia said, tilting her head in thought. "Male or female?"

Audrey picked up her clipboard and eyed her client's name. "Female." The name caught her attention and she glanced at it once more. Rain. Why did that sound so familiar?

"Don't get involved with this one," Olivia said.

Audrey ignored her as her heart began to beat faster. Her mind raced as she placed Rain's name. She looked to the parking lot again and saw two figures. She easily made out Rain and then the other. She recalled the conversation she'd had with Rain when she'd first called. She'd said she wanted the sessions for herself and a friend.

"You okay?" Olivia asked. "Audrey?"

"Oh wow."

"Huh?"

Rain moved closer and waved. Audrey waved back briefly and then dropped her hand as her suspicion was confirmed. It was Lillian. She was there. In the flesh.

Lillian met her gaze and recognition fell across her face. She froze mid-stride and reached for Rain's arm. Audrey moved forward quickly, crossing the park in record time.

Don't leave.

Don't leave.

"Audrey?" Olivia called after her.

"Hi!" Rain said with enthusiasm as Audrey approached.

"Hello," Audrey said, holding Lillian's cool gaze. "How are you?" She smiled, unable not to. She was so excited to see her she could hardly contain herself.

"I'm fine." Her eyes traveled down Audrey's body oh-so-briefly before she turned away in obvious embarrassment. "I think I should go," she said to Rain.

"No," Audrey said before she could stop herself. "Stay."

Lillian crossed her arms over her chest. "I don't think this is a good idea," she whispered to Rain.

Rain smiled at Audrey before whispering back. "But you promised."

"That was before I knew—"

"Why don't you guys join us?" Audrey asked, trying to think fast. She looked back to Olivia and began leading them toward her, near the center of the grassy park. "We were just getting ready to stretch."

"You've just finished your workout?" Lillian asked, arms still crossed.

"Yes, and I like to stretch as both a cooldown and a warm-up for my arriving clients."

"That's a good idea," Rain said. She held out her hand to Olivia. "Hi, I'm Rain."

Olivia gripped it with a smile. "Olivia." She did the same with Lillian.

"Olivia's an old client of mine," Audrey said, wrapping an arm around her.

"That's right. This woman busted eighty pounds off me. And I'm still around to talk about it. Barely." She laughed and squeezed Audrey playfully.

"Wow," Rain said. "Sounds great. Doesn't it, Lil?"

"Hmm? Sure, yeah. Sounds great."

Audrey could tell she didn't mean it. She was ready to flee.

"Why don't we all sit and stretch?" Audrey asked, encouraging them to settle in. They all sat in a circle, Lillian doing so reluctantly. Her eyes drifted over to Audrey every now and then, burning Audrey's skin with their heated caress. She always looked away just as quickly, her face giving away nothing.

Was she still interested? Her eyes said yes while her body said no.

Maybe she was confused as to what she wanted. Maybe she was fighting it. Audrey would have to try to change that.

Olivia gave Audrey an odd look, letting her know she knew

something was up. The air hung heavy with silence, broken every now and then with only the hurried whispers between Lillian and Rain.

Audrey merely shrugged at Olivia as if she had no idea what was going on, but Olivia didn't seem to buy it. Instead, she broke the silence like only Olivia could.

"So I was just telling Audrey here that she sounded like my kid when she talked."

Audrey looked at her and shook her head in disapproval.

Olivia mouthed the word *what* and smiled. "You do. You sound just like her."

Audrey forced a smile. "Maybe that's because you let her hang around me."

"Yeah, I know. What am I thinking?"

Audrey glared at her, silently warning her of an impending ass kicking.

"I'm not a bad influence," Audrey said, showing them all a good hamstring stretch.

"Oh, God. Yes, you are. You're too damn wild."

"Am not." What the hell was she doing?

"Are too."

They partnered up, placing the bottoms of their shoes together. Audrey took Olivia's hands to pull her for a gentle hamstring stretch. She squeezed hard as she did so, trying to get her to back off with the information leaking.

"I am not too wild for your kid."

Olivia laughed, oblivious. "She's thirteen, Audrey, not three. She notices things."

"Like what?"

Audrey turned, surprised to hear Lillian's voice. Her pale eyes were keen and seeking and she was suddenly very interested in the conversation. Olivia ate it right up.

"Like her driving around in that black Jeep with no doors or windows, for one thing."

"So?" Audrey spotted her Jeep across the street and smiled.

She loved its black shiny gleam and big rugged tires. Doors and windows were for wimps or for those unfortunate enough to live in bad weather. This was Phoenix, for fuck's sake. Air-conditioning was still a month away. "So don't let her ride with me."

"I don't. Haven't you noticed?" Olivia wiped her red face. Her smile was as bright as the missing sun. She had no idea she was driving the nails into Audrey's coffin when it came to Lillian. None. She was just being Olivia.

"Not really," Audrey said firmly.

Olivia slugged her in the arm. "Figures."

"What else?" Lillian asked, this time meeting Audrey's gaze. Her eyes bored right into her, and for an instant, Audrey sensed the powerfulness she'd felt with her the other night. Her body trembled as she remembered what the look preceded.

"Well," Olivia said, straining into the stretch. "There's your hickeys."

"Hickeys?" Rain asked and then laughed.

Audrey blushed profusely. "I think a change of subject is in order."

"No, no," Olivia said. "You need to hear this. We can see the hickeys when you wear your sports bra, Aud."

Audrey clenched her jaw in frustration as she heard Rain laugh softly. Then she panicked. Did she have a hickey today? She rarely looked above her abs in the mirror after a shower. All she cared about were those sweet etchings defining her six-pack.

She glanced down, seeing nothing but her black sports bra.

"Yes, you have one today," Olivia said. "Right here." She touched her neck and Audrey flushed again.

"Will you please stop?" Audrey whispered angrily, finally catching her attention.

Olivia blinked in confusion. "I'm only playing around, Aud."

Audrey looked over to Lillian and Rain. They were both watching her intently.

"Just…never mind." Audrey stood and retrieved her water. She tried to look calm and unaffected, but she could still feel her skin burning.

"What else?" Lillian asked, standing along with her.

Olivia looked between them and then settled on Audrey. Her eyes were full of questions, and Audrey had no idea how to begin to answer. Lillian didn't let up.

"I've heard you're wild in other ways," she said, tugging her foot back for a quad stretch.

Olivia nodded as if she couldn't help it.

Audrey stared at her, mouth agape.

"I didn't say anything," Olivia said.

"You might as well have."

"I'm sorry. It's just that I happen to agree with her."

"You don't even know her!"

"No, but I do know you. And Kelsey does notice these things."

"This has nothing to do with Kelsey."

Olivia crinkled her pale face, marked here and there with red from her workout. "Again, she's thirteen, not three. Besides, you aren't exactly quiet about it."

"I'm not? Because I sure as hell am trying to be right now."

Olivia gave her a look and cocked her head. They always talked like this. Her giving Audrey a hard time over her lifestyle. It had never bothered Audrey before. Not even in front of others. It had always been a running joke. So it was no surprise to Audrey to see the confusion on her face. She just didn't have time to explain.

Okay, maybe she did talk about women an awful lot. Maybe she'd have to be more careful what she said around Kelsey. Point taken. But could she please shut up?

"Everybody already knows," Lillian said coolly. She was standing with her hands on her hips, staring Audrey down.

Audrey faced Lillian and tried to ignore the delicate bones of her face, the full pout to her lips, and the sensuous curve of her exposed neck.

"Knows what?"

Lillian blinked once. "That you sleep around."

Rain stood and looked panicked. Olivia let out a whistle of

surprise. Audrey searched Lillian's face but found nothing. Nothing but contempt.

"If everybody already knows, then why do you seem so interested?"

Why was she asking all these questions? And why at Audrey's expense?

"I just wanted to make sure there was some truth to all that I'd heard." Her eyes dropped to Audrey's neck, the spot Olivia had touched only moments before. "I can see that there is."

Audrey stood very still, completely gobsmacked. She kept opening and closing her fists, feeling like she'd just been attacked. Finally and with her voice shaking, she spoke. "There's a lot more to a person than what meets the eye."

Lillian's eyes had lost their ferocity. Now they just appeared reflective and almost sad. "Is that so?"

Audrey was surprised at the sincerity she heard in the question. She swallowed with difficulty and fought crossing her arms. "Sometimes."

Lillian seemed to think for a moment. "Is that the case here?"

Audrey straightened her back, trying to look confident. "Yes."

Lillian nodded, letting her know she heard, and then she turned toward Rain as they busied themselves with more stretching.

Olivia came to her side. "What's going on?" she whispered.

"Nothing." She looked to Lillian and offered a smile of surrender. "Maybe I really am bad."

Rain smiled in return as Olivia chuckled. "To the bone, I'm afraid."

Audrey sank to the ground and picked at the grass, which still smelled strong despite needing a good rain.

"But you're good inside," Olivia added.

Lillian once again looked very interested.

Audrey scoffed. "Thanks."

"No, really, Aud. You've helped me through so much. I can finally move thanks to you."

"You did it all. I just made you."

They both laughed.

"No, seriously, you're a good woman, Audrey. Truly. You're just a little wild." She directed the comment toward Lillian and Rain, as if she needed to let them know.

Audrey appreciated the gesture, but to her dismay, the topic didn't change.

"Have you tried, you know, toning it down a little?" Rain asked.

Audrey thought of her longtime friends and fought a scowl. Why did it always come to this? And even if she wanted to, would she know how?

"How?"

"Getting a girlfriend, for starters," Olivia said.

Audrey stiffened, growing even more uncomfortable. A fucking relationship. "Here we go again."

Olivia sat next to her. "Why don't you ever want to talk about it?"

"I talk about it."

"No, you don't. You never have. I always ask, but you never give me a straight answer."

"Good, then I'm not going to today." She offered Lillian and Rain a smile.

"Why not?" Olivia asked, sounding almost hurt. She positioned herself for another series of stretches that Audrey helped her with, despite not liking the topic of conversation.

"I don't know. I don't feel like going into all of it."

Olivia seemed to sense her discomfort, and she didn't push it any further with more questions. "I just think it would be so good for you to meet someone special is all. You deserve that."

"Yeah," Rain said. "I mean, I don't know you that well, but we all deserve that. Right, Lillian?"

Lillian stared at Audrey for a moment before speaking softly. "Yes, I suppose we do."

Audrey looked away. No one understood why she didn't want a relationship. She hardly understood it herself. But like her mother always said, she just wasn't good enough. She was just like her father, and he took off. No one sticks around. So why waste your time?

But she wasn't just upset over her past or her mother and father and their fucked-up relationship. She was upset about the whole damn thing with Lillian. "You want to know my luck, Olivia? You want to know about my life? I'll tell you. I did meet someone. Well, someone I at least want to see again."

Audrey saw Lillian stiffen from the corner of her eye.

"You did?" Olivia tightened her ponytail and wrapped her arms around her knees. "Why didn't you tell me?"

"Because there's nothing to tell."

"How do you mean?"

"She wants nothing to do with me."

"What happened?" Olivia finally asked.

Lillian reddened and Rain kept looking between her and Audrey. Audrey shook her head and picked at the grass. "She's unlike anyone I've ever met. She's, I don't know, so sure of herself and she took control and made me feel things I've never felt…haven't felt in a really long time."

"Like what?"

"Like—I don't know. Moved. Excited. Crazy."

Lillian shifted, but her eyes were glued to Audrey, as if unable to break away.

"Crazy?"

"Yeah. I felt crazy and I liked it."

"I don't think that's a good thing, Audrey."

"Oh, but it was. She took control, took me, all of it on her terms, and yet she was there. She was really there, really into it. I could tell because she wouldn't kiss me."

"You're right. Sounds crazy as hell to me."

"No, you don't understand. I think she wanted to kiss me, but she felt something when she did. So she didn't."

"Then why did she do you at all?"

Audrey smiled, remembering. "Because she couldn't totally say no."

Lillian stood and Rain followed. "I think we should go."

"But I already paid for these sessions."

"I can't, Rain. Not today."

Audrey rose and brushed off her backside. "Please don't go."

Lillian gave her a half smile, one that looked forced. "Thank you very much for your time. We'll have to do this another day."

"Anytime," she said, meaning it. She chided herself for saying too much. She should've kept her mouth shut. But she was just so tired of being picked on for her choices.

She watched helplessly as Lillian and Rain walked away, back toward the parking lot.

Olivia rolled her eyes. "You slept with her, didn't you?"

Audrey finally turned away and faced her. "Yes."

"Good heavens, Audrey."

"But she was the one I was talking about."

Olivia raised an eyebrow.

"I've never heard you talk like that about anyone before," Olivia said.

"I know."

"I can see why you like her. Beautiful yet brave. She really put it to you."

"She thinks I'm a player."

"You are a player."

Audrey didn't reply. Obviously, her lifestyle was disapproved of by Lillian.

"So I guess this means you've got to go after her."

"Yes."

"You've got an uphill battle, my friend."

Audrey nodded.

Olivia touched her arm. "The truth may hurt, Audrey. I know you're used to women liking you, but this woman may not."

"I just want to know if I'm the only one that felt something different."

Olivia stopped her again.

"What if she felt it too? Did you ever consider what that might mean?"

Audrey stopped, the sun suddenly fiercely bright. "It won't mean what you think."

"Uh-huh."

"No, really. I won't let it. I just want to have fun."

"We all know that."

"Don't be like that."

"You confuse me, Audrey."

"I just want to have fun. Why is that so confusing?"

Olivia turned. "Because you're not playing a board game, Audrey. You're playing with people. And people have emotions."

"You think I'm going to hurt her?"

"Not intentionally."

"Damn it, I just want to get to know her. We could have such a great time. Why the fuck does everyone want to complicate things?"

"Maybe you're the one who's complicated."

Audrey considered that for a moment. She recalled the look on Lillian's face only moments before when she'd accused her of sleeping around. Maybe she was the one who was complicated. Maybe the things that didn't bother her bothered others.

They reached their vehicles and Audrey reached inside to retrieve her sunglasses. Olivia squinted at her.

"Wait, did you just tell me a woman made love to you and you let her have control?"

Audrey blushed a little, the notion still startling to her as well. "Maybe."

"What? Why? Why would you do such a thing when the mere thought sends you running for the hills?"

Audrey shrugged and gave a half smile, knowing it sounded crazy. "Because I just couldn't say no."

CHAPTER FIVE

Lillian drove straight home from work, weaving through traffic, cursing at herself and others. She'd made herself mad on so many different occasions lately it was a miracle she hadn't thrown herself off a cliff. First with Holly, and then with Audrey, and now with work. She was doing nothing but thinking about both women when she should be listening to clients.

"Damn it!"

She jammed on the brake, nearly rear-ending someone.

"It's okay. It's okay. I just have to calm down." She'd get home, relax, maybe work on some crafts, go to church. It would be okay. She didn't have to think about Audrey and how good she'd looked standing there all sweaty in a black sports bra and shorts. She didn't have to think about the hickey or her last words, telling her just what their brief encounter had meant to her. The confession had been shocking, taking her completely aback. What did it mean? Was there more to Audrey McCarthy? Didn't she want to find out?

The prospect was tempting, damn tempting. But she couldn't let it lure her in. She could force her mind to do anything. She had done so the past six months with her sobriety. She breathed deeply, in and out, soothing herself.

She was just about totally relaxed when her cell phone rang. It was Carmen, and Lillian was in no mood for any more berating. She was doing a good enough job of that herself.

"Hello?"

"Lil?"

"Yeah?"

"Can you—" But she was breaking up.

"Carmen, I can't hear you."

"I'm at—"

"Carmen, I'll have to call you back."

Lillian pulled the phone away and looked at the screen. She'd already missed three calls from her while she was in session. What in the world was wrong? It wasn't like Carmen to act so strangely, and she rarely ever called like that during work hours. She hoped she was okay.

She was dialing her back when she pulled onto her street and spotted her car in the driveway.

"What the hell?" As close as they were, it was unlike Carmen or any of her friends to just show up unannounced. And so soon after work? Obviously, she really did need to talk.

Lillian parked and hurriedly exited her vehicle. She found Carmen still in her car sitting quietly behind the wheel.

"What's going on?" Lillian asked, knocking on the window, concern turning to panic.

Carmen sat still for a moment before looking over. When she did, she opened the door and climbed out quickly.

"What's going on? You're scaring me."

Carmen slammed the door shut. "Sorry. Wouldn't want to scare you. Can we go inside?"

"Are you okay?"

"No. Yes. It's nothing…like that."

Lillian lightly touched her elbow to lead her inside, but Carmen stopped her.

"I'm not going to fall over."

"Okay."

Lillian allowed Carmen to walk slightly ahead of her, still concerned about her physical well-being. Her back was ramrod straight and her eyes looked fierce, like someone was trying to pick a fight with her and she was trying to decide whether or not to hold back.

Lillian didn't like the look; it unnerved her, especially knowing it probably had something to do with her. After all, why else would Carmen be there?

Lillian quickly unlocked the door and led them inside, where she offered Carmen a seat on the couch. The low-hanging sun was angling in through the back patio door, giving the room a warm golden feel. The ticking of her large mantel clock tried to soothe her and welcome her home, but it was useless. The day had been long and trying, and it seemed it was just getting started. So she busied herself making them some iced tea, wishing she had something stronger to offer Carmen, who definitely looked like she could use it.

"First of all," Lillian said, walking over to the couch with their glasses, "tell me you're okay. Tell me everyone's okay."

"I'm okay. So is everyone else, as far as I know," Carmen said, thanking her for the drink.

"Phew." Lillian kicked off her shoes and sat, sipping her iced tea. "That's good to know."

Carmen brushed back her thick hair and then wrung her hands. Why was she so worked up?

"I tried to call," Carmen said shortly.

"Yeah, I know. I saw that. I'm sorry. I was still at work."

Carmen gulped at her tea. "How did that go?"

Lillian groaned and tucked her feet under her. "Work? It didn't go well at all."

"Has it been going well?"

Lillian shook her head. "Not really." But she didn't want to get into why. She wasn't about to admit thinking about Holly and Audrey during her sessions. She just wanted to know what was wrong.

"So what's the deal, Carmen? What's the urgency?"

Carmen sighed and suddenly looked like she didn't want to talk. "I don't exactly know how to say it without sounding like a bitch."

"Try me."

"Okay." She breathed deeply and then placed her hands on her thighs. "Lillian, you're scaring the hell out of me."

Lillian reared back. "What?"

"The pining over Holly and now this...this Audrey thing. I mean, what the hell were you thinking?"

"I don't understand. You're this upset over me? Why haven't you told me you were this upset?"

"Because..." She paced back and forth. "I mean, I've been different, you know? I know you've noticed."

Lillian thought for a moment. "Yes, I have noticed. You've been sort of—"

"Bitchy?"

"I was going to say high-strung and distant."

"I've...yeah, I've been different because I've been trying to work things out. I was only going to approach you about Holly, but then this thing with Audrey happened and it scared me. Seriously, Lil? A one-night stand? With Audrey McCarthy?"

Lillian felt attacked and defensive even though she knew Carmen meant well. "First of all, what I do is my business. Second of all, it wasn't a one-night stand. You have no idea what happened back there. It wasn't even an hour, for God's sake."

"So you're saying you didn't have sex?"

Lillian fought to speak but couldn't think of the right words quickly enough.

"So you did."

"Carmen, it's my business."

"Like hell it is. I'm your friend. I've watched you mope around for a long damn time over a woman who's not even worthy of you, and now this? Wild sex in the Midnight Room? What's come over you?"

"Well, if anything, Carmen, this should please you. You always said I needed to move on from Holly."

Carmen looked incredulous. "Not like this! I mean, Jesus." She paced harder. Faster. Shoving her hands into her jeans pockets. "Are you saying you don't want Holly back now?"

Lillian brought a throw pillow up to her chest and squeezed. "No, I'm not saying that."

"Then what is going on?"

"I don't know, okay?"

"How can you not know? Rain told me about the meeting in the park. About how shook up you were afterward. Are you really going to let her train you after what went on between you two?"

"Carmen, I don't know. I'm really confused right now, okay? And with you guys always ragging on me about Holly, I guess it just got to me. I saw Audrey. I've always found her attractive, and I guess I wanted to forget for a little while. Is that so awful?"

"So you're attracted to her?"

Lillian looked away, feeling herself flush. "Yes."

Carmen sighed and sat down. "Are you still?"

Lillian met her gaze, knowing she could tell her anything despite her keyed-up attitude. "Yes. But I'm going to try real hard not to act on it."

"How can you still want Holly, then? If you're into Audrey?"

"Because Holly was stable! Holly was my life. Audrey was— is—I don't know." She couldn't get her out of her mind. It was even encroaching on Holly.

She rose and busied herself making them more iced tea. She fumbled with the sweaty glasses a bit, nervous about the topic.

Carmen softened her tone. "Audrey's just so wild."

"Mmm, so I've heard," Lillian said, knowing it was true.

"I don't have anything against her or anything. I just don't think she's right for you."

"My head tells me the same. I'm scared shitless of her ways. But..."

"But what?"

"I'm still drawn to her." She felt incredibly guilty in confessing it, but it was the truth. And the way Carmen was looking at her, she knew she could see it too.

"That's just because she's hot."

"No, it's more than that. There's something there, something more that no one else sees."

"You're not falling for her, are you? Please, God, tell me you aren't."

Lillian shook her head, contemplating in silence. "No. Of course

not. It's nothing like that." But who was she trying to convince—
Carmen or herself?

"Then why all the avoidance? You haven't been back to the club
yet. You've just been sitting here at home, like a hermit. Scaring the
hell out of me."

"I didn't mean to scare you," she said, gripping her hand. "I'm
just not ready to see her yet." It had all been so confusing. She'd
wanted her so badly and then she'd freaked and run out, too afraid
of just how much she did enjoy it. And after the confrontation at the
park... What would she say to her?

"God, I was so pissed when you went off with her. I thought
you had lost your damn mind for good. And then she came out and
said that she liked you—"

"She really said that?" Lillian's heart fluttered. She had hardly
believed it when Rain had told her the same thing.

Carmen nodded. "Afraid so."

"Maybe she says that about all the girls."

Carmen smiled. "Heh, I don't think so. I think you've got her.
Whatever having her means."

"Yes, whatever that means."

"Look, I'm just going to say be careful. And if she hurts
you..."

"Thank you." It was nice to have someone just care and nothing
more.

"And just stay off Holly, okay? I mean it's time, Lil. You're
worth so much more. I love you and you deserve happiness. Holly
wasn't happiness. You just think it was because you didn't know
any different."

Lillian nodded but said nothing. She couldn't help how she felt
about the Holly situation. Holly was what she knew. She was safe.
She was home base.

"And I think you should date."

"You think so." Lillian wasn't sure if she was ready for that.

"Yeah, just not Audrey."

They laughed softly, though Lillian did ponder it for a bit longer
than she should have. Who was this woman who had encroached on

Holly when no one else could? Did that mean something or was it her long-starved libido talking? The questions left her feeling alone and confused and she didn't want to feel either. Suddenly, she couldn't bear the night before her. She'd think about Audrey and she'd want to drink her away. There was only one solution. She needed her friends.

"Can we make tonight a movie night? Call Rain and invite her over?"

Carmen seemed surprised, but she nodded slowly. "Sure. We haven't had one of those in a long while."

Lillian nodded. "I know. I think I just really need you guys right now."

Carmen leaned over and embraced her. "You'll always have us. No matter what."

Lillian sighed and fought off tears. "Thanks. That means more than you know."

❖

The Griffin was Saturday-night crowded, the walls nearly bursting with people. Lillian could almost feel the building groan with each thump of the heavy bass. She loathed nights like these anymore and wished once again her friends would call it quits with the bar scene. But they'd spent the night and given her the same old lecture about how she was a hermit and that avoidance would do her no good as far as Audrey McCarthy went.

So here she was again, ambling through a crazy crowd, searching for the overwhelmed bar, in need of a good strong alcoholic beverage. Tonight, she would've chosen vodka. Straight up. Or maybe Patron. Some lime to go with it. Either would've done her just fine, and either would've helped her through this soon-to-be nerve-wracking night. But alas, she was all alone in her anxiety and she had to face it sans alcohol. Besides, she wanted to be on her toes and on the lookout for Audrey.

It had been two weeks since she'd been to The Griffin, and Audrey was exactly the reason why. She didn't want to see her or deal with her. It was just easier to forget, though doing so was easier said than done. The reprieve, however, had done her some good. She'd started walking again in the evenings and even swimming some late afternoons when it'd been warm enough. A long trip to the craft store had started her in on some creative work, and she'd greatly enjoyed her nights alone. Even if she did just sit and think of Audrey while making a blanket with colorful yarn. It was still better than being at The Griffin.

Bodies bumped her on her way to the bar, making her feel like a damn pinball. When she arrived, she felt bruised and disheveled, not at all as beautiful as Brea the bartender seemed to think she was.

"Welcome back," she said, smiling and slinging her bar towel over her shoulder.

"Uh, thanks, I guess." Lillian squeezed onto a stool, causing the woman next to her to frown.

"Don't want to be back?"

"Not really."

"So why are you?"

Lillian pointed. "Friends."

"Ah, right. They keep holding that gun to your head."

"'Fraid so."

She chuckled. "Well, here's one on the house." She handed over a club soda and flicked the little umbrella she'd placed inside, clearly a new touch. "Just for you."

"Thanks, but you don't have to." Lillian didn't want to give her the wrong idea. She still felt like shit after their last encounter.

"No sweat." She smiled. "Really." She leaned in closer as if she didn't want anyone else to hear. "And no strings."

Lillian smiled in return. "Thank you."

Brea remained close, glancing around the club. "You know, FYI, Audrey McCarthy's been looking for you." Her face crinkled at the mention of Audrey's name.

It startled Lillian and she looked behind her. "She's here?" Her friends had said she was a no-show so far tonight.

"I don't know about tonight, but every other night she's been here she's been looking for you." She studied Lillian closely, waiting for a response. It was obvious she wanted Lillian to react negatively to Audrey, and knowing so made Lillian uneasy.

What was she supposed to say?

She quickly excused herself. "Thanks again for the drink."

"Yeah, no problem."

Lillian didn't look back, unwilling to see the sting that was no doubt on Brea's face. She didn't want to deal with that issue when she had Audrey McCarthy to worry about. And she hadn't liked the scowl that had come over her face when she'd said Audrey's name. What was that about? Was she really that jealous? Or was it just general dislike for Audrey?

What *did* people think of Audrey?

More importantly, why did she care?

"Hey, girl!" Rain said, coming up to her immediately, beer in hand. "I'm so glad you came!"

"Hey, yes, I'm here," Lillian breathed, a little overwhelmed at the big greeting. She sat quickly, carefully glancing around as she did so. She feared the whole club would be staring at her, but to her relief, no one seemed to be paying attention.

"She's not here," Carmen said, spinning her beer bottle. "So no need to hide away or anything." She winked at her.

Lillian tucked her hair behind her ears nervously. "Oh, well, that's good."

"You wouldn't have come otherwise, right?" This time she met Lillian's gaze and raised an eyebrow.

"You know me so well it's scary."

"I knew it." She leaned over and patted her hand. "It's going to be all right. We're here to protect you."

"That's even scarier," Lillian said, causing them all to laugh.

"So tell us," Rain started. "What's been going on at home? That blanket you showed us was amazing. Have you finished it yet?"

Lillian toyed with her drink, scanning the club every now and then, searching for Audrey. And every time she did, her heart rate increased and the anxious knots started. She was sure she would spot her on the dance floor, moving seductively with two or three women, sweat coating her gorgeous body and gleaming off her chiseled face.

"Lil?"

"Huh?" She blinked back to the present, but her stomach sank at the loss of the image. "Sorry."

"Where were you?" Rain asked, waving a hand in front of her face.

"Nowhere."

"You know," Rain said. "I really don't think Audrey's here."

Lillian tried to laugh it off. "That's fine. Whatever."

Rain looked concerned. "If she does come, you won't leave, will you?"

Carmen squeezed Lillian's hand. "No, she won't leave. Right, Lil?"

Lillian cleared her throat and did her best to speak loudly over the music and laughing women.

"I'm not upset, okay? I just don't know if I want to see her again." In fact, she knew she didn't want to see her again, mainly because she did. But try explaining that one to anyone when she didn't understand it herself.

"Why not?" Rain asked. "I mean, if you don't mind my asking."

"I'm just not ready for more. And I think that's what she wants."

"Get outta here!" Rain said. "Audrey McCarthy finally interested in someone."

"She's not interested," Carmen said. "She's playing."

"You don't know that for sure," Rain said.

"It doesn't take a genius to figure it out," Carmen said. "McCarthy plays. She has fun. End of story. Lillian was probably a good lay."

"Were you?" Rain asked.

Lillian shook her head, refusing to answer. She hadn't been a good lay. It had been totally one-sided. Was that why Audrey wanted more? To get to the other side? Was it a game? She feared it was, which was why she didn't want to deal with it. The game of life was difficult enough without having a wild woman on her heels or in her bed.

"It's almost Midnight Room time," Rain said, clapping her hands. "I promise I didn't pay to have your name called this time."

They all looked to Carmen. "What? Like I would? Please."

"So you can relax." Rain patted her leg as the festivities began. "Just enjoy your night out."

But it was easier said than done. Lillian again scanned the club, sinking lower in her chair. The lights dimmed. "Let's Get It On" began to play. The strobes searched along with the spotlights as the deejay spoke. Women cheered. Rain went wild, waving her hand in the air, begging to be chosen.

Lillian downed her drink, feeling the déjà vu from hell. She could just hear her name being called over the loudspeakers. Lillian Gray. Lillian Gray. Lillian Gray.

She plugged her ears, hoping to douse the memory. She recalled the way everyone cheered, stared, and egged her on. The way the bright light had sought her out and illuminated everything she felt inside.

She didn't want to be here. It was a mistake to have come. She closed her eyes and dropped her hands, trying to breathe deep.

And then the first name was called.

"Lillian Gray!"

Lillian's mind went blank and then fuzzy. She sank into herself and saw the world from another angle. Rain was looking at her, complete shock on her face. Carmen had stood, beer angrily grasped in her hand. People were cheering; the music continued.

The spotlight found her and she felt like she was burning under its glare.

"Lil." Rain was in her face, tapping her cheek. "Lil."

Carmen was in her ear. "We didn't do this, Lil. We didn't do this."

The next name was called.

"Audrey McCarthy!"

Lillian stood on wobbly legs. This wasn't happening. It couldn't be happening. The knots inside twisted and twisted, wrapping up her internal organs, cutting off her blood supply.

She was going to faint. Oh God, she was going to faint right there onto the floor in the middle of "Let's Get It On."

She leaned on Carmen, almost unable to stand.

And then she saw Audrey's face move through the parting crowd. That gorgeous face with that jet-black hair and black-as-ink eyes. She came at her in slow motion, a look of pure desperation on her face. There was no cocky smile or confident walk. There was just a strong stride headed right for her with nonthreatening purpose.

Suddenly, she wanted to be in her arms. She wanted Audrey to take her away.

"Audrey," she whispered as she reached her.

"Please," Audrey said in return. "Talk to me."

Audrey touched Lillian's arms oh so gently, looking deep into her eyes.

"Please."

But Lillian nearly sank to the ground, the heat from everyone's stare getting to her.

"Take me away from all this."

CHAPTER SIX

Y ou okay?" Audrey asked over the loud music. Lillian stumbled along after her, her legs having gone numb with fright.
She shook her head. "No, but I will be."
Audrey seemed to like the sound of that because she smiled and draped a secure-feeling arm around Lillian's shoulder. Lillian felt strangely safe in her arms, protected somehow, but from what she didn't know. It seemed ridiculous because the whole thing she'd feared had come true. Audrey had found her and was leading her toward the Midnight Room. How she could feel safe at that moment was beyond her. And yet she did.

Audrey moved them through the crowd expertly, shouting at people to move, keeping them at bay with her free arm. Despite feeling safe, Lillian was briefly reminded of a lioness protecting her prey so she could finish off the kill alone. Was this what was happening? Was Audrey merely leading her away so she could have her all to herself? Or was she as sincere as she had seemed just moments ago?

Lillian was so confused and so weak, she just wanted to stop thinking. She just wanted to lie down, to pretend she'd never stepped foot in the club at all, yet it all still spun around her like a maddening carnival of sorts. Around and around it went. Lights, strobes, lasers, music, laughs.

She leaned into Audrey, not for affection but for need. Audrey mistook the gesture and pulled her closer, nodding at the decjay as if to say, "Yeah, this is my girl." As uncomfortable as that was to Lillian, the comments from the surrounding women were even worse. They wanted Audrey and they didn't seem to care that Lillian was right there with her, causing Lillian to feel embarrassed and completely ignored. It was as if she didn't matter or even exist at all.

What a wonderful feeling to pile onto the near-debilitating anxiety she already felt.

Audrey, however, didn't seem to notice any of it—the women's comments or Lillian's reaction. She just kept plowing through, her sole focus on getting to the Midnight Room. It was as if it was her mission in life. Grab woman. Walk directly to Midnight Room.

"Almost there," she said.

Lillian thought about stopping and turning to leave. She didn't want to be another plaything or another conquest, but Audrey felt so good, so strong, and the club seemed so out of control and crazy. The Midnight Room, much to her trepidation, would have to do for now.

They walked between the glass partitions and directly up to the woman Audrey called Beastly. Music pounded around her, the song having gone from "Let's Get it On" to a popular Pink track.

"Wait," Beastly said loudly, holding up her hand.

"No sex, got it," Audrey said, just as loudly back. She didn't release Lillian as she stared directly into Beastly's face.

"Apparently not. I shouldn't even let you in. After last time—"

"Aw, fuck off." Audrey shouldered past her and off they went through the tassels and into the red velvet room. It would have been warm and somewhat peaceful if Beastly hadn't followed them inside.

"No sex." Beastly pointed at them like a scolding teacher. "I know you know that," she said, directing the comment toward Audrey. "But you girls never listen."

"Look at her," Audrey said, pointing to Lillian. "She can hardly walk."

Beastly started to speak but then clammed up when she took a look at Lillian. After a brief pause, and much to her obvious chagrin, she left them alone.

"Finally," Audrey said as she sat Lillian down on the couch and knelt at her knees. "Are you sure you're okay?" She lightly touched her face and smiled so sweetly.

Lillian had never seen her like this. So soft and kind. God, she could really melt in her hands if this kept up.

"I think I will be." She had to look away from the dark eyes, afraid she'd get lost in them, never to return.

"You didn't look so good out there. I thought you were going to pass out."

"I felt like it." She ran her hand through her hair. The room seemed considerably warmer than it had before.

"Do you want some water?"

Lillian shook her head. "No, I'm fine. Really."

"Are you sure? Because I could run to the bar and get some."

"No, that's not necessary. I'm okay."

Audrey sank to a knee and rubbed her hand. "What happened back there?"

Lillian considered how much to tell her. "I just got a little freaked out."

"Because of the drawing?"

Lillian closed her eyes. "Yes. And because…"

"It was me."

She opened her eyes. "Yes."

"Here you are trying to avoid me and I go and do this. Bet you're pissed." Audrey sighed and clenched a fistful of dark hair in frustration.

"I'm not pissed." She wasn't. Being pissed off was the furthest thing from her mind.

"You have every right to be."

"Well, I'm not. I just—I guess I just don't understand."

Audrey released her hair and fingered through it. Lillian could tell she was nervous. It was written in her eyes and evident in the pulse jumping in her neck.

"I just didn't know any other way to get you alone. All I wanted to do was talk."

Lillian wanted desperately to reach out and touch her, but she didn't dare. "I—I don't like this place very much. It makes me… anxious."

"I'm sorry. God, I must really seem like an ass. Honestly, I thought you'd bolt the second your name was called."

Lillian laughed softly. "I would've if I could've."

Audrey took her hand and held it in front of her. For a second, Lillian thought she might propose marriage. The idea made her laugh with nerves. She covered her mouth, making herself stop.

"What?" Audrey asked, smiling.

"Nothing."

"You can tell me."

"No, I can't. It's stupid."

"Come on. Please?"

Lillian gathered her thoughts as best she could with Audrey so close. She looked so damn good in the tight gray T-shirt, faded jeans, and boots. And she smelled like heaven itself.

"Your position."

"My position?" Audrey looked down at herself and laughed. Then she quickly stood.

"I thought you were going to propose," Lillian said, trying to keep the mood light.

"Yeah, well. We wouldn't want that, would we?" She cleared her throat and chose to sit next to Lillian on the couch. The romantic lighting kissed the edge of her jaw and reflected off her hair. The muscles in her arm moved as she rested it along the back of the sofa. She was absolutely breathtaking, and Lillian felt light-headed again.

"Of course, I would've almost done anything in order to talk to you," Audrey said, smiling.

Lillian felt her face fall. They needed to talk. This little charade in a romantic velvet room couldn't go on.

"I can't see you, Audrey," she said softly. "I'm sorry, but I can't." She stared at her hands as they twisted into each other, much like how her organs had felt.

Audrey studied her for a long moment. "Why not?" she asked just as softly in return.

Lillian sighed. "I just can't."

"Because?"

"Because I don't do relationships."

Audrey threw her head back and laughed.

"What's so funny?" Lillian asked.

"You're worried about a relationship?" She sounded cocky again, sure of herself and of what she intended to have.

"Well, I don't know. What is it that you want?"

"I can assure you, it's not a relationship."

Lillian chewed her lower lip, Carmen's words heating her mind. What happened to the soft, sincere Audrey who was here just seconds ago?

"Because you're a player, right?"

Audrey's smile vanished. She blinked and glanced away, obviously distraught. "I guess that's the term these days."

She sounded offended, yet she had admitted to it.

"So you want to play me, then?" Lillian was regaining some of her strength, some of her nerve. She had to know.

Audrey shifted. "No."

"Then what?"

"I just thought we could, you know—"

"Have sex?" Lillian asked.

"Is that so terrible?"

"It is for me." Lillian stood, slowly but firmly. She was ready to go now.

Audrey joined her. "Why? Tell me why it's so terrible."

"Because I don't do that."

"But you don't do relationships either."

"No, I don't."

"Then what do you do?"

"Not this." She tried to walk away, but Audrey held her hand.

"I won't do anything you don't want me to do."

"Then where's the fun for you?"

"Are you kidding? I had a great time the other night. Didn't you?" Audrey looked completely serious.

Lillian pulled away, afraid to answer.

Audrey gently caught her chin and turned it so Lillian would look at her. "Tell me you didn't."

"I don't have to tell you anything."

"You did enjoy it. I know you did. I could feel it in your every touch, hear it in your every word, taste it in your kiss."

"Audrey, I—" But Audrey leaned in and captured her mouth in an impossibly soft kiss.

Lillian reacted with alarm at first, but as soon as she felt the soft, warm lips, she melted, allowing Audrey to kiss her further, to seek her with her hot tongue. Lillian clung to her, felt the rippling muscles in her back and then a rush of heat came, nearly knocking her right off her feet. It gathered in her center, pulsed at her flesh. It was as if Audrey's tongue was stroking her down there, swirl after swirl after swirl.

"Audrey," she whispered. "I c—"

"Shh."

Audrey lifted her and carried her to the couch. She sat with Lillian straddling her lap. The next kiss came before Lillian could protest. It deepened quickly with Audrey knotting her hand in the base of Lillian's hair, holding her to her. The sensation caused another flood of arousal to rush between Lillian's legs. So much so that she began to gyrate against Audrey's thigh.

"Yes, baby. Oh, yes," Audrey whispered, running her hands up Lillian's back as she sucked on her neck. Lillian moaned, the hot mouth feeling so good on her awakening skin. She called out softly as her eyes threatened to fall closed.

"I think—"

"Shh," Audrey protested.

"But—"

"Don't think."

Audrey nibbled just below her jaw, and Lillian lost it. She wrapped her arms around Audrey's head and moved her hips faster, loving the way Audrey's firm thigh felt between her legs.

Oh God, oh God. It felt so good. Don't let it stop. Just please don't let it stop.

She moved quicker, harder, unable to stop. Audrey encouraged her, trailing her short nails down her back, running them up and down and up and down, oh so painfully gentle. Then she moved her talented hands forward and caressed her taut breasts, pinching her nipples oh so slightly.

"Oh fuck yes, Lillian," Audrey said. "Look into my eyes."

Lillian moaned and looked down into her eyes. The black irises were churning with passion, mirroring Lillian's every move. She saw fire in there, wanting, yearning, and something else. Something else entirely. What was it? Lillian couldn't place it, but it made her feel warm and safe and wanted. It sent her over the edge, and she came hard atop her, riding her leg and falling apart in her arms. She kept her cries soft and throaty, her eyes clenched in a last effort to grasp control.

Audrey spoke to her, encouraged her, loved every second. Lillian couldn't allow herself to make sense of the words, for she knew at once what she'd done and with whom. The last time she'd come like that had been with Holly. In their bed. In their home. Safe and secure.

This was not Holly and she wasn't at home.

Lillian caught her breath as she inhaled the sweet scent of Audrey's hair. Audrey's face and hands were warm, but they were not what she needed. Had they been what she wanted? She refused to answer her own question, instead unwrapping herself from Audrey quickly.

"I have to go," she said, carefully standing.

Audrey stood as well, completely flustered. "No, you don't."

"Yes, I do." Lillian straightened her hair and smoothed her clothes. Her body was trembling, still craving the spent climax.

"Oh, of course you do," Audrey said, raising and dropping her hands. "Any time we experience any kind of intimacy, you have to go."

Lillian clenched her jaw, the words stinging. "Then it should come as no surprise."

"Well, it does."

"That's not my fault."

Audrey touched her hand. "You really don't have to go. We have time. We could still have some more fun."

"I told you I'm not interested in fun."

"What do you call what just happened? A bad time?"

"I call it a mistake."

Audrey flopped back down onto the couch. "You're unbelievable."

"So are you."

"Why? Because I want more of you?"

"Yes. Because you just want to get off with me, nothing more." Lillian turned away, knowing she'd said too much.

"Whoa, wait a minute. You said you didn't want more."

"I need to go."

Audrey stood and stumbled into her path. "Wait a minute. Is that what this is about? You wanting more with me?" Her eyes flashed with curiosity.

Lillian couldn't hold her gaze. "No. And even if I did, it absolutely wouldn't be with someone like you."

"Right, because I'm a player."

Lillian took another step. Audrey mirrored it.

"Why can't you just admit you want me too?" Audrey asked.

"I have to go."

"Is it because the feeling scares you? Because I scare you? Well, you scare me too, but I'm not running."

Lillian pushed past her and hurried through the tasseled doorway.

Audrey was asking too many questions. Getting too close to the answers she'd rather not face. She had to run. Far and fast.

She had to get away.

Far away from Audrey McCarthy.

CHAPTER SEVEN

I don't understand," Audrey said, bending her knees for her twentieth freestanding squat. "Why is she running from me?" She continued on quickly to twenty-five and then stopped to wipe her face with her towel. Olivia stopped along with her, shaking her legs out.

"She didn't say?"

They were doing cross fit again, this time indoors at Audrey's favorite gym. It was Sunday afternoon, and Audrey still couldn't shake the memory of the night before.

"Well, sort of. She said I'm a player."

Olivia snorted. "Well, duh, there's your answer."

"But she says she doesn't want a relationship either."

Olivia wiped her face and neck and then set her jaw as they started in on another set of twenty-five. "Correction. She doesn't want one with you."

"You think?"

"Uh-huh. But she definitely wants one."

"How do you know?"

"Because she's a woman, honey. A careful woman. Trust me, she wants love. So you better run for the hills."

Audrey considered this as a few men moved in closer, wanting to stretch on the mats. Audrey didn't care, though; she was all about Lillian. Nothing would stop her conversation.

"She wasn't careful that first night. She was fierce and in control and so damn confident," Audrey said.

"That was a ruse. All women need to let loose now and then. She used you to do it."

"She used me?"

"Oh sure." Olivia began to gasp for breath as they neared the teen mark, her purple tank top soaked through. "She'd probably heard you were up for some fun, so she let loose. Kept things one-sided, though, so she couldn't get too close."

Olivia stopped at twenty, but Audrey kept going, needing to feel a real burn. "How do you know this?" she said, clenching her teeth as the burn came.

"Women 101, silly. And, oh yeah, I am one."

"I'm one too, and I never would've come up with that shit."

"You're not a woman, honey. You're a player."

Audrey collapsed onto the bench behind them and swatted Olivia with her towel.

Olivia laughed at her own comment for far too long. "I'm sorry. I had to say it."

"Go ahead. Everyone else does." Frankly, she was getting tired of hearing it. She eyed the men on the floor who were trying hard not to make eye contact. She almost dared one of them to call her a player too.

"If the shoe fits." Olivia laughed.

"Whatever."

Olivia sat next to her, taking a quick breather. "You're still coming to the track meet, right?"

Audrey nodded. "Wouldn't miss it for the world." Once or twice a month, she worked for a program at the local schools where disabled children got to compete in athletics. She'd been doing it for a while now, and she absolutely loved it.

"Good, those kids love you."

"I love them."

"You love something?" She slung an arm around her shoulder. "Who woulda thought?"

Audrey shook it off. "I'm not that bad, Olivia. Even you say so."

"Honey, to see you work with those kids, you'd never know just how bad you are."

"Thanks. Now can we get back to my crisis?"

"You mean about the woman?"

"Yes."

"Well, tell me something, stud. Have you slept with anyone else since you've met her?"

Audrey stood and groaned. "Olivia, please."

"Just answer the question."

"Why?"

"You have, haven't you?"

"So what?"

"See what I mean? You're all about you."

"I'm not committed to her."

"No, but most people, when they meet someone they really like, they tend to focus on them and worry less about getting others into their bed."

Audrey strode across the gym, irritation tickling her skin. Olivia was making sense, and she didn't like it. Not one little bit. When she reached the hand weights, she grabbed two twenties and began doing bicep curls. They had fifty of these, and she was determined to go hard.

"I'm not committed to anyone," she repeated as Olivia approached and grabbed two tens.

"No, you're not. And that's exactly why she's steering clear."

"She likes me, though. I know it."

"Physically, yes. Honey, who wouldn't?"

"No, it's more than that."

"And you're okay with it?"

Audrey focused on herself in the mirror. Was she okay with that? "No. Yes. I don't know."

"Well, you need to find out. Otherwise, just get the girl out of your head."

Audrey knew she was right. But she also knew that getting Lillian out of her head was an impossibility.

"She was different last night. She was…vulnerable."

Olivia looked over at her with concern. "And…"

"And I felt like I needed to protect her."

"Audrey, are you sure you're not falling for this girl?"

Audrey laughed, causing the woman next to them to stare. She didn't, however, answer the question.

"Uh-huh."

"It was just different is all. I liked it. I felt like she showed me a piece of herself. A hidden piece."

"And you still just want to fuck her?"

"I don't want to fuck her. I want to…"

"What? Make love?"

The woman about dropped her curling bar, and Olivia gave her the evil eye. "Do you mind? My friend's in a crisis here."

"I don't know, Olivia. Yeah, I guess. I just know I want to be with her."

"More than a few times?"

She set down the weights and shrugged. "I don't know. I guess if it goes well."

"So your perfect fantasy is to have this girl, mind, soul, and body, but only until you get tired?"

Audrey looked at her in shock. "No, not like that."

Olivia set down her weights. "I think it's exactly like that."

"Well, what if things went bad? It would be good that we weren't attached, right?"

"Audrey, honey, she's never going to go for this."

"No?"

"No."

"Then what do I do?"

"You really want to keep seeing her?"

"Yes."

"Really really?" Olivia asked.

"Yes."

"Then there's only one thing you can do."

"What's that?"

"Change."

Audrey laughed again.

"Then you can kiss her good-bye."

Audrey paced, avoiding the weights. She wanted to throw them through the damned mirror. Why the hell couldn't she have it her way? She didn't want to hurt Lillian. Had no intention of doing so. As long as they were honest, no one would get hurt.

"I'm going to go after her."

"You're falling for her."

This time, Audrey did pick up the weights. But she replaced them for a heavier set and started in on her remaining set. "I am not."

"Are too."

"Shut up."

"Gladly. And when you get rejected, I won't even say 'I told you so.'"

Audrey pumped the weights, staring at the veins in her neck as she did so. She was going to go after Lillian. She was going to go after her with full force, no holds barred. She had to get Lillian to see how much she wanted her.

It didn't take changing her ways to do it. Lillian knew who she was, and she'd accept that. Why couldn't Audrey be who she was but be caring and attentive at the same time? Did sleeping with different women make her an ogre somehow? She was still a good person. A caring person. She just had to get Lillian to see that.

With her set finished, she caught her breath, stretched her arms, and glanced at her watch. She knew just where to start too.

"I gotta go," she said hurriedly to Olivia.

"What?"

"Got something I gotta do."

"Like hell. You never bail on a workout." She set down her weights and placed her hands on her hips.

"I am today," Audrey said.

"What about my workout?" She looked incredulous and so not happy.

"Finish these, then do your sit-ups and pull-ups. Then do your time on the treadmill. Incline this time. Fifteen minutes. No cheating."

She found her small sport backpack with the strings and pulled it on over her shoulders.

"You're really leaving, Audrey McCarthy?"

"Yes, I am."

"Well, screw you." Olivia turned and sought her water bottle.

"You'll be okay."

"I'm not paying you for this session, you know."

"You haven't paid me in over a year."

"Well, that's beside the point."

"Bye, Olivia."

Audrey turned to leave. As she pushed her way past the gawking woman, she heard Olivia say, "I hope she's worth it!"

❖

Audrey pulled into the church parking lot ten minutes before evening services. Her palms were sweaty and her mind raced with possibilities. Could Lillian see her already? Would she flee the second she did see her?

How was she going to go about this? She'd never chased a woman before, and never had she set foot in a church. Just what the hell was she doing?

Her blood pulsed in her head as she quickly found a parking space near the back. She turned off the engine and sank lower in her seat, terrified her cover would be blown before she even got close to the church. But luckily, a couple dozen people milled from their cars to head inside, paying her no mind. They moved like calm insects, drawn to the light. Slow, peaceful, focused. She cracked her knuckles and checked her reflection in the rearview mirror. She supposed she looked nice enough in dark slacks and a gray long-sleeved oxford. But she felt a little too stuffy, so she rolled up the sleeves to her forearms and untucked the shirt a little.

After breathing into her hand to check her breath, she inhaled deeply and stepped from her Jeep. Her hair was a bit windblown, but she drove her fingers into it, taming it as best she could. She'd never been so nervous before, and she tried to laugh it off, but the attempt failed and only brought her unwanted attention from a couple nearby.

"Sorry," she said, feeling like an ass. To her relief, they only smiled and moved farther ahead. Nerves got the better of her, and Audrey quickened her pace, afraid of being late. Hopefully, she could squeeze into the back somewhere and watch Lillian from afar. Maybe catch her on her way out. Maybe go somewhere for a talk. Maybe have coffee.

Coffee? Since when did she go have coffee?

She shook the thought away. Okay, maybe not. But they would have to find somewhere to talk and hopefully do a little more.

The stairs to the main entrance were grand and quite steep. She walked up them with a surprising spring in her step as if she were a kid headed for the Easter egg hunt after Sunday service. She wished she'd been able to do that as a child. She wished she'd been able to do a lot of things. The closest she'd come to church was her uncle Dale's funeral. She remembered because her father had held her hand during the service and left right afterward, never to be seen again. She could still hear her mother blaming her for his absence. And she would still do it today; Audrey had no doubt.

A large smiling man greeted her politely at the big arched doors, having no clue into her psyche. He seemed genuinely happy, and she was glad for him. A fucked-up mother and father probably didn't play into his background. Or maybe it did. Maybe that's why he was at church rather than at some bar. Maybe he was trying his best to carry on in a positive way. She wished she could do that.

She forced a smile in return and stepped inside. The feeling was immediate. Warm, kind, peaceful. The smell of polished wood and old books. Soft music came from the front where a man with an acoustic guitar sat on a stool strumming and humming to his heart's content. People stood in the pews, shaking hands and talking quietly. Most seemed at ease and were eagerly friendly to one another. As if it had only been days since they'd last spoken. Audrey felt a little out of place, and she sank quickly into a pew near the back. She picked up a hymn book and began flipping through the pages. She recognized none of the songs but hadn't expected to. She continued to study it, hoping it would help her blend in.

Her mother had never attended church, and her father— she didn't know much about him. But she could remember the neighborhood kids all going every Sunday, and somehow she'd felt left out, like maybe she was missing something. "Spiritual guidance" was how one girl had put it. Audrey had none. And it seemed to this day, she lacked the gist of it.

The man playing the guitar stopped and motioned for everyone to take their seats. Audrey returned the book, grateful to have her thoughts back on the present. Lillian was nowhere to be seen. Maybe she didn't attend the night service. Maybe Audrey was too late. A part of her was disappointed, but another part of her was relieved. This place was making her think about her childhood and about internal peace in general. Two things she'd rather not ponder.

She wanted to rise to leave but felt glued to her seat. If she stood, people would see, and everyone seemed so nice. She didn't want to be rude. No, she couldn't be rude, so now she was obligated to stay. The pastor started in with greetings, trapping her for good.

"Shit," she whispered. She fingered the red velvet of the pew and thought about the Midnight Room. Who knew two totally different places would have something so romantic in common? She wondered what people would think if they knew.

She glanced up as someone entered. It was Lillian, and she was sliding down her pew, completely oblivious. Audrey froze, unsure what to do. All her suave comments were out the door. They just fluttered away like butterflies in a breeze. She swallowed hard as Lillian looked up and caught sight of her.

Her face said it all. A good dose of shock and then the bloom of anger.

She stalked toward Audrey as the lights dimmed. She sat in a huff and leaned in.

"What the hell are you doing here?" she whispered angrily.

A spotlight focused on the man with the guitar again as he and a small child began to sing. The congregation stood and sang along with them. Audrey tried to stand, but Lillian gripped her arm and kept her sitting.

"Answer me!" Lillian continued to whisper, her blue eyes wide.

"I came to see you."

"I don't want to see you."

"Yes, you do," Audrey said.

"No, I don't!"

"Well, I'm not leaving unless you promise to talk to me."

"There's nothing to say."

"There's a lot to say. I want to see you, to be with you. I know you want it too. You're just afraid I'll hurt you. But I don't see how that's possible if we're both honest."

Lillian released her arm and looked away. Audrey could sense her racing heart and smell her light perfume. She wanted to hold her hand and lean in to gently kiss her. She wanted to slowly unbutton her cream-colored blouse and kiss the tip of the lace of her camisole. She wanted to hear her moan again, hear her strangled cries of passion as she came on top of her.

"How dare you come here," Lillian said, shaking. She looked directly at Audrey and repeated her words. "How dare you."

Audrey took her hand. This was going wrong. So terribly wrong. "I had to see you. You just don't understand."

"I understand perfectly. You're stalking me now."

Audrey laughed, truly offended. "I'm not stalking you, for fuck's sake. I just want to talk. And you know, you never considered that I may just want to go to church."

Lillian scoffed and removed her hands. "Hell would freeze over first."

Audrey could tell she wasn't reaching her. Lillian was pissed, seriously so. And she was losing her only chance.

Audrey stood and held out her hand. "Come with me."

"Where?"

"To talk."

"No."

"If you do, I'll leave." She raised an eyebrow, knowing that might do the trick. Lillian wanted her gone.

Lillian seemed to think for a moment, and as the song ended, she stood, refused Audrey's hand, but led them out of the church and back into the twilight. She didn't stop until she reached her car, unlocked it, and threw in her purse. Then she turned to Audrey and glared at her.

"Do you know why I come here?"

Audrey blinked, confused. "To—"

"I come here because it's the only peaceful and meaningful thing I have in my life. My faith is all I have. Without it, I'm lost. Without it, I drink. Did you know that?"

Audrey pressed her lips together, her own wants and needs instantly meaningless. "No."

"I didn't think so."

"I—I'm sorry, I had no idea."

"Well, now you do."

She looked away, sighing into the oncoming night. "And to know that you came here, interrupting my peace and tranquility only so you could try and talk me into bed with you—"

"Wait, no." Audrey shook her head. "It's not like that." Audrey knew something had switched on inside her the moment Lillian blurted out her confession. She saw her heart then, her fears, her faith, her vulnerability. She'd never seen or felt anything so beautiful. So raw. She reached out and touched her face. She skimmed her pale skin with the backs of her fingers, feeling the warmth of her anger where her cheek crimsoned slightly.

"I didn't mean to upset you."

Lillian closed her eyes. "So talk, then. Tell me what you want."

"I want to see you," Audrey said.

"I've already told you, no."

"I'll keep asking, then."

She opened her eyes but she didn't pull away. "Why?"

"Because I don't believe you when you say no."

"Well, believe me now."

Audrey leaned in closer. "Kiss me."

"What?"

"Kiss me and tell me you don't feel anything."

"No."

"Then I'll keep trying."

"Why?"

"Because I like you." Audrey smiled. "And I know you like me too."

"I do not."

"So kiss me."

"Right here?"

"Yeah, why not? No one's around. Of course, we could go back inside and do it there if you prefer."

"Shut up," Lillian breathed. "God, you're the biggest pain in the ass."

"I'll take that as a compliment."

"You would."

"Are you going to kiss me?"

"If I do, you'll promise to leave me alone?"

"If you say you don't feel anything."

Lillian seemed to think long and hard. There was an awkward pause as she stared at first the church, then the awakening street lamp, and then at her feet. Finally, she said, "Okay."

Audrey slowly came around the open car door and slipped a hand around her waist. With her other hand she smoothed back her hair and gently stroked her face.

"You are so beautiful, Lillian," she said. "So delicately beautiful. And you don't even know it, do you?" She lightly kissed her cheek, her lower jaw, and then her lips. When she heard and felt Lillian inhale sharply with desire, she kissed her fully on the lips, tugging slightly and sucking here and there.

She groaned at the taste of her, forcing herself to remain calm and not deepen the kiss. Lillian moaned too, and she seemed to relax in her arms, nearly going limp. Audrey could feel her skin alight with fire and her heart beat against her chest. She kept kissing her, kept tasting that sweet, sweet nectar until her head spun with her growing passion.

Lillian made a whimpering sound as she pulled away slightly. She breathed, "I don't feel anything."

Audrey didn't stop, knowing it wasn't true. "No?"

Lillian kissed her again. "No."

"Then we'd better stop."

Another long kiss, this one Audrey's doing.

"Yes," Lillian said.

"Come on. Let's go to my place," Audrey said, unable to take much more without totally losing control.

Lillian halted. "What? No."

"Come on. Don't be ridiculous. We both feel this."

"I'm being ridiculous?"

"Yes."

"This whole thing is ridiculous!"

"Really?" Audrey kissed her again. Deeper, with more passion. She held her tightly and refused to let go. Not until Lillian went soft in her arms and returned the kiss.

"Is this what you want?" Lillian finally asked when they pulled apart. "You want me kissing you back?"

"Yes. Because I know you feel something. Don't you?"

Lillian touched her lips as if to analyze the situation. "Maybe," she said defiantly.

Audrey couldn't help but smile. "Then yes, that's what I like."

"Then get in the car," Lillian said, her voice lowered and more determined.

Audrey hesitated slightly but then eagerly started to climb in, thinking they were going to her place.

"In the back," Lillian said. "Hurry."

The backseat wasn't very big, but Lillian scrambled in after her, shoving Audrey against it.

"There," Lillian said after yanking the door closed and pressing the button on her keyless remote. "The doors are locked. You can't get out."

"Why would I want to?"

"Because I'm about to attack you."

"You are?" She grinned as she held Lillian's hips.

"This is what you want, isn't it?" Lillian asked, taking her arms by the wrist to pin them. "Me, like this?"

"I want you any way I can get you."

"Well, this will have to do." She leaned forward and tore open Audrey's shirt.

"Whoa!" Audrey wasn't sure if she should be shocked or totally turned on.

"Sorry, no time to play nice."

"Why do you always say we haven't got time? We have plenty of time."

"No. No, we don't. We only have now."

"What happens after now?"

Lillian was leaning in, nibbling on her neck. Audrey had to fight from closing her eyes and groaning.

"Lillian?"

"Shut up."

"No, I want to know."

She stopped and pulled back. "Can't you just enjoy this?"

"Yes, I should be able to, but honestly, I can't. I want to know."

Lillian sighed. "I change my mind is what."

"You change your mind? You mean you run from me again and say no."

"Yes."

"So we'll repeat the whole cycle."

Lillian looked confused. "You mean this time still wouldn't be enough? You'd still come after me?"

Audrey thought about it, looking into her mesmerizing eyes awash with passion and heat in having just torn her shirt open.

"Oh, yes."

Lillian sighed again and laughed. "Then how is this going to stop, Audrey?"

"Who says it has to?"

"Me."

"But you were just willing…"

"Because I thought this would be the last time."

Audrey felt herself blink with surprise. What was happening here? Tables were turning and she was having a hard time getting on board. "You did it to get rid of me?"

Lillian crawled over her into the front seat.

"Is that why?" Audrey hated the way she sounded. But she couldn't help herself.

Lillian straightened her hair in the rearview mirror. "I can't keep doing this."

Audrey had never had a woman's words hurt her before, but Lillian's nonchalance and admission were punching her in the gut. She felt short of breath and sick, like maybe she might retch. She struggled to open the door and climb out. When she did, she took deep breaths and rested with her hands on her knees.

"Are you okay?" Lillian asked.

Audrey waved her off. "Fine."

"Are you sure?"

Her shirt was hanging loosely from her body, but she didn't care. She focused on a single hanging button and tried to calm herself. She didn't understand what was happening to her. Maybe she was getting ill. She definitely didn't want to be doing it in front of Lillian.

"Get in. I'll drop you home," Lillian said.

"No, it's okay."

Lillian climbed from the car. She rounded the front and came to stand by her side. "Audrey, I'm sorry. I just can't do this anymore. It's not you…well, not really."

Audrey straightened and tried to walk. The pain just kept coming. It was coming directly from Lillian's words and straight into her physically. Relentlessly.

"Please just stop," she said. "Stop talking."

"But I don't want to, you know…hurt you."

Audrey turned, hand on her stomach. "Hurt me? You think I'm sick because of you?"

Lillian seemed at a loss. "Well, yes, I—"

"I'm fine."

"You mean you're not upset?"

"Because of you? No. No one can hurt me like that." She was lying. The pain had Lillian's name written all over it. Signed, stamped, delivered. It was Lillian. She was tearing her insides out, and Audrey hated everything about it.

Lillian appeared stunned. "Forgive me, then. It's just you usually get so upset when I tell you no."

"Yeah, well, I've gotten used to it." She fumbled for her keys in her pocket. She had to get out of there.

"At least let me see you home," Lillian said, following her to her Jeep. "I'll follow you."

"I don't need you to, thanks."

"I'm doing it regardless. Call it penance for showing up at my church."

She hurried back to her car as Audrey climbed into her Jeep, not giving her time to argue. Audrey watched her crank her car and put it in gear. She was waiting for Audrey's move. Another wave of pain came over her as Lillian's words replayed in her mind.

And for the first time ever, Audrey wished like hell that Lillian would just go away.

Chapter Eight

Lillian sped up as Audrey's Jeep quickly rounded corners and sprinted down the straightaways. It was obvious Audrey was trying to lose her, but Lillian was intent on giving chase. She'd hurt Audrey's feelings, and for that she needed to apologize. Sure, it would be easy to turn around and go home. To leave Audrey to fend for herself with her hurt feelings. Hell, Audrey would no doubt leave her alone now. But Lillian just couldn't do it.

She was upset at herself for not handling the situation better, and honestly, she was still turned on. She'd been serious when she'd shoved Audrey against the backseat. She'd wanted her, and when she allowed those feelings to overtake her, there was no stopping her. It had happened twice before, and tonight was no different. She needed to act on it before her conscience got the better of her.

God, she should turn the car around. Right now, before this went any further. Right now, before she saw where Audrey lived. That way she wouldn't be tempted to drive over in the middle of the night to see her. To touch her, to taste her, to take her.

"This is madness," she said, but she didn't stop the car. She kept on driving, chasing Audrey's Jeep, swerving past clueless drivers who had no idea what she was chasing or why.

If they knew, she'd stop to ask them because she had little clue herself. She only knew her body was demanding she follow, and her heart was demanding she apologize.

Audrey's Jeep finally slowed and pulled into a large apartment complex. Lillian gunned the engine and pulled in after her, only to find Audrey's Jeep awkwardly parked up onto the curb with the lights killed. Audrey wasn't inside.

Panicked, Lillian parked, climbed out, and began looking around. The complex was full of silent cars and quiet lights, both telling her nothing. Finally, she heard someone cuss as she dropped her keys. It was Audrey and she was heading up a flight of stairs.

"Audrey!" She hurried after her, afraid she'd go inside and lock her out. "Audrey, wait." She sprinted up the stairs and clung to Audrey as she hastily unlocked the door.

"Go away," Audrey said, shouldering her off. "I don't need any help."

"Yes, you do," Lillian breathed. "And I need to talk to you."

"I'm not in the mood." She opened the door and stepped inside, turning on Lillian. "Good night." She tried to close the door, but Lillian jammed her foot against it.

"Don't you do this to me, Audrey McCarthy. Not after the way you've come after me. You owe me more than that."

Audrey's drawn face showed nothing. She stood there holding the door with her shirt hanging open, hair disheveled, taut abs moving as she breathed. She was a goddess, even like this.

"Please."

Audrey finally released the door and turned to walk inside. She did so silently, leaving Lillian on her own. Lillian followed carefully, closing and locking the door behind her. Audrey disappeared farther into the apartment, and Lillian looked around, more than curious.

She saw a small kitchen, a dinette, and a living room. All were connected, giving the apartment a feeling of open space. The place felt warm, lived in, and Lillian at once felt calm and secure. What had she been so afraid of? A part of her had imagined Audrey living in some sort of sex dungeon with whips and chains and handcuffs and a plethora of leather-clad women lounging about awaiting her every command.

But it was just an apartment. An average, comfortable apartment. Not overly clean, not overly messy. It was just a home.

She sat on the couch and noted the scent of lavender. She thought about cuddling up there and drifting to sleep with Audrey spooning her from behind. How nice that would be sometime. But Audrey reemerged wearing gray sweatpants and a T-shirt.

"What do you want?" Audrey asked, her forehead creased with obvious annoyance.

"Why don't you come sit?"

"I don't want to."

"Well, how are you feeling?" She still looked like hell. Like she might pass out or flee at any second. Lillian knew that feeling all too well.

"Fine."

Lillian stood. "Look, Audrey, I know you're not fine. So please stop saying that."

"What do you want me to say?"

"How about the truth? You're angry and hurt because of what I said."

She didn't speak, just stood very still.

"I told you, I'm fine. I just feel a little sick is all."

"I hurt you, didn't I?"

"No."

"I know I did. And for that, I'm sorry. But you said we needed to be honest—"

"Why are you here?" Audrey asked. "I mean, this is obviously the one place you've been trying to avoid."

Lillian moved toward her. "Because I wanted to tell you I was sorry."

"For what?"

"For, you know, saying what I said."

"But it was the truth."

Lillian stopped in front of her. She looked into her eyes and saw searching and pain. It was so evident she had hurt her. It nearly took her breath away.

"Yes."

"Then there's nothing more to say."

"But I wanted to be with you."

Audrey searched her face as if she disbelieved but wanted desperately not to.

"I did, Audrey. I do."

"But—"

"But nothing."

"You mean you haven't changed your mind yet."

Lillian blinked, surprised at how correct she was. "No."

"You want me."

"Yes."

"Here. In my home."

"Yes."

Lillian reached out to her to touch her face, but Audrey caught her by the wrist.

"I don't want to think about anything," she said, deadly serious. "Or talk about anything."

"Then we won't."

Lillian reached up with her other hand and touched her face. Audrey angled her head into it and closed her eyes. But when she opened them, she looked hungry and focused. She tugged Lillian into her and kissed her deeply, fiercely. So passionately Lillian had to pry herself away just to breathe.

"My God," Lillian said. "You sure know how to kiss."

Audrey grinned slightly and tugged on her again. "Then this time, don't pull away."

Their lips met again, and Lillian melted into her, loving every tug of her lips, every shot of her slick tongue. She moaned with delight when Audrey kept kissing her, unrelenting, like a starving being.

Lillian felt completely hopeless, powerless to fight her should she want to. But she didn't care. This was what she came for.

Audrey released her wrist and lifted her with ease. She carried her into the bedroom and set her on the unmade bed. She eased her back onto the fluffy white duvet and kissed her again, this time capturing her completely, swirling her tongue around and around inside her mouth.

Lillian arched up into her, loving the feel of her muscular body atop her. She wrapped her legs around her and reached for her ass.

"You want me," Audrey said again, lifting herself to stare down into her.

"Yes. God, yes."

Audrey's eyes flashed with need, and she tore open Lillian's shirt and fastened herself to her neck. Lillian gasped in surprise and then in ecstasy as Audrey's hot mouth devoured her. First her neck and then her chest, and finally, oh God, finally her breasts, where Audrey teased through the clothing. But then Lillian's camisole was torn and thrown aside, and her bra was unlatched quickly with masterful hands. Soon her bare breasts were ready, and Audrey took them mercilessly, first one and then the other, sucking on them hard and licking them long.

Lillian cried out and clung to her head, loving every second. Loving how she seemed to suck the pleasure right out of her through the tips of her nipples, and yet more always came. And more and more and more, each wave better than the one before.

It left Lillian panting with need, pleading for more. Audrey knew it; it was evident in the way she began to nibble on her nipples, holding them captive with her teeth while flicking them with her tongue.

"Audrey, please," Lillian begged her.

"Please, what?"

"Touch me."

"Where? Tell me where."

Lillian opened her eyes and found Audrey looking down at her. Her face was tinged with red and her pulse jumped in her neck. Her eyes were hungrier than ever and flashing with intent. Lillian wanted to remember that look forever.

"Tell me," Audrey repeated.

Lillian, still breathing hard, moved her hands slowly over her body and down to her pulsing center.

Audrey grinned. "That's where?" she said coyly.

Lillian nodded, not trusting her voice. "Mmm-hmm."

"You want my mouth there?"

"Y-yes."

Audrey slowly unfastened her pants and pulled them down. Lillian lifted her hips and helped, Audrey only allowing so much. Once the pants were gone, she kept Lillian's hands at bay by her sides while she lowered herself to her panties.

"These are nice panties," she said. "Not exactly churchgoing panties."

Lillian laughed at her black satin lacy panties and even blushed a little. Audrey hadn't found the best part yet.

"I expected—I expected anything but these."

"I like nice lingerie."

"Yes, you obviously do. And I'm glad you do." She placed gentle kisses on Audrey's thighs, then licked her way up to the crotch of her panties. She pulled back when she realized there was no crotch.

"What the hell? Crotchless?"

Lillian blushed for real this time. "Uh-huh."

"To church?"

"Well, no one sees them at church."

"Why are you wearing crotchless panties?"

Lillian considered making something up, but nothing crazy enough came to mind. So she told her the truth.

"These are what I wear at night."

"Why?"

"So I can touch myself."

This time Audrey blushed. "Oh."

"Every night I do it. And every night, I think about you."

Audrey stared at her. "You think about me?"

"Yes."

She crawled atop her and kissed her hard, this time placing her thigh between her legs and grinding. Lillian clawed her back and arched into her, moving her hips against the motion of her leg.

"Fuck me, Lillian," Audrey said breathlessly into her ear. "Fucking come against me."

Lillian rode against her as Audrey devoured her neck and pumped her harder.

"Fuck yeah, baby. Come. Come so I can put my mouth on you and taste it all."

Lillian clenched her eyes and dug her hands up under Audrey's shirt. She scraped her nails across the rippling muscles and bit her lower lip in hot, maddening pleasure. She came as Audrey licked her ear, telling her all the things she was going to do to her.

She came loudly, calling out to God and everything holy, nearly ripping Audrey apart in the process. Audrey urged her on, licking her ear and biting down on her neck. She cried out as well, Lillian's nails doing a number on her back. But she seemed to like it, laughing in an evil way as if the pain was bad in a very good way.

"You are one hot woman," Audrey said, trailing her way down with kisses. "So responsive."

Lillian sat up on her elbows. She reached for Audrey's T-shirt, but Audrey refused.

"No, no," she said, settling between Lillian's thighs.

"I want to see you. Feel you against me."

"Not now."

Audrey began kissing her thighs again. Gently at first and then with more vigor. Lillian jerked at the feel of her breath and mouth, anticipating each move. She knotted her hands once again in Audrey's hair, and she found herself urging her toward her center.

"You're hot here too," Audrey said, breathing on her bare crotch. She inched out her tongue and eased it into Lillian's folds, lapping at her flesh in slow, long strides.

Lillian gasped and lifted her shoulders off the bed, holding fast to Audrey's head. She was so sensitive now, her clit full and reeling from the climax. Anything at all touching it would send her over, and Audrey's tongue was just, oh God, right there, touching the very tip.

"Audrey," she panted. "Oh God, Audrey. Yes. Right there. Oh, more. Oh God, please more." She tried rocking her hips into her. Tried pulling on her hair. But Audrey held fast, teasing her wickedly.

"Tell me what you want," Audrey said, still teasing with her tongue.

"Touch me," she breathed. "Please."

"Where?"

"There. Where your mouth is."

"I want you to say it."

"Say what? I want you to touch me."

"Tell me you want me to put my mouth on you."

Lillian hesitated slightly. She'd never said such words, not to anyone. She flushed and then saw the look on Audrey's face. She saw the need and the hunger, the pure wanton lust. The words were getting her off. Getting them both off.

Lillian spoke softly, so moved by Audrey's gaze. "I want you to put your mouth on me."

"Louder."

"I want you to put your mouth on me."

"Good, now make me."

Lillian tightened her hands in her hair and tugged her closer.

"Spread me open," Lillian said, desperate.

Audrey laughed wickedly. "Yes, tell me. Tell me how it feels when I bathe you with my tongue." She spread Lillian carefully with her fingers and then plunged with her tongue, lapping full and strong.

The sensation sent Lillian into a tailspin of ecstasy and she came up off the bed again, clinging to Audrey's head.

"Yes, oh yes. Oh fuck yes."

"Feels good?" Audrey asked as she continued.

"Mmm-hmm. So good."

"It can't feel as good as you taste." She licked her some more and then removed her underwear with her teeth. "Those were getting in the way," she said as she came back up. "Now, where was I? Oh yeah, right here." She spread her again, this time further, and snaked out her tongue to flick at her clit.

Lillian bucked at the sensation and cried out, so close to the edge. She moved her hands to clutch at the bedcovers. Her head moved from side to side. Beads of sweat formed on her abdomen and her heart was beating right out of her chest.

Faster and faster Audrey flicked, licking at her clit in an insanely quick and agile motion.

"Audrey," Lillian panted. "Audrey, God. Feels so good. Feels so fucking good."

Audrey moaned into her and then took her clit into her mouth to suck.

Lillian bucked wildly and came all over her, holding her head again and fucking her face, groaning in a guttural way, a primal way.

Audrey stayed with her, wrapping her arms around her hips to hold her tightly, smothering her clit with her mouth, sending her over yet again, this time softer but no less powerful. Lillian could feel herself pushing, pulsing, her body trying to take in and push out at the same time. She wanted more but couldn't stand another touch. She wanted to shout hoarsely for joy but then collapse into tears.

Instead, she lay very still and stared at the ceiling. Audrey came up beside her and stroked her face. She was still fully clothed, so there was no skin-on-skin connection. Lillian looked into her face and saw amusement along with a small spark of compassion.

"You proud of yourself, McCarthy?" Lillian asked, wishing there were stars on the ceiling.

"Would it be horrible of me to say yes?"

"Yes."

"Then no, I'm definitely not proud."

"Then what are you? Amused?"

"I'm…just pretty damn good at the moment, if that's okay."

Lillian pulled the covers up over her, feeling exposed all of a sudden.

"How are you?"

Lillian shrugged. *Emotional. Light-headed. Moved.* "Exhausted, I think."

"I imagine so." Audrey stroked her hair and kissed her softly on the lips. "I've never met a woman so responsive, and, you know, into it."

Lillian wanted to bathe in the bliss she felt, but her mind wouldn't let her. It played instead on the words Audrey had just spoken. She glanced around the room and looked down at the duvet. "Just how many women are we talking about here?"

"What?"

"When you say you've never met someone so responsive, I find that hard to believe. Mainly because I know you've slept with what? Dozens of women?"

Audrey shifted but didn't answer right away. "Why does that matter?"

"So it's dozens, then?"

Audrey pulled away and sat up on her elbow. "Maybe. But it doesn't mean I didn't mean what I said."

"I'm the only one so responsive."

"Yes."

"Ha."

"You are."

"You've had crazy, wild sex, Audrey."

"Maybe."

"So don't bullshit me."

"I'm not. And I don't appreciate the accusation."

Lillian decided to let it go. Audrey was obviously convinced that what Lillian had just shared was something special, if not rare.

Is that why I'm so afraid? Because I secretly agree?

Maybe Audrey didn't have a plethora of crazy lovers after all. But still, there were just so many of them. How could she be anything special?

Lillian's eyes settled on a bra hanging from a knob on the dresser. It was bright red with lace. She had a feeling it wasn't Audrey's, and the thought made her insides twist, but still, she had to ask.

"Whose is that?" She pointed as she sat up and hugged the covers to herself.

Audrey followed her line of sight and rose hurriedly. She tucked the bra into a drawer and slammed it, almost jamming her fingers. "It's nothing. No one's."

Lillian's eyes fell to the top of the dresser where a handful of small pieces of paper were strewn. "What are those?" Some were folded; some were torn. As she rose to stand, she could see that all had writing on them.

Audrey turned and quickly swept them into a drawer.

"Were those phone numbers?" Lillian approached, needing to see. Audrey kept her away though, backing up to the closed drawers.

"It's none of your business."

"Just how many women are there, Audrey?" She looked around the room and noted the unmade bed, the black satin sheet she'd just lain on, the clothes strewn about, the— She looked closer. The satin wrist cuff hanging from the far corner of the bed?

"Oh my God." She felt dirty, used, embarrassed. Panicked, she began searching for her clothes.

"What are you doing?" Audrey asked, her voice high-pitched with nerves.

"I'm getting dressed and I'm getting the hell out of here."

"Why? We were having a good time."

"Because I'm freaking out, Audrey. I'm realizing what I am. And that's just another notch on your well-used bedpost."

"You are not. I've told you that. I—I want more with you."

"How can you say that when you've got women's underwear hanging about, along with numerous phone numbers piled high on your dresser?"

"I just haven't tidied up in a while."

Lillian yanked on her pants and stuffed her panties into her pocket. When she found her bra, she double-checked to make sure it was her own. "I need a shirt. Something to wear home, and preferably one that doesn't belong to a strange woman. I already feel creepy enough having been in that bed."

Audrey pushed off from the dresser angrily. "That's about enough."

"Is it? Did I strike a nerve, Audrey?" She trembled as she tried stupidly to button her shirt.

"You're about to strike my last one."

"Well, I would hate to do that."

"Hey, you're the one who came here."

"Yes, and that was obviously a mistake. I didn't know the damn bed would have a turnstile on it."

Audrey's face was red and her jaw clenched. She angrily pulled off her T-shirt and tossed it at Lillian. "Take this and get out."

Lillian caught the shirt and stared momentarily at Audrey's heaving bare chest. She was still just as gorgeous as ever, with her etched abs and beautiful apple-sized breasts. But Lillian had to let that go. Audrey was into women. A lot of women. And no matter how sweet and sincere she seemed, she was dangerous.

Dear God, what had she done? And where? It might not be a sex dungeon, but it was definitely not an average bedroom with her own things. What was in the drawers? A dozen dildos? Condoms? K-Y Jelly?

She cringed at the thought and tugged on the T-shirt. She tried to ignore Audrey's scent as she strode from the bedroom. "Where's my purse?" she asked when she reached the front door.

"You didn't bring it in."

Lillian reached into her pants and fumbled for her keys. Her heart raced as she considered what to say. "This was a mistake."

"Isn't that what you always think?"

"Well, it was. Is."

"For once, I agree."

"You do?" The words stung harshly, but at least they were on the same page.

"You don't accept me," Audrey said. "You judge me. You're just turning me away again. So you should go." She sounded angry and her eyes were as black as coal and just as cold.

"I—" Lillian wanted to explain but realized she didn't have to. Audrey was who she was, and it would never work out.

"Just go." Audrey pulled open the door and refused to look at her.

Lillian reached out to touch her arm but then thought better of it. She walked out the door without saying good-bye.

❖

Lillian drove home quickly, cursing herself for her stupidity. Never in her life had she been so reckless. She just wanted to get home, shower, and curl up in bed. No more thinking about Audrey McCarthy. No more dreaming, no more touching herself, no more reliving every kiss or every touch. It was time to let it go.

"I screwed up," she said, smacking her steering wheel. She winced at the pain and shook her hand. "I seriously screwed up."

What was wrong with her? Did she need some therapy, for God's sake? It sure sounded like it. Losing your long-time lover for reasons unclear and then sleeping with the city's biggest get-around girl sure sounded like a good reason for therapy. But she knew she'd never go. She *was* a therapist, for God's sake.

What she needed was to get her life back to normal. With Audrey now agreeing that their encounters had been a mistake, maybe she could actually do it. It would be nice to go to the club and not have to worry about anything. She needed to just hang with her friends and at least pretend like things were halfway okay.

But who was she kidding? What she really needed was a damn drink. And as soon as she pulled into the garage and killed her engine, she was off for the second fridge, the one she kept extra soda and water in. The fridge hummed and stung her eyes as she opened it. She felt naughty and stealthy, out in the middle of the garage at night, huddled over in the near darkness digging through her freezer. She found it rather quickly though. A half-full bottle of raspberry vodka. Every once in a while when she would get to missing Holly, she'd come outside and open up the freezer and stare at it for a long moment before returning it to its home next to the frozen Thin Mint Girl Scout cookies. She liked to just hold it in her hand, feel its chill, look at the beautiful clear liquid as she imagined how it would feel to swallow it. First, the freeze and then the beautiful burn. Sip after blissful sip.

Tonight, however, was different. Tonight, she *needed* the alcohol more than she just wanted it.

She walked inside and stood at the kitchen sink. A clean glass sat on the counter near the dish drainer. She opened the bottle and poured herself a swallow. She held it up to the light and studied it.

This would make Audrey McCarthy way less of a threat. This would make her sweet, sincere, monogamous. This would make her the perfect woman for Lillian. Just like Holly, only with more passion. She could down this drink, have herself two or three more, and she could drive right back over there and fuck Audrey's brains out. They could do it all the time. Every night. Three times a day. They could fuck in the Midnight Room, on the floor, on the couch, up against the wall. Then they'd fuck again when they got home. Life would be good. Fun. Audrey liked fun.

She brought the glass to her lips and inhaled. Oh, how she wanted those things. She wanted them so badly. But even if she did swallow the vodka, it didn't change the fact that now Audrey no longer wanted her. She'd blown it for good. She'd opened her big mouth and insulted her. Right in her own home.

So now, even if she took that sip, it would do nothing but make things fuzzy. Take the edges off, make them seem less painful or unimportant. Probably what she needed. God, she could already smell the raspberry, taste that tartness. Just one sip. Just one tiny sip.

But no. A sip wouldn't be enough. It would take the glass. Then another and another, until she was down near the bottom of the bottle. It would be never-ending. A sick cycle just like she and Audrey had fallen into. There would never be a good ending. Those were strictly for fairy tales.

She closed her eyes and fought herself. She prayed for the reason inside to win out. When it didn't, she forced its hand by pouring the vodka in the glass down the sink. Then she did the same with the remainder in the bottle. She did it quickly before she had a chance to change her mind.

Time seemed to tick by slowly as she stood and stared into the sink. She wondered if her life was much like that vodka. If it had gone down the drain in a clear and quick spiral never to return again. She thought back to that first night when she'd met Audrey. The woman outside had been talking on the phone. She'd said, "There are some that come broken, but they can be repaired."

What had she been talking about?

Was she broken? Yes, she was. Was she repairable? No, she didn't think she was.

The woman had been wrong. Some things were not repairable. Not even when you stood up for your morals and said no to your addictions. Some things were meant to lie on a table with their pieces strewn apart. A puzzle never to be put back together.

She was one of those things.

Irreparable. She repeated the word as she made her way into her bedroom. The shower called and she answered, ready to wash away all that had been and never would be again. But she froze when she went to remove Audrey's shirt.

Her reflection showed the mint green tee fitting a little loose on her, accenting her light eyes. She recalled how Audrey had looked wearing it, and she preferred that image to her own. She gathered the front of it and brought it to her nose. It smelled of Audrey's cologne, and she knew at that moment that she was going to sleep in it.

And she knew she wouldn't be able to stop thinking about her. That just as with alcohol, she could think all she wanted; she just couldn't act.

She switched off the bathroom light, took off her pants, and climbed into bed. Her freshly clean sheets felt good, smelled good even, but it wasn't what she wanted. She brought the shirt up to her nose again and stroked her body long and slow, awakening her nipples. Audrey had touched her there, had put her mouth here. She didn't want to let that go, not just yet. She needed to fall asleep with Audrey on her. Just for the night. One last night.

She curled up on her side and inhaled. Just for tonight, she could have good dreams.

Tomorrow would bring new things. New beginnings. And for the first time in a long time, she considered moving on with her life.

CHAPTER NINE

Audrey usually loved nights like these. The club so full you could hardly move, the music so loud you could hardly hear. The strobes slicing through the crowd, sweat reflecting off red, blue, and green lit skin. It all felt so primal to her, women dancing and moving, trying to lure a partner, the beat encouraging them all. She usually loved it. Most nights even lived for it.

But tonight and every night since she'd last seen Lillian had been different. She felt defeated, uninspired, lost. What was the point of it all?

Was she just going to go through the motions until she finally found someone else she liked? What were the odds of that happening considering it had never happened until Lillian?

She was at a complete loss, and yet all she could do was return to the club and try to behave as if everything were okay. At least here she could see Lillian, pretend things were different, live in a fantasy world. She could catch a glimpse of her and try not to remember the hurtful things she'd said. But then again she was good at that. Hurtful things had been said to her all her life. She was good at pushing past them and moving on.

So she entered with her head held high, wearing a tight black T-shirt and worn jeans. Her motorcycle boots matched her belt and thick wristband. All purposely done, of course. As was her carefully sprayed-on cologne, black thong underwear, and lack of a bra. Though she wasn't on the hunt tonight, she wanted to make damn sure it looked like she was.

She made her way to the bar and ordered a beer. She positioned herself on the stool and stared across the bar trying not to look into the far corner where Lillian usually sat. But she did a brief scan anyway. Lillian was nowhere to be seen. She blew out a long breath and focused on the bartender, motioning her over.

"Beer," she said. "Heineken."

The beer was slid across the bar to her and her gaze traveled back over to Lillian's table. Lillian's friends were there, talking and laughing as usual. It was getting late, though, and she wondered if Lillian was coming tonight at all.

She downed her beer quickly, taking in nearly half the bottle. She had to do something to get her mind off Lillian. Where the hell was she?

"Be careful with that one," the bartender said, getting in her line of sight.

Audrey leaned the other direction in order to keep looking. "What?" She was only half-paying attention.

"I said—" the bartender said again.

"I heard you. I just didn't understand."

A thick hand encircled Audrey's wrist. "No, I don't think you heard me."

Audrey yanked her arm away and glared into her eyes. It was the same bartender who had given her countless dirty looks.

"What's your problem?" Audrey asked, ready to fight if need be even if the bartender had way more muscle than she did.

"You." She yanked her thumb back toward Lillian's group. "And Lillian. She doesn't need you messing with her."

"I'm not messing with her." What the fuck? Who was this chick?

"The hell you aren't. I've seen you in here looking for her, asking about her."

"So? What's it to you?" She could damn well do as she pleased.

"She's not interested."

Audrey fought not to look stunned. "How would you know?"

"Because she told me so."

"Yeah, right." Was Lillian talking about her? It seemed unlikely. She didn't seem to be the gossip type.

"Seriously. She did."

"Yeah, well, whatever. You need to mind your own business."

"Lillian is my business," the bartender said.

"Since when?"

"Since last night."

"What happened last night?" Bile began to rise in her throat as she considered the possibilities. But no, not Lillian. She wasn't the type.

"We got together. Went out."

Audrey felt like she'd been smacked.

"Lillian doesn't date." She tried to act cool and downed the rest of her beer.

"She does now." The bartender smiled, pretty damn proud of herself. It made Audrey want to rip her head off. She continued, rubbing the salt in the wound. Fucking grinding it in.

"You see, I'm stable. I'm sober. And I'm not a whore."

Audrey rose and grabbed the bartender by the shirt collar. She merely smiled.

"I'm also very levelheaded. But if you don't take your hands off me, I'll have you thrown out of here so fast your head will spin."

"Go ahead."

"Make your day? I would, but that would upset Lillian." Her eyes drifted and locked onto someone. Audrey released her and turned to look.

Lillian had entered and was stopped near the bar at the edge of the dance floor watching them. Her face was paler than usual and her mouth was slightly open in shock. She was staring at Audrey as if she were a wild animal, totally out of control.

Audrey stalked toward her, furious. "You really need to tame that hunk of meat," she said, gesturing back toward the bar.

"Looks like you're the one who needs taming. How could you?"

"How could I? What the fuck, Lillian? You're dating now? Her?"

"Brea's nice. And yes, I can choose to date if I want to." But her eyes told a different story. One Audrey couldn't read but desperately wanted to hear.

"But what about us? You said—"

"You said you didn't date either. So would it have mattered?"

Audrey wanted to say yes, but she just couldn't bring herself to do it. And besides, it was no use. Lillian was lost to her. She could tell by the way her eyes kept drifting over to the bartender.

"Forget it."

Audrey shouldered past her and went to find her seat near the Midnight Room. She sank into the plush chair and buried her head in her hands. A few of her friends tried to say hello, but Audrey ignored them, unable to look up. When she finally did, she saw Lillian at the bar, talking to the bartender. They were both looking at her.

Something stung her eyes then. Something that burned. She reached up and found warm tears.

She stood and wiped her face angrily. This wasn't her. She didn't cry. Not in years. No one got to her like this anymore. Not her mother, her absent father. Especially a woman. It didn't matter that it was Lillian. It didn't matter that she was unlike everyone else.

Crying simply wasn't her.

"Hi."

Audrey rubbed her cheeks and focused. A good-looking young blonde was smiling at her. She was nearly Audrey's height. She looked familiar. Too familiar. Audrey knew that she'd been with her.

"Not now." She was in no mood for small talk. In less of a mood for fun. She tried desperately to remember the woman's name.

"I think you should talk now," she said. "Before you cry some more."

"Look, I just can't. And I'm not crying."

"Sure looks that way to me." She took her hand. "Come on."

"No, thanks."

"No, really, you won't be sorry." She led them back to the plush chair where she encouraged Audrey to sit.

Audrey did so, too vulnerable to fight. Her mind was in a fog and she let it overtake her. The buzz from the beer had started and she wanted another. She wanted all the beer in the world so she wouldn't have to see what was standing across the dance floor.

She motioned to the cocktail waitress and grabbed herself a Miller Lite.

"Who are you?" Audrey tried to look at the blonde, but she had moved behind her where she began to massage Audrey's shoulders.

"You mean you don't recognize me?"

"Yeah, I've—I remember you. Sort of."

"It's okay. I can hardly remember that night myself. We were both pretty drunk. But still, I have been saying hi to you for like a month straight."

Audrey laughed. "I don't do anything straight."

"Funny."

"No, seriously, who are you and why are you rubbing me down?" She tried to sound tough, but goddamn, it felt good. It burned just a little and then warmed all down through her muscles.

"I'm Janis. As in Joplin. My mom had a thing for her when I was born."

"Oh. Janis. Right. You left me a note. And your bra."

"My bra? Wow, I've been wondering where that went."

"I've still got it."

"Good. I hope you've enjoyed it."

"So why are you rubbing me down?"

"I'm rubbing your shoulders because you look like you need a good rubdown. That and another few beers."

"I look that good, huh?" She winced as she watched Lillian move away from the bar. She was headed toward her friends at the far table in the corner.

"She broke your heart, didn't she?"

Audrey tensed. "No."

"It's okay. Everyone here knows it."

"What?"

"I wouldn't worry about it, though. No one is surprised. You're hot to trot and she's way too uppity."

"She didn't break my—where did you hear this?"

"Around."

"Well, don't believe everything you hear."

"I don't. But I did find you crying."

"I wasn't crying. I just don't feel well."

Janis came around the chair and dropped her ass on the armrest, draping an arm around Audrey.

"You must not have felt good for a while. You just haven't seemed yourself."

"How would you know?" She looked into her brown eyes and found herself amused at the way they sparkled.

"Because I've liked you for a while now."

Audrey fought rolling her eyes. "That's nice."

"Well, don't get all excited or anything."

Audrey laughed.

"Don't you like me? I mean, I did just rescue you and give you a mind-blowing massage." She smiled, showing she wasn't serious. "I mean doesn't that mean we get married next?"

"You're funny."

"I knew you liked me."

"Don't call the preacher yet. I don't do marriage."

She batted her eyes dramatically. "Oh, please say it isn't so." She grinned. "Why would you want to be miserable? Who in their right mind actually signs up for that?"

Audrey shrugged. "People do."

"Well, people are nuts, if you ask me."

"I don't think I actually asked." This time Audrey smiled. She was feeling a little bit better.

"Too bad." She took her hand and tugged. "Come on. Let's dance." Audrey stumbled along after her to the dance floor. They managed to squeeze into a spot between a clamor of sweaty women where they began to move to the powerful music.

"You're a good dancer," she said, not moving badly herself.

Audrey allowed herself to take her in for the first time, and she didn't mind what she saw. Janis had a young appeal to her, though Audrey didn't think she was as young as she appeared to be. With her nice long legs, firm buttocks, and the smooth planes of a nice waist, Audrey didn't care how old she was.

"I like your shirt," Audrey said. It was a Western-style red-and-black checkered shirt with the sleeves torn off. Very lesbian. But Janis, or the manufacturer, had replaced the buttons with red sequins, giving it a nice femme flair.

"I like the buttons," Audrey said, trying not to stare at her ample cleavage.

"Uh-huh. I get that a lot." She was grinning again, and Audrey noticed a dimple and a cute little freckle right near it.

"I like your shirt too. Especially your bra."

Audrey laughed. "Thanks. I was hoping someone would notice it. I just got it."

"It's nice. So…what's the word? Natural."

"Thank you. Exactly what I was going for."

"I thought so."

They continued to dance, and Audrey, despite beginning to relax and have a good time, couldn't help peering over at Lillian. She did it so often that Janis took notice.

"So who is she?"

"Who's who?"

"Don't play coy. Who's the chick? The one that had you in tears."

Audrey stopped dancing, losing her good mood. "No one."

"Just a girl, right? Didn't mean a thing?"

Audrey started to walk off, but Janis stopped her by gently touching her wrist. "They're watching us, you know." She motioned with her head, looking back toward Lillian's table.

Though she knew she shouldn't, Audrey turned to look. What she saw tore a hole right through her heart. Lillian was staring directly at her with her piercing blue eyes. Looking at her like she'd just torn a hole right through *her* heart. The look lasted an instant and was then quickly replaced with anger and what could only be disgust as her friend Carmen leaned in and said something to her. Lillian nodded, looked Audrey up and down, and then looked away.

"I have to go," Audrey said.

"Don't let them get to you," Janis said, squeezing her wrist. "Fuck 'em."

But Audrey didn't feel like sticking around. She didn't feel like being anywhere near the club at the moment.

"I don't even know you," she said, realizing just how alone she was.

"Yes. You do." Janis leaned in and whispered to her, "I'm you."

Audrey laughed a little, growing even more uncomfortable. She turned to look at Lillian again and saw the bartender leaning down, chatting her up, placing a hand on her shoulder. Lillian laughed up at her and sipped her drink slowly as if to say, "Why, yes, I am available. Won't you sit down?"

Audrey couldn't take anymore. She had to bolt. She moved again and Janis tugged on her.

"Don't run, Audrey. Stay and have fun."

"I can't."

"Yes, you can. You're stronger than this."

"You don't even know me."

"Yes, I do."

Audrey faced off with her in the middle of the dance floor. "That's right. Because you're me."

Janis smiled.

Audrey looked back one last time at Lillian.

I'll show you.

Then she tugged on Janis's hand. "Let's go."

❖

Audrey let Janis ride with her. Normally, she wouldn't allow such a thing, but she was too upset to really think about it. She just wanted to get home and get her booze on. If Janis wanted to come along for the ride, then fine. And if Lillian saw it and thought ill of it, even better. If Lillian could date, then so could she.

They rode in silence save for the radio, which Janis kept tuned to a popular country station. She kicked her brown cowboy boots up onto the dash and leaned back to relax, obviously loving the way the whipping wind blew through her hair.

She was a wild girl; Audrey could tell that much. She knew them when she saw them, and for the moment, it felt a little freeing. Like maybe she could latch on to her free spirit and fly away with her. It was such a nice change from the feelings of turmoil that always arose with Lillian, she almost wasn't sure what to do with herself.

If Janis had no worries, why should she?

"This feels good," she said, accelerating into the night.

Janis whooped into the wind. "It sure does. I'm going to have to get me one of these."

"Jeeps are great. You'd love one."

"I sure would." She turned up the radio and danced as Audrey drove.

When they pulled into her apartment complex, Audrey's ears felt fuzzy from the lack of wind just as they always did when she slowed her Jeep from a high speed. Her skin tingled and her mind slowed back down into reality. She parked in her spot and climbed down to lead the way. Janis hopped out quickly and stood by her side.

"I remember now. This looks a lot like my place, you know."

"It's okay," Audrey said.

"I bet it's cozy."

"It does the job."

They walked up the stairs and Audrey shooed away the neighbor's cat who loved to linger by her door. He always mewed like he was starving when she knew better.

"He's cute," Janis said.

"He's a pain."

They stepped inside.

"You don't have animals?" Janis asked, almost sounding disappointed.

"No."

"How sad. They liven up your life."

"Yeah, my life doesn't need livening, trust me."

Janis slinked toward her. "I bet not."

Audrey stopped her when she was a mere breath away. "Not now." She hadn't really considered getting it on with Janis. When she thought about it now, she wasn't opposed to it; she just wasn't ready.

"I need a drink," she said as she moved toward the fridge.

"Beer's fine with me."

"Haven't got any. Jack will have to do."

"That's fine."

"Straight up?" Audrey asked, pouring herself a hefty shot.

"Thought you didn't do anything straight?" Janis leaned on the bar, once again showing off her cleavage.

"You're right. How could I forget?" She slammed back the shot and offered Janis a Coke while she poured them both a nice amount of Jack Daniel's into a pair of tumblers.

Janis mixed hers with the Coke and sipped while Audrey downed a bit more and winced as she headed for the couch. The whiskey was strong and distasteful but just what she needed. She had hoped it would wash Lillian away quickly, but the images still came.

She sat with a groan and thought about the look Lillian had given her. It was filled with such hurt and disapproval. Did Lillian really think that awfully of her? She supposed dancing with a new woman didn't help matters any, but what was she supposed to do? Live how she felt? Like total and complete shit? So badly that she didn't even want to go out anymore? There was no way she was going to give in to that. She had to go on, and if Lillian could suddenly start dating, then she could dance with a new woman.

"You're thinking about her again," Janis said.

Audrey reached for the whiskey bottle and drank straight from the lip, tired of thinking at all.

"What exactly happened?"

"I don't want to talk about it."

"You should. At least a little. It might make you feel better."

"I thought everyone already knew?"

Janis raised an eyebrow. "I know what I figured out. Everything else is speculation."

Audrey considered that a moment, and then, just as she was about to say no, she didn't want to talk about it, the words just tumbled out. "She doesn't accept me. Not at all. She thinks I sleep around. Have too much fun. She doesn't take me seriously."

"Should she?" Janis edged closer to her and placed a warm hand on her leg.

"You sound like everyone else."

"It's an honest question."

Audrey didn't like the answer. "I suppose from the outside looking in, she shouldn't. But I was honest with her. Very honest. I told her I just wanted to have fun."

"You can see why that scared her."

"But she said she doesn't want a relationship either."

Janis looked perplexed. "Really?"

"Yeah." She was starting to feel the whiskey now. The lines of life blurred and she felt warm and uninhibited.

"That is confusing. I can see why you're upset."

"Yeah, tell me about it. She doesn't want to see me, but now she's seeing the damn bartender. The fucking bartender. Who suddenly acts like she knows Lillian so well. She's all protective of her and everything."

"That must've been hard."

Audrey nodded. It had been hard. One of the hardest nights of her life. How could Lillian make her feel so torn up inside? They'd only been together a few times. There was no relationship, no anything. So why did she feel like she wanted to cry again?

"I should—" She stood and the room moved a little.

"We should get you to bed."

"Yes."

"Now, before you take a spill."

She rose to help her, but Audrey fought her at first.

"I don't even know you."

"Since when does that matter?"

"Since…I don't know." She laughed. "Yeah, you're right. Who gives a fuck?" They headed into the short hallway and into the bedroom.

Audrey felt sad but giddy. As if she might laugh at any second just thinking about how tough the bartender tried to act. It all seemed so asinine now. Why hadn't she just hit her? One quick blow to the face to shut her up? That would've done the trick. But she also would've been thrown out of the club. Maybe that wouldn't have been so bad. She might've missed the awful look from Lillian. She would've given anything to not have seen that look.

"Why don't you take off your clothes?" Janis said, already helping her with her shirt.

Audrey didn't fight it; she just closed her eyes and let it fall to the floor.

"Now your pants." She undid those and helped Audrey step out of them, Audrey carefully bracing herself on her shoulders. "Nice panties."

"These stay on," Audrey said, collapsing onto the bed.

"Okay. Whatever you want. Do you mind if I get naked?"

Audrey turned her head into her pillow as she hugged it. "No."

"Good." Janis stripped slowly, as if she were merely getting ready for bed with no one else in the room. She even hummed as she did so. Then she climbed in and helped herself to the lotion on the night table, rubbing it furiously between her hands.

"Come here," she said. "Let me have your back."

Audrey moved over a little and then groaned as Janis placed her hot hands on her muscles and began to rub. She worked her good and hard, massaging those muscles with her thumb and fingers and then using the heel of her palms to smooth it out. It felt so good Audrey nearly fell asleep.

"Now roll over," Janis said softly, like a lover's whisper. "I want to touch your front."

Audrey thought about it only briefly and then rolled over, liking the way the cool air felt on her bare breasts. Janis stared down at her, her full breasts heaving slightly as her excitement grew. She licked her lips as she rubbed more lotion between her hands. And when she touched Audrey's breasts, she groaned.

"Oh, these are nice. Mmm."

"Feels good," Audrey mumbled, closing her eyes. "Feels really good."

"Good," she purred. "I don't want you to think about anything. Just close your eyes and think about how good it feels."

Audrey did and her mind swam in the whiskey, like a peaceful little boat out in the middle of the ocean. The waves were small but continuous, rocking her to sleep.

"Oh God, Audrey," she said. "You're so incredible."

"Mmm."

Audrey felt her kneel and capture a nipple in her furnace-like mouth. The sensation was insanely wonderful and Audrey arched up into her.

"Can you?" Janis asked.

Audrey shook her head, watching her crimsoned face. "No."

"Can I?"

She had straddled Audrey's thigh and was moving back and forth. Audrey could feel her hot slickness and she knew she must be close. "Yeah."

"Okay," she said breathlessly. She began to buck wildly like a cowgirl on a crazy horse. Up and back and up and back. She gripped Audrey's hands and held them to her breasts. Audrey squeezed and played with the large nipples. Flashes came into her mind as Janis called out again and again.

Audrey shook her head, trying to shake the images. She saw Lillian's face in place of Janis's. Heard Lillian's cries, looked into Lillian's eyes.

"Oh, Audrey," but it was Lillian's voice.

It was Lillian. Oh fuck, it was Lillian.

Audrey called out too, groaning into the night as Janis came all over her leg, panting and convulsing like a madwoman.

As Audrey drifted off to sleep, she said the word that had been playing on her tongue all along.

"Lillian."

CHAPTER TEN

Lillian poured herself another cup of coffee and then settled into her office chair. It had been a quiet Monday so far, and for that, she was thankful. The weekend had been long and downright torturous. She'd done nothing but think about Audrey and the way she looked dancing with that blonde. She couldn't care less about her scuffle with Brea the bartender. As far as she was concerned, it just proved Brea right. Audrey was bad news. But still she wondered, what really had transpired and why had she looked so devastated while dancing with a new woman? One minute they look connected and seductive, and the next, Audrey was looking over at her as if her heart had been dug out with a spoon.

How could she tell Audrey she was only dating so she wouldn't think of her? How could she even admit that to herself?

"It will be good for you," Carmen had said. "A new start. A new person. Someone normal, like Brea, who understands your addiction. Do it, Lil. Do it for you."

So she'd done it. She'd called Brea and accepted her offer for coffee and they'd gone out and had an okay time. She wasn't keen on seeing her again, but she wanted to give her a fair shot, despite the lingering thoughts of Audrey.

She thought back to Audrey dancing with the new woman and how jealous she'd felt even with Brea standing right there with her. She'd had to leave soon after Audrey did in order not to drink every beer sitting on her table. Brea had offered to drive her home, but she'd refused, needing to be alone. Unfortunately, the alone time hadn't helped. She'd done nothing but toss and turn all night long, thinking about things.

First Audrey, then Holly.

Then Audrey again.

Rain had been bugging her about going to another training session. She'd already paid and she really wanted Lillian to make up with Audrey to at least be friends. She kept saying what a good person Audrey was. And while she wasn't sure what Rain was basing this on, she knew enough to know it to be true. Audrey was just different than she was. She chose to live her life differently and it was no reason not to be friends. Besides, she owed her an apology. She should've never spoken to her that way. Audrey had been nothing but nice to her. Sincere even.

She made a note to call Rain to set up a time with Audrey.

At the very least she'd get to see her again. This time without the bouncing blonde.

She took a long sip of her coffee and forced a smile as her clients entered. First, the woman, Barb, then her husband, Frank. Frank always held the door for his wife. Even on the way out and even when they entered their vehicle. She found it amusing considering he didn't like to do much else for her.

They said good morning and settled into their position on the sofa. Frank always sat next to her and held her hand. He was all about appearances.

"How are we today?" she asked, readying her laptop for notes.

"Fine, good," Frank said, looking to his wife and squeezing her hand.

"How have things been going?" she asked, knowing he would answer first.

"Really well." He nodded as if proud of himself for something.

"Barb?" Lillian asked softly. "How do you think things have been going?"

Barb shifted slightly and smiled carefully. Lillian could already feel the tension building. Frank was watching her closely, squeezing her hand, readying himself for the blow. It happened like this every single time.

"Well, okay, I guess," Barb said.

He sighed heavily and rubbed his forehead.

"Just okay?" Lillian asked.

"Okay is good, I guess," he said quickly, as if trying to stop her from saying more.

"Yeah, just okay." She was a meek woman both in build and in personality. Lillian wished she would meet with her alone, or seek someone else for personal therapy, but Barb always politely refused.

"Tell me what's happened since I last saw you two." It was always like pulling teeth. Frank never wanted to 'fess up and Barb always seemed a little afraid to.

"Not much," Frank said, smiling, showing off his perfect pearly whites.

"Barb?"

"Why do you always ask her? I just answered the question." His temper was showing again.

"Because this is couples therapy," she said calmly. "I need to hear both of you."

Barb refused to look at her or Frank. She just stared at the carpet. Finally, she decided to speak and it came out softly, just like her demeanor.

"I caught him online again."

Lillian pressed her lips together and made a note. She'd suspected as much.

"Tell me about that."

"It was no big deal. I was just chatting," he said.

Barb composed herself, straightening her back. This time she looked at Lillian as if gaining strength from her.

"She called you sexy," Barb said. "She continuously referred to you as sexy."

"So? I've never met her. She must've just liked my picture."

"Tell me about this, Frank," Lillian said gently. "She was what? A friend?"

"Just someone I met online."

"Have you chatted with her before?"

"No."

"Yes," Barb piped in. "The woman referred to a previous chat."

Frank shook his head. "Fine, yes, once before."

"Who is she?" Lillian asked.

"I don't know. Just a woman."

"Have you met up with her in person?"

"No." He clenched his jaw and gave Lillian a warning look.

"Did you intend to?"

"Yes, he did," Barb said. "They had exchanged phone numbers."

"That doesn't mean we were going to meet," Frank said, releasing her hand.

"What does it mean?" Lillian asked, keeping her voice soft and calm.

"It means—it means we might talk. You know, on the phone. Or text. Yeah, you know, text. Just see how she's doing rather than having to log on to the computer."

"I see."

"So you see, it was no big deal."

Lillian paused a moment to let all the details sink in.

"But it was a big deal to you, wasn't it, Barb?"

"Yes."

"Tell him why."

"Because it went against our agreement."

"Do you remember the agreement, Frank?"

"Of course I do."

"No chatting online with strange women? Wasn't that part of it?"

He didn't answer.

"So how does it make you feel to know he did this, Barb?"

"Hurt, betrayed. Like I can't trust him."

"So it brings up all those same feelings, right?"

"Yes."

Frank sighed again and shifted uncomfortably in his seat. "Look, women like me. I can't help that. They see me, they like me. They talk to me, they like me. I have no control over that. So to say all these things are my fault, it's, well, it's ridiculous."

Lillian chewed on her pen. She thought of Audrey and could easily imagine her saying the same things. *Women like me. It's not my fault. What do you want me to do?*

"It's how you react to that," Barb said, "That's the problem."

Frank whipped his head around to look at her. "What are you, the fucking therapist now?"

Lillian closed her eyes, trying to get Audrey out of her mind. But she could easily see herself having the same conversation with her. This is what their life would've been like.

"Let's calm down a moment," she forced herself to say.

Frank eased back against the couch and crossed his legs, one foot bouncing rapidly. "I just don't understand why she doesn't understand. I mean, I'm a man, for God's sake."

"What do you mean by that?" Lillian asked.

"I'm a man. When women hit on me, it's hard not to react."

"What about your marriage?"

"What about it?"

Lillian wanted to roll her eyes at him. "Your commitment to Barb. That has to come first."

"It—" But he shook his head as if too frustrated to talk.

"It always has to. Always."

"I know," he said.

"Even though you may think it's okay to exchange phone numbers with a woman, it's not."

"Why?"

"Because even if you have no intention of doing anything inappropriate initially, that could easily change. It's the second step in your cycle. The first being flirting."

"Oh, that's right. My fucking cycle. I'm like a woman with a period now. I cheat a couple of times and now I have a cycle."

Barb looked away, obviously hurt. Lillian felt for her, truly felt for her.

"Frank, have you considered going to those meetings I referred you to?"

"No."

"What about seeing my colleague? Have you made that appointment?"

"No."

"Why not?"

"Because I don't need any more help. If you can't fix us, then no one can."

"You have to want the help, Frank. And you have to be willing to change and to put in the work. Otherwise, nothing will help, not even these sessions."

"What if I don't want the help?"

Yes, what if. What if Audrey never wanted to change? How would they have had anything special? Why was she still thinking about it?

"Then I would ask you how important your marriage is to you. Because I know suggesting that you just stop is out of the question."

"Why is that?"

"Because you have an addiction. We've talked about that before."

Frank stared her down, and for a second she grew uncomfortable. "Remember, I'm here to help."

He continued to look at her in silence. Eventually, he spoke. "So help."

"Okay." She let out a long breath and then breathed deeply. "Firstly, I would like it if you made those appointments. Then you should focus on your marriage and on Barb. Ask yourself what her needs are. Are you truly being the best husband you can be? Talk to her. Tell her about your feelings. She wants to help you. She's accepted that you have a problem and she's willing to stick by you and help."

"What else?"

"You have to become you without the addiction. Find out who you are, what you like, what you need. It's not easy, and that's why I want you to get some additional help. Remember, you and Barb are two different people leading different lives. Your relationship is only a part of that. So it's important for you both to be healthy and whole.

"Here, let me show you." On a nearby notepad, she drew two circles intersecting. She pointed to the two individual circles. This is you and this is Barb. This," she said, pointing to the intersected piece, "is your relationship."

He nodded and the tension eased out of him a little. "So I guess I need to work on me, huh?"

"I think so. And I also think that a simple 'I won't do it anymore' isn't enough. It isn't working, is it?" She'd told him more than a few times that it wouldn't work, but he'd refused to listen, insisting that a simple agreement and "Scout's honor" were enough for him.

He shook his head.

"What do you think about all this, Barb?"

She smiled. "I think it's…great. I know I could use some work myself. And if he works on him, then hopefully, we will get somewhere." It was a big step. Frank actually admitting that the agreements weren't working obviously made Barb feel better too. Maybe now they could get somewhere with therapy.

"I think we will." She made some more notes and thought back to Audrey. Why did she do what she did? Could she be helped?

She chewed on her pen, wishing she had the answers and then reminding herself that she didn't care.

"Will he always, you know, need attention?" Barb asked, bringing her back into focus.

"It's hard to say. It depends on what the root causes are and whether or not he can overcome them."

She closed her laptop and rested her pen.
She'd just answered her own question.

❖

"That guy seems like a real sleazeball," Nadine said as they closed up shop for the evening. Frank and Barb had just walked out with Frank holding the door for Barb, a big shit-eating grin on his face for all to see.

"Who, Frank?" This time Lillian did roll her eyes at the sight of him.

"Yes. What a creeper. With that nasally voice and cheesy grin. Ugh. And he's always leaning on the front counter talking to me like we have some sort of connection. He does it right in front of his wife. Sickening."

"He needs some work." To say the least. He was one of her most difficult clients. He had to see things for himself before he would take her word for it.

"I'll say. I know you can't tell me anything about it, but I can guess what they're here for."

"You probably could."

"God, what's the world coming to? What's marriage coming to?"

They turned off the lights, set the alarm, and locked up. "I don't think marriage has necessarily changed," Lillian said.

"You don't?" They headed for Nadine's vehicle.

"No, I think it's always been shitty. It's just that now people complain about it and want changes. Back in the day, you didn't complain, you just put up with it."

"Are you saying you would just grin and bear it?"

Lillian laughed. "No."

"I think you are. Look at you and Holly."

"What about me and Holly?"

"You two hung on forever when it wasn't good."

"Wasn't good? Who says it wasn't good?" Her pulse began to

race just like it did when she and Holly were together and she'd found out Holly had been talking about her.

Nadine looked incredulous. "Um, Holly for one."

"Holly?" Oh God. She forced herself to breathe deeply. It had been two years; how could she still react this way?

They climbed in the vehicle and headed for Lillian's home. They often carpooled on Mondays and Tuesdays. Nights when Lillian didn't have church.

"Yes, Holly. She always complained. I remember because all I ever did was secretly roll my eyes at her."

"When did she do this?" How could she not have known? Lillian was so shocked she had trouble getting her seat belt on. "This fucking thing." She jerked at it.

"Easy there," Nadine said. "Maybe we better change the topic."

"No, no. This is fine. I want to know."

Nadine pulled into traffic and immediately honked her horn at a slow driver.

"What did she say?" Lillian asked, dying to know.

"Oh, just the usual. She wasn't happy. You guys weren't happy. She was bored. You were passionless."

"Passionless?" She gasped, offended and hurt. The comment stung. Deeply.

"Her word, not mine."

Passionless? She thought of Audrey. Would she say the same thing? How could Holly? Granted, they hadn't made love much in the end, but it was usually Holly who was turning away.

"Why didn't you ever tell me?" Lillian asked.

Nadine looked over at her with surprise. "She said you knew. That you two talked about it all the time."

Lillian stared straight ahead, unsure what to say.

"Are you telling me you didn't know?"

"How she felt?"

Nadine nodded.

"I knew…some of it."

"Then why so shocked?"

Lillian blinked back tears. "Because I didn't know she was literally telling the world."

"Oh, honey, it was just me. I'm hardly the world."

"No, she was obviously telling everyone, and I was apparently the last one to know. And you know what else? I wasn't unhappy."

Nadine slowed for a red light and patted her hand. She didn't seem to know what to say to that.

"So there you have it. I made my lover unhappy and I did nothing about it."

"Oh, come on now. That's not true."

"No, it is true. Apparently, she was miserable."

"You really weren't unhappy?"

"I thought we were...okay. Doing fine."

"There was no trouble?"

"We had arguments and all, but nothing awful. I thought, you know, she just complained a lot."

"Well, if a damn couples therapist can't make it work, then I guess no one can."

"That's just it, Nadine. I don't think I'm very good at evaluating myself and my situations." It was the first time she'd admitted that to anyone.

"Why would you think that?"

"Holly's a perfect example. I didn't see that one coming. At all. And everyone else could. Even you."

Nadine nodded. "Well, yeah. Why do you think you can't see it when it's you?"

"I don't know. Can't see the forest for the trees, I guess."

"Sounds about right." She drove in silence for a beat and then patted her hand again. "Don't beat yourself up over it. It's over."

Lillian swallowed hard and decided to voice her deepest, most hopeful secret. It was there, swimming just beneath all the other emotions flowing like a tidal wave through her mind. "What if... what if it isn't over? What if she comes back?"

"Oh, honey," Nadine said as if she were talking to a small child.

"You can't think like that. You'll torture yourself. Is that why you haven't been dating?"

Lillian felt a fool, completely let down. There was no one willing to support her dream. Not even Nadine. "Yes."

Nadine slowed the car, turned left, and sighed. "You have to let her go. It's the only way. And get out there and date someone. There are lots of beautiful fish in the sea."

Lillian thought of Audrey and considered telling Nadine about her, but she'd just think she was crazy to date someone like her. Just like everyone else did.

She looked over at her longtime friend and knew Nadine wanted the best for her. Maybe she should start listening more to her friends and less to her heart.

"I think I finally get the saying 'Listen with your head, not your heart.'"

Nadine found it amusing. "They didn't teach you that in school?"

"If they did, I was absent that day."

"We can't all be perfect."

"I'm certainly far from perfect."

Nadine made a noise of disagreement. "You're the closest to perfect that I know of."

"Oh, please. I am not." If only she knew about Audrey and the wild sex. She'd change her mind for sure then.

They slowed as they pulled into Lillian's driveway. Nadine put the car in park and switched off the engine.

Lillian asked the expected question. "Iced tea?"

"Thought you'd never ask."

They followed the cement path to the front door where Lillian stopped to dig for her keys. She'd just unlocked the front door when she heard a vehicle behind them.

"Who's that?" Nadine asked, turning to look at what appeared to be a delivery van.

"I don't know." Despite the logo on the van and the enormous bouquet bobbing in front of the small man walking toward her, it took her a while to catch up.

"Lillian Gray?" he asked behind the bouquet of fresh white roses.

"Yes."

He pushed them forward and had her sign a small clipboard. Then he left her with nothing but questions.

"My my my," Nadine said as she touched the tight blooms. "Looks like somebody doesn't need my advice."

Lillian turned and fumbled with the door. She had no idea who they were from, but they made her heart race nonetheless. She hurried through the door and placed the flowers, which came in a glass vase, on the kitchen counter. She searched for a card and found only a small one with a single line.

It said "More."

"What does it say? Nadine asked.

Lillian studied the card, hoping more words would appear. When they didn't, she handed the card over to Nadine, who whistled.

"Damn, Lillian. Who have you been seeing?"

Lillian crossed her arms over her chest and paced. She wasn't sure how to answer the question. Could Audrey have sent the flowers? Why would she when they ended on such bad terms? More importantly, why would she when she'd already been with other women?

The only one it left was Brea. She obviously wanted another date.

"I think they're from my friend Brea. I had coffee with her the other night."

Nadine helped herself to some iced tea, pouring them both a glass. They functioned just as they did at the office, Lillian often deep in thought and Nadine doing the small things.

"Oh?"

Lillian sat on the sofa, thinking of Brea.

"Is she nice?" Nadine asked.

Lillian shrugged. "Seems to be."

"But…"

"But what?"

"Something's wrong. I can tell. You're not all excited and everything."

"I just...she just...I don't know. Maybe I just don't know her well enough yet."

"No spark, huh?" Nadine got it. She always did.

"Not outrageously, no." *Not like with Audrey.*

"What's wrong with her?"

She's not Audrey.

"Nothing really. I guess she's just a little aggressive." *Aggressive Audrey I can handle. Aggressive Brea is less appetizing.*

"You're comparing her to Holly, aren't you?"

Lillian almost laughed into her iced tea. "Mmm."

"I knew it." She walked the length of the room. "I mean you've still got all these photos of her everywhere. The house looks exactly the same. Lillian, baby, you've got to move on."

"I know, I know." She understood but she just didn't want to hear it. Move on, move on, blah blah blah. Well, what if she had moved on? And what if now she needed to move on from the one she moved on to? Only she couldn't.

"I'm fucking insane," she said as she rose from the couch. She truly was.

Nadine reacted, coming at her with a glass half-full of iced tea. "No, you're not," she said softly as if she were indeed insane. "You're just having a hard time letting go and starting anew. It happens to everyone." She eased her back down onto the couch, and Lillian couldn't help but laugh.

"Nadine, you have no idea."

"Yes, I do. I've been through it. Remember Pete? That rat bastard? It took a while, but I got over him with your help. You'll get through this too."

She wiped her eyes, trying not to laugh at her fucked-up little world, about which Nadine had no clue.

"Okay, you're right." She just wanted her to leave so she could go curl up in bed and pretend things were totally and completely different.

"Good. Now, let's leave you on a positive note." She retrieved Lillian's cell phone and handed it over just as she did at the office. "Call her."

"Call who?"

"Who? Brea! Call Brea and thank her for the flowers." She nudged her with her elbow.

"Oh." Call Brea. "Okay."

"You do want to see her again, don't you?"

Lillian widened her eyes in response. "Mmm-hmm."

She did need to see her at least one more time to apologize for the way she'd last left the club.

"Oh good. Okay, I'll leave you to it." She patted her leg.

As she left the room, Lillian eyed her phone and considered what she would say. She looked at the card as the phone rang. The word "more" played in her mind.

CHAPTER ELEVEN

Audrey awoke and stretched languidly on her bed. She turned on her side and yawned, happy to find that she was alone. She vaguely recalled Janis being there the night before, wanting to stay. Audrey couldn't remember what had been said, but whatever it was, it had left her there alone. Thankfully.

The sunlight didn't stream in through the blinds anymore because she'd covered the window with a dark blanket. So the room was dark and cool, cavelike. She could lie there all day and not think twice about it. This feeling had come a lot lately, and it was becoming a struggle to even get out of bed. All she wanted to do was stretch out on her bed, listen to music, and drink. Even Janis seemed to be losing her charm.

Audrey had been seeing a lot of her lately, and she had to admit, they did have a lot of fun. If you considered mindless drinking and sex fun. Janis didn't expect anything from her or nag her about this or that. In fact, it was quite the contrary. Janis actually had to calm Audrey down and tell her there were no worries when subjects that were normally touchy arose. Like when Audrey didn't want to go on a dinner date, or stay over at Janis's place. Most women freaked out on her or nagged her to death over why and when. But Janis wasn't like that. And the change, she had to admit, was really nice.

Still, there was something missing. Something off. It wasn't Janis's doing; it was hers. She just wasn't right inside. She knew why. Janis wasn't Lillian. And if she were honest with herself, she'd admit the only reason she was becoming serious with Janis was to prove to Lillian and to herself that she could.

She turned again, languishing in the dark, groaning as she stretched. God, just thirty more minutes. Thirty more minutes of sleep and she'd be ready to go. Today, she got to see Lillian. They were supposed to meet for a session. Rain couldn't make it, and Audrey had been more than surprised when Lillian had called. She eyed her alarm clock and decided against resetting it. She was more than awake now in thinking about some alone time with Lillian. Hopefully, Lillian had seen her with Janis. Maybe now she'd believe her when she said she wanted more with her. That now she was capable of offering more.

She was just about to head for the shower when her phone rang. After fumbling for it on the nightstand, she managed to answer in a groggy voice.

"Yeah, Audrey here."

"McCarthy."

"Viv?" Christ, she hadn't heard from her in what felt like ages. She wondered if Becky and Gail were there with her, anxiously waiting to talk to her like they used to do, sometimes losing their patience and yelling over Viv. The memory made her smile, but her smile fell when she remembered her friends all had lives now. Married lives. Now the calls came once in a blue moon and individually. And most definitely not from crowded bars.

"Yeah, it's me. The one and only. How you been?" She sounded the same, and Audrey could picture her sitting on an old leather chair, feet up and crossed on the ottoman. She wondered if she was wearing her trademark basketball shorts and T-shirt. Probably not. It was rather early. She was probably in dress slacks and a button-down, all ready for work in a day of sales.

"Oh, you know, same old same old." It was rather easy to lie, but she knew she didn't sound convincing.

"I bet." She laughed a little. "Did I wake you?"

"Nah."

"Bullshit. I did. You're still lounging in bed sleeping off a bender."

"Am not." She even rose, trying to convince herself that she was up.

"You got a woman next to you?" She still knew her so well.

Audrey actually checked. "No."

"Good, good." She cleared her throat. "Listen, I called because I ran into your mom the other day."

Audrey's heart sank to her stomach. What? What the hell? She sank back onto the bed. "Yeah? So? This is why you called?" Her mother was an off topic. Everyone knew it, especially Viv. How could she?

"I know you've got some bad blood between you and your mom and all, but—"

"But what?"

"She's not looking so good, Aud. Not looking good at all. And I thought maybe you might know what's going on."

Audrey stood and began to pace, looking for something to put on. Unfortunately, the bits of clothes she did find weren't hers. Panic was beginning to consume her, and she felt betrayal on so many levels.

"What do you mean?" She was growing angry, impatient.

"She looks bad. Like maybe she's sick."

"Well, did you ask her?" Jesus, what was she supposed to do about it? The woman never called her either.

"I did, but she gave me the runaround. Then complained about how you never call or stop by."

"I see." It was the usual. Bitch, bitch, bitch, and guilt, guilt, guilt.

"Listen, Aud, I know how you feel about her."

"You have no idea." She could barely get the words out.

"I just thought you might want to know."

"Yeah, well, I don't. Honestly, I don't."

She sat on the bed and dropped the pair of sweatpants in her hand to run her fingers through her hair.

Viv was silent on the other end for a long while. So long, Audrey wondered if she were in fact still there. "I can go with you if you want."

Audrey laughed. Right. "Nah, that's okay. I do things alone, remember?" She'd been alone the past three years without her friends while they went on with their own lives. So now she called, bringing up her mother and wanting to help?

"You don't have to." She sounded soft and sincere and it only angered Audrey all the more. "I still care, Audrey. We all do."

Audrey didn't speak.

"I love you. And I'll help you if you want it."

"I got it, thanks."

There was another long silence. Then Viv finally spoke.

"I'm having a birthday party for Kayla two weeks from Friday. I really would love it if you would come."

"I don't know Kayla." She knew she sounded like a child, but she didn't care. She knew Kayla just fine, but she didn't consider her a friend. She was just Viv's wife.

"Yes, you know Kayla. And she likes you. So please come. And bring a date."

"Since when?" They'd never asked her to bring a date before because they knew she didn't date.

"Since now. Bring a date if you want to. Your friends are as welcome as ours."

"Is this you feeling guilty over this phone call?" Audrey tried to stay mad at her, but the feeling was wearing off. Now she was more upset over her mother.

"Maybe."

"Figures. Kayla loathes me, Viv. So spare me the feel-good routine."

"No, she doesn't. She just doesn't understand all the reckless… you know…partying."

"Well, tell her not to hold her breath. I doubt I'll come."

"Oh, come on, Aud. We haven't seen you in forever. And I miss you."

"I'm real busy."

"You're not that busy. Come on. I'm making my famous margaritas."

Audrey rolled her eyes. There were so many memories with

the margaritas. Viv knew it and she was playing the card no holds barred.

"We'll see."

"You're always welcome. You know that."

"Yeah yeah." Always welcome at a home where one person loathes you. Sounded so inviting.

She ended the call and tossed the cell phone onto the dresser. Fucking Viv. Fucking phone call. The nerve of her to call her about her own mother. *Well, have you seen her lately?* No. *Well, do you know what's going on?* No. *In other words, don't you care?* No!

Her mother didn't care about her, so why the hell should she care in return? Couldn't everyone just leave her the hell alone?

She rose and headed bare ass naked into the kitchen.

"Jesus Christ!"

Janis was standing there cooking, naked as a jaybird, pan in hand.

"Morning," she said.

Audrey grabbed her own face in torment. "Fuck." Not this. Not right now.

"I see I'm not a welcome sight."

"Not exactly."

"That's cool. I'll just finish making breakfast and be gone."

Audrey didn't argue, too pent up to play nice. She dug in the fridge for some orange juice.

"I would ask what's wrong, but I can tell that wouldn't be a good idea," Janis said.

"You'd be right." Audrey found the juice and grabbed a glass from the sink. It smelled like whiskey. "What are you doing here?"

Janis stirred the egg whites while salting and peppering them. "I spent the night, remember?"

"No."

"Well, I did. We had sex and you said I could stay, but only on the couch."

"Oh." It still wasn't coming back to her.

"Your couch sucks, by the way. Way too small to sleep on."

"You didn't have to stay."

She flexed her ass and pushed back her hair. "You were really drunk."

"So?" What else was new? They were always drunk.

"So I felt obligated."

Audrey chugged her juice, unusually thirsty. She didn't like what she'd just heard. Even if it was bullshit. "Whoa. There is no obligation here, got it? Next time, go home."

Janis turned and slid the egg whites onto two plates next to some whole wheat toast.

"You don't have to tell me, Audrey. I know."

"Then what are you doing here?"

She shrugged and drank the juice from Audrey's glass. "I think I like you."

Audrey took her glass back defiantly. "Oh no. Oh no, you don't. There's no liking anyone here."

"Just like there's no obligation?"

"Exactly."

Janis laughed. "Relax. I'm not going all Kathy Bates on you. I just…I don't know. Think you're cute with all your dysfunction."

"Jesus." She didn't need this now. Not in any way.

"Oh, come off it. I just like you, okay? So get over it."

Audrey panicked, the thought of Viv's phone call not helping. "Maybe we should stop seeing each other."

Janis shrugged. "Okay. Whatever." She tossed the pan in the sink. "Can we at least eat first?" She drank more of Audrey's juice, acting like she didn't have a care in the world. Audrey wondered if she did.

"I'm not hungry," Audrey said. The last thing on her mind was a healthy breakfast.

"I know you're going to go work out, so you better eat."

"I can grab a protein shake."

"The food's already ready." She took both plates and sat at the kitchen table, where she dug in heartily.

Audrey stared at her for a moment, confused and somewhat amused by the sight of her sitting there naked at the kitchen table, eating like she hadn't eaten in days.

"You're driving me fucking nuts today," Audrey said.

Janis continued to eat. "You'll get over it."

Audrey walked slowly to the table and sat, unsure what else to do. She dabbed at her eggs and then took a small bite. Janis had been paying attention. Audrey ate egg whites and half a piece of whole wheat toast every morning. She wasn't sure how Janis preparing the meal made her feel.

"I've got to be at work in an hour," Janis said, mouth full of toast. "I need a ride."

Audrey paused mid-bite, remembering they'd again left Janis's car at The Griffin.

"Next time, bring your car." She took another bite. The egg whites weren't bad. Weren't bad at all.

"Yeah." She drank more juice, then rose to get the jug from the fridge.

She didn't mention the fact that Audrey suggested they stop seeing each other, then the next instant suggested she bring her own car when they hooked up again.

"You know, you said her name again last night," Janis said, pouring more juice.

"What?"

Audrey was busy thinking about Viv, her mother, and all the other shit in the world. Bringing up Lillian definitely topped it off.

"Lillian."

Audrey blinked a few times, knowing damn well who she meant.

"You say it almost every time we're together. And the funny thing is, you don't even come. You just say her name when I come."

Audrey pushed her food away. She could feel herself flush with anger and embarrassment.

"Why are you bringing this up?"

Janis shrugged again. "Why not? I thought you might want to know."

"Well, I don't."

"You're obviously not over her. It's kind of sad really."

"Is it?"

"Yeah." She met her eyes and Audrey could tell she was sincere. Sincere yet blunt. That was the thing about Janis. Sweet and sour.

Audrey rose, needing to leave her behind for the time being. She needed to leave it all behind. "Remember to bring your own car from now on."

"You going to shower?" Janis asked.

"Yeah." Audrey hurried down the hallway and into the bathroom. She turned on the shower and stepped inside while it was still cold. The shock of it took her breath away, and she had to steady herself with her palm to the wall until it grew warmer. She soaped her hair and again considered telling Janis to get lost. But when she thought of reasons why, she couldn't really come up with one. They had an easy agreement. Neither was willing to commit to anything. They were both just content in being. Still, the bluntness was starting to get to her. Maybe they should see less of each other.

Audrey leaned back to rinse her hair as the shower curtain opened. Janis entered with a soft smile, almost shy.

"Sorry, but I've got to get ready for work," Audrey said.

"And I didn't want to leave things, you know, like they are." She pulled the curtain closed and enveloped Audrey in a hug.

"Things are what they are." Audrey fought telling the truth, not wanting to regret anything she might say. She also didn't want to sugarcoat the situation any. So instead she closed her eyes and began to like Janis's presence more and more as she slid her body against hers.

"I think I freaked you out, didn't I?"

Audrey allowed her to run her fingers through her hair, completely rinsing the soap away.

"Maybe a little."

She laughed softly. "Maybe a lot."

Janis turned them and put herself directly under the spray. "Why don't you soap me up?"

"I thought you were in a hurry?"

"I am. So hurry."

Audrey squirted shower gel into her hands and rubbed it on her body. Janis purred and moved against her. She was an incredibly sexy woman. There was no denying that.

"Give me some." She held out her hands and Audrey dispensed more shower, which that Janis applied to her. Audrey shuddered under her hands and felt her body awaken despite the contents of her mind.

"This is the best shower ever," Janis said wickedly. "I think we'll both get thoroughly clean."

Audrey closed her eyes and inhaled the fresh scent of the soap. Then she watched as Janis tilted her head back and rinsed shampoo from her hair. The water sloughed off her body smoothly, rounding her breasts and dripping down onto her abdomen. The sight was more than Audrey could bear and she had the urge to just leave all the shit behind. Leave it all behind for pleasure. She traced the water on Janis's breasts with her fingertips and then roughly pinched her nipples.

"Oh, baby," Janis said with a grin. "You keep doing that and—oh God. God, it's going right to me." She leaned forward and grabbed Audrey's pussy. "It's going right here."

Audrey didn't grin, didn't say a word. She just kept doing it. Harder and longer. Quicker and rougher. Until Janis was calling out her name and coming up to her tiptoes in ecstasy.

"I can't take anymore," she finally said, pushing Audrey's hands away.

She knelt and spread Audrey with her thumbs.

Audrey grabbed her head and clenched her jaw as she tried to pull her away. But as soon as she felt the pressure of her tongue, she nearly buckled with pleasure.

"I can't—" she tried to say, but Janis kept flicking her tongue across her clit, pleasuring her in a frenzy of hard, wet licks.

"Janis, I—" But Janis only moaned and continued, wrapping her hands around Audrey's legs to ensure she stay still.

"Oh—ah—oh fuck." Audrey closed her eyes and focused on the pleasure. The water beat down on her stomach and on the back of Janis's head, flecking her face. Steam rose before her; she could feel it as she breathed it into her tightening chest. She clutched Janis's hair and held fast to her, her legs beginning to shake. "Jan—" But it wasn't the name she wanted to say. It wasn't the name she was thinking of. The last woman who had given her this kind of pleasure had been Lillian.

Oh, Lillian.

She opened her eyes and stared into the mist. The orgasm was looming, marching toward her quickly. There was no way she could stop it, not when Lillian was on the forefront of her mind. She thought of her piercing blue eyes and pale skin. The way her sharp cheekbones crimsoned when she was turned on. She remembered the look on her face when she'd shoved Audrey up against the wall in the Midnight Room.

The way she came at her all hungry and fierce, refusing to take no for an answer.

"Ah God!" Audrey came, convulsing all over Janis, holding her head and smashing herself into her. It was a long and beautifully rich orgasm, one that lasted for what felt like an eternity. She clung to Janis for a long while.

"Ah fuck," she breathed, too shaken to stand on her own yet.

"Yeah, baby." Janis laughed and stood alongside her, holding her tightly.

Audrey rested her chin on her shoulder, trying to catch her breath. She stared into the mist again, lost in her own world. Questions came, one right after the other.

What was she doing? Why? And who with?

Why couldn't she answer the questions and do exactly what she should do? What she truly wanted to do?

"Hey." Janis turned off the water and handed her a towel. She gently touched her face with it. "That was fun," she said.

Audrey nodded and slowly dried herself off. She caught her reflection in the mirror as Janis wiped away the steam. She looked hollow, felt hollow. What had happened to her happy-go-lucky life?

Janis turned and embraced her, nibbling on her neck. "That really was fun," she said. "And look on the bright side. At least you didn't say her name." She gave her a peck on the cheek and walked briskly from the bathroom.

Audrey sat on the toilet and rested her head in her hands.

Yeah. At least she hadn't said her name.

❖

"So how have you been?" Lillian asked as they walked the dirt path at a nearby desert park. The surrounding mountains stood archaically with their sharp edges and serrations cutting deep brown into a pale blue sky. Overhead, hawks flew like kites, gliding and swooping, looking for a meal. The air was no longer fresh and cool, having warmed a little in the awakening sun. If Audrey hadn't had such an atrocious morning already, she would've thoroughly enjoyed the view.

"Fine." She sped up a little and wiped the sweat from her brow, in little mood for talking. She was upset over the phone call and over Janis. She should've never let her touch her like that. She felt like she was losing control. And she felt like she'd betrayed Lillian even though she'd made it clear she wanted nothing to do with her as far as a relationship.

Lillian picked up her pace as well and took a deep breath as she stared up into the blue sky. "I've been fine too. Thanks for asking."

Audrey glanced over at her, noting her short running shorts and tight tank. Her hair was pulled back into a tight ponytail, covered by a Breast Cancer Awareness ball cap. Her skin glistened with sweat, and Audrey could smell the light scent of her perfume.

"I'm sorry," Audrey said, knowing she was being an ass. "How are you?"

"I'm okay." She smiled. "Thanks for meeting with me. I know it's kind of weird after, you know."

"No, I understand."

"No, I was wrong to say what I said to you, Audrey. I'm sorry." She looked over at her with serious eyes. "Sincerely."

Audrey couldn't hold her gaze, the pain of that last encounter fresher than ever. "You told me how you really felt. Now I know."

"No, I was a jerk. You just choose to live your life differently than me. That's all. I had no right to attack you over it. You don't need my approval to be who you are."

Audrey shook her head. Lillian still didn't understand. Why couldn't anyone understand her? Was she that messed up?

Lillian saw her. "What? What's wrong?"

"Nothing."

"No, tell me. Please."

"No."

"Audrey." She touched her arm and they stopped their brisk walk. "I'm trying to make this right. I'm sorry I hurt you."

Audrey drew a deep breath, wanting nothing more than to just run away. "You don't get it, do you?"

Lillian's face showed her confusion.

"I'm not upset over what you said. Yeah, it hurt me, but you spoke the truth and I got over it. I'm upset because you wouldn't even give me a chance. I was willing to change for you."

Audrey started walking again, her breath feeling tight in her chest.

"And I'm not surprised you're doing okay," Audrey added, her emotions beginning to swirl hotly inside. "I'm sure the bartender is making you very happy."

"Audrey," Lillian said, hurrying to catch up. "It's not like that."

"It's not?" She kept walking, looking straight ahead.

"No. And what about you and the girl you've been seeing?"

Audrey laughed. "I don't want to talk about it."

"Why not?"

"Because you wouldn't understand."

"So it's okay for you to see someone but I can't?"

"You can and are doing as you please."

"And so are you."

"No, I'm not. I'm doing what I have to do. There's a difference."

"What does that mean?"

How could she tell her she was only seeing Janis to prove that she could?

A hawk called out overhead and Audrey looked up, yearning to join it, to be able to soar overhead, leaving everything else behind.

"I need to run," she said, walking faster.

"I thought you just finished."

Audrey had arrived a little before Lillian for a quick run up and around the mountain. She'd actually done it twice. It hadn't helped a damn bit.

"It didn't help."

"Help with what?"

"Stress."

"Should I run with you?"

"If you want."

"I mean, is this part of my workout?"

"It can be."

"Audrey, are you even here?" Lillian stopped and put her hands on her hips. She looked so beautiful under the high sky with the desert mountains surrounding her.

"I'm just thinking about my workout," Audrey said. She had her whole regimen planned. "I've doubled up on everything." She had to do something to help with the impending anxiety, and lying in her cave with a bottle of whiskey wouldn't cut it twenty-four seven. She needed something more, and exercise had always been her savior.

"Why?"

"Because I have to."

"Because of stress?"

Audrey finally stopped and walked back toward her. "Yes."

"Audrey, that's too much. Even for you."

"I'm fine." She was working out stronger and longer, but she'd had a lot on her mind. Janis, Lillian, her friends, her life, and now… her mother.

"No, you're not. You don't even look fine anymore. Your face is all sunken-looking."

Audrey stopped, taken aback.

"I'm serious, you don't look well."

"I'm fine. Besides, what does it matter?"

"It does. Are you eating?"

"Yes."

"What did you have this morning?"

Audrey paced, wishing Lillian would walk again. She needed to move. "Egg whites and toast."

"Bullshit."

Lillian looked concerned and even a little ticked off. "It's not bullshit. Janis made it." She should've refused breakfast, walked out without showering. She was letting Janis get too close.

"So she's…spending the night?" Her jaw dropped slightly, but she recovered quickly. "Making breakfast and everything?"

Audrey felt like she needed to explain and she hurried to do so. "It's not like that. She—she slept on the couch. And I didn't ask for breakfast."

"I'm just surprised is all." Her voice fell as her words trailed off.

"I've had women stay over before."

"I'm sure you have."

"It's no big deal."

Lillian lifted her chin slightly. "You're right, it's not." But she was shaken up, Audrey could see it. And she didn't need this. God, she just wanted to focus on the beautiful amber mountains and pinpoint each large dark-purple rock and wonder how old it was. She didn't want to think about the phone call, about Janis, and especially about Lillian.

"I didn't ask her to stay, okay? She just left her car at the club, so she was sort of stuck."

"You don't have to explain."

"Yes, I do."

"Why?"

"Because I don't want you to get the wrong idea."

"Who cares what I think?"

Audrey kicked a small pebble. "I do."

"Well, you shouldn't. All that matters is your own happiness."

Audrey laughed. "You think I'm happy?"

Lillian tugged on her cap and looked at her. "Honestly? No. You are so not happy."

Audrey wiped her brow and studied her Adidas trail shoes.

"Are you?" Audrey finally asked, pointing the question back to her.

Lillian didn't seem to want to answer. "It doesn't matter."

Audrey could see the answer. She wasn't happy. Audrey wondered why.

"I think it's because you're too afraid to try," she finally said.

Lillian whipped her head up. "Excuse me?"

"You're too afraid to try. With me."

Lillian laughed a little, but Audrey knew she'd hit home with her point.

Lillian, however, wasn't about to admit it.

"Know why I think you're unhappy? Because you're too afraid to change."

Audrey pushed on her sunglasses as her heart rate tripled in pace. "Me? I have changed. I'm seeing someone exclusively—"

"Who? The blonde? Please, Audrey. That's not a relationship."

"At least I'm trying."

"Trying? Trying for what?"

"For—" She kicked the ground again. "Nothing. Jesus."

"Don't tell me you're serious with that girl. Don't even. I see you two. Getting drunk, so drunk you can barely stand. Both of you flirting with anything that moves. If you call that trying—"

Audrey ripped off her sunglasses and stopped walking. "Look, can we just stop with the bullshit?" She stared her down. "I came to work out. That's it. I don't need to hear about how fucked up I am, okay?" She dug her fingers into her hair and fought pulling it out. "I know I'm fucked up. I don't need to hear it from you. Goddammit, why is nothing ever good enough? Not for you, not for my mother, not for anyone!"

Lillian took a step back, obviously startled. She looked like she might flee.

"Go ahead," Audrey said, lowering her voice to a mere whisper. "Tell me I'm no good and then run off. Fucking run away."

Lillian took off her sunglasses and stepped toward her. She searched her face with true concern, but Audrey backed away. She couldn't take anymore. She just couldn't take it.

"Audrey," Lillian said, reaching out to touch her. "Audrey, please."

"Just go."

"I'm not going anywhere, Audrey," she said carefully. She tried to place a hand on her shoulder, but Audrey shook it off.

"Well, maybe you should."

"No. I don't want to. I'm going to stay right here with you." She was speaking softly, so softly it made Audrey's eyes well up with painful tears. "Why do you feel this way, Audrey? Did I make you feel this way?"

Audrey fought to breathe. "No. Yes. I don't know."

"Audrey?"

"I know I'm fucked up."

"Audrey, you aren't fucked up. You're just lost."

"I'm no good. I ruin everything."

"Who has said this stuff to you?"

"I've heard it all my life, okay? I'm used to it."

"Your mother, father?"

Audrey felt the sting in her eyes again.

"Just fucking go." She returned her sunglasses to her face and tried to fight off the tears. "I don't need you or anybody else."

"You do, Audrey. You need people in your life. And you have me. You deserve happiness. All the happiness in the world. You are worth it."

She tried to touch her, but Audrey turned away, breaking down into tears. Lillian embraced her from behind. "You're a good person, Audrey, and I care about you."

Audrey felt the warmth. Warmth she'd never felt from her mother. The sensation overwhelmed her, and she turned into it and fell into Lillian with sobs.

Lillian held her and let her cry, saying nothing. When Audrey finally pulled away, she felt drained and embarrassed. She wiped her eyes beneath her sunglasses. "I have to go," she said. "I need to run." She had to get away, just forget everything.

"Okay," Lillian said softly. "You go run. Will I see you again soon?"

Audrey nodded. She couldn't get any more embarrassed than she already was.

Lillian squeezed Audrey's shoulder.

Audrey turned one last time before running up the trail. She felt lost, embarrassed, confused. But she did feel calmer. She had Lillian to thank for that. Lillian hadn't run from her. She'd stayed and she'd tried to help her.

"Thanks," Audrey said, meaning it.

Lillian smiled. "Anytime."

CHAPTER TWELVE

Y̶ou look nice this evening," Brea said, settling into the table across from Lillian. They were at a trendy Italian restaurant, the kind that served wine in the port bottles and left it along with a fresh loaf of bread on the table before the meal. The light was dim, the tablecloths white—a perfect setting for a nice romantic meal.

But Lillian wasn't much in the mood for a date, nice place or not. Audrey had overpowered her thoughts, and she found herself not only thinking about her, but worrying about her as well. She'd told her she cared, and she'd meant it. Now she was finding that she cared more than she realized. She'd fought calling her even though it was really what she wanted to do. She wanted to talk to her, to listen, to experience the real Audrey. Not the cocky dream girl everyone seemed to want and admire. That wasn't the Audrey she was drawn to. She wanted the Audrey who felt, the Audrey who cared. That was the Audrey she wanted and needed to spend more time with.

Lillian took a sip of water and tried to refocus.

Work had been long and difficult too, and she'd had more déjà vu feelings with another couple, reminding her of Holly all over again. One person seemed perfectly happy, the other totally miserable. Had she missed a major clue with Holly? Could she have had her head that far off in the clouds?

Brea was looking at her expectantly, making Lillian realize she hadn't responded to the nice compliment she'd given her.

"I'm sorry," she said. "You look very nice as well." She smiled and hoped she looked the part. The last thing she wanted to be was rude.

"Only say it if you mean it," Brea said with a smile.

Lillian nodded and refilled her glass of water. "I mean it."

Brea had on dark jeans, a black button-down, and a skinny white tie. Her hair had been recently highlighted and she wore it swept up and over in front, giving her a very modern, punk-like look. Lillian smiled at her, noting again that she did indeed find her attractive. Even if she had a more notable look than Lillian's plain Jane.

Brea held up her glass of water for a toast. "As did I."

"I don't know about that," Lillian said, laughing as she looked down at her jeans and white sleeveless sweater. "I feel a bit old these days."

Brea dismissed her with a wave of her hand. "No way. You look great. Trust me."

"Well, thank you."

"My pleasure," she said with a grin.

Lillian fought staring at her mouth as the words breezed out. As nice as it was, she noted that it wasn't as full as Audrey's. But still she wondered if she was a good kisser. She flushed as she recalled how Audrey's mouth felt on hers. The heat of it. The moisture, the tugging and taking. Audrey had been the best kisser she'd ever had the pleasure of knowing. How could anyone else ever compare to that?

"You doing all right?" Brea asked, smoothing down her tie. She was smiling as if she assumed Lillian's fond look was solely because of her. "You got kind of red."

"I'm fine," Lillian said quickly. She'd promised herself she wouldn't think of Audrey on this date, and she was already blowing it.

Thank God, Brea couldn't tell. Thank God, no one could. After all, what would Audrey do if she knew just how much she thought of her? The consequences wouldn't be good. Audrey would come at her full force then.

Oh God, wait. That did sound good.

She wondered what Audrey was doing at that moment. Was she on a date too? Hadn't they both said they didn't date? Yet here she was, and no doubt Audrey was out with that blonde. What was the deal there? Had Audrey found someone she considered good enough to change for? And so soon after Lillian? She chugged her water as the idea stung up through her chest and into her throat.

"Lillian?"

"Hmm?"

"Wow, penny for your thoughts right now."

"No, oh no. Trust me. You don't want to know."

Brea leaned forward. "I think I do."

Lillian searched desperately for a change in topic and decided to butter some bread for distraction.

"You don't have to tell me," Brea finally said, still grinning. "No pressure. I'll just continue to assume they were good thoughts."

"Okay," Lillian breathed, relief rushing through her. "Bread?"

"No, thanks. I'm doing the low-carb thing."

"Oh."

"I know it sounds crazy coming to an Italian restaurant, but I hear the place is good and I only want the best for you." She winked. "Besides, I can have some chicken and a salad."

Lillian thought right through her words, not even hearing them until she finished. Then she had to hurry to catch up.

"I hope your meal is as good as mine is going to be." She bit into the bread, actually beginning to look forward to a small serving of lasagna.

"Me too."

Lillian smiled, already feeling like she'd have to force her way through conversation. Why was she here again? Oh yes, Nadine had made her call. Of course.

"Thank you for the flowers, by the way," Lillian said, glad to have something of relevance to say. "That was very nice of you."

Brea's smile fell, and this time she flushed. "Um, flowers?"

Lillian nodded. "Yes, the white roses?" Something was wrong. She could tell by the shocked look on her face. What had she said?

Brea sat back and crossed her arms over her chest. "Well, I

wish I could say they were from me, but…" She held up her hands. "No can do."

Oh no. Lillian struggled for words, unable to find a way out. "You didn't send them?"

"No."

Lillian looked away as her mind raced. One name came to mind. The name she'd been trying to avoid.

"Audrey," Brea said it for her, and she didn't sound happy about it. She pointed a stern look at Lillian waiting for her to respond.

"I don't know," Lillian said, shook up. "I just don't have any idea at this point."

"There was no card?"

"Yes, there was a card."

"What did it say?"

Lillian patted her mouth with her napkin. Brea was obviously upset, and Lillian didn't particularly like her tone. If she hadn't sent the flowers, then the contents of the card were no business of hers.

"I'd rather not discuss it."

Brea appeared more shocked than before. She blinked a few times and then drummed her fingers along the tabletop. When she spoke again, she tried to sound calm and indifferent.

"So you called me because you thought I sent the flowers, didn't you?" The disappointment clouded her face and she looked for a second like she might get up and walk away.

Lillian hesitated, feeling like she had that first night when she'd turned Brea down for a date. She felt like shit and she hadn't even meant to hurt her.

"I called. I called to say thank you, yes."

"But we got to talking and you forgot."

"Yes, I guess I did."

Brea nodded and tightened her lips.

"It doesn't mean we can't have a good time," Lillian tried.

Brea licked her lips and took a sip of her water. "I don't know about that," she said.

"Oh." Lillian was afraid to ask why. Instead, they sat in silence for a long while, politely refusing an appetizer from the waiter, putting off their order for dinner. Lillian had hoped they could salvage dinner, but it didn't seem like Brea was willing.

"Fucking McCarthy," Brea finally whispered, turning red again. "Are you still seeing her?"

Lillian felt her eyes go wide, and she looked around to make sure no one could hear them. "What? No. I'm not."

Brea continued, her rage full on. "You don't understand what it's like competing with her. She's not good for you, Lillian. Not good at all."

"I think I can be the judge of who's good for me and who's not, thank you." The nerve. She heard this all day long from controlling partners. She wasn't about to put up with it in her personal life.

"I'm not sure you can," Brea said.

"Excuse me?"

"Just knowing you've been with her—" But she couldn't finish her statement, the topic obviously too upsetting for her to even verbalize.

"Then why are you here?" Lillian felt herself growing angry. Her voice had raised an octave, and she could feel the pulse jumping in her neck.

"I thought—" Brea shook her head. "I thought you were different. Not like everyone else at the club."

"I am different. And if you can't see that, then—"

"You were with Audrey McCarthy."

What the hell?

"First of all, I don't have to defend myself to you, and second of all, so what?" Her private life was none of Brea's business, and she didn't like the way she was speaking about Audrey. "Just what the hell is wrong with Audrey?"

Brea's jaw dropped. "Are you serious? She's the biggest whore in Phoenix, for starters."

Lillian tossed her napkin onto the table, having enough. "You don't even know her, do you?"

"I know her well enough."

"You obviously don't know her at all or you wouldn't talk like that."

Brea's face contorted in confusion and what could only be anger. "Why are you defending her?"

Lillian let her have it with both barrels, not giving a damn who could hear. "I'm just telling it like it is. Audrey's a good person. A human being. And you know what I think? I think you're jealous."

"Jealous?" Brea whispered between clenched teeth. "Of what?"

"Of Audrey. Because she can and does get anyone she wants. And you can't stand that."

"Please." But anger tinged her cheeks, and she began to flex her jaw, staring Lillian down.

"What I was about to say before you so rudely made your assumptions was that Audrey and I have agreed to go our separate ways. I don't know who the flowers are from, but I seriously doubt they are from her." She didn't owe her any explanation, but it felt good to give one. Even if she didn't quite believe it herself.

Brea breathed deeply, listening. "I understand."

"Good." Lillian controlled her own breathing and downed the rest of her water.

"I just can't stand to think of her with you."

Lillian studied her. "Why?"

"Because I've seen her going from woman to woman, and you deserve better than that."

"Well, thank you, but I don't need protecting. And I really don't like the way you spoke about Audrey."

Brea held up her hands. "I'm sorry. I just have seen her night after night—"

"It doesn't matter. That has nothing to do with me, and it has nothing to do with you either."

Brea clamped her mouth shut.

"Now if you'll excuse me, I need to get to church."

"I thought you weren't going tonight."

"I changed my mind."

Brea stood along with her. "Don't leave like this. We can at least have dinner, can't we?"

Lillian slung her purse over her shoulder, her stomach in knots. "I'm not hungry."

"Let's just let it go, okay?" Brea tried.

Lillian decided to be honest with her, wanting nothing more to do with her. "Look, Brea, had I not gotten the flowers, I wouldn't have called you."

The words took their time sinking in, and when they finally did, Brea paled.

"Seriously? I thought we had a good time the other night when we went for coffee and talked and—"

"We did. It was nice. But I just—I'm sorry. I told you before, I just don't date. This is why. Someone always gets hurt or it ends in disaster."

"So you don't like me. That's what you're really saying."

Lillian closed her eyes. "Please don't do this." She had to listen to people and their insecurities all day long, and frankly, she just couldn't take any more. Not at that moment or any moment soon after.

"Then just tell me."

"I did." She started to walk away. "I just don't date."

CHAPTER THIRTEEN

Yeah, baby, do it. Do it harder," Janis said from her position against the red velvet wall, one leg up, arms thrown around Audrey's neck. "Fuck me harder."

Audrey pushed her fingers farther up and in, jamming into her harder, feeling her soft, wet walls tighten around her, wishing she'd hurry and come. They'd been going at it for ten minutes already, and she just knew Beastly was going to poke her head in at any minute.

"What's wrong?" Janis breathed.

"Huh?" She looked back into her eyes. "Nothing."

"You're not into this."

Audrey pumped her quicker, harder. "Yes, I am." But she wasn't. In fact, she'd just been thinking that she didn't want to fuck Janis again ever.

"Prove it."

Audrey strained, her arm and wrist beginning to hurt. "What?"

"Bite my neck."

"No."

"Why not?"

Because she didn't want to smell her hair, her skin, and feel her soft flesh under her teeth. It would only remind her that she wasn't Lillian. That she didn't smell the same, feel the same, sound the same. All she could think about was Lillian, especially in this fucking room.

"Look at me," Janis said. Panting.

"I am."

"That's it, get mad. Fuck me mad."

"You want me mad?"

"I want you feeling something."

Audrey grit her teeth and continued fucking her. "Then hurry the fuck up."

"Yeah, that's it. Oh God."

"Fucking come. Fucking well come."

"Oh God, Audrey. Yes." She closed her eyes, and when Audrey flicked her clit with her thumb, she spilled over into orgasm, screaming into the Midnight Room. It assaulted Audrey's ears and she turned away, no longer wanting to be a part of the spectacle.

"Yeeees," she said when she finally came down, laughing throatily. "That was great."

"Good," Audrey said not really caring one way or the other. She pulled herself from her slowly and backed away, not liking the smell of alcohol on her breath even though she was damn sure hers smelled the same way.

She went to the bar and washed her hands and then sat on the couch, digging her fingers through her hair. She was drunk, exhausted, and dying to see Lillian, who had yet to show up to the club.

Janis smoothed down her skirt and came to sit next to her, trailing her hand along Audrey's shoulder and neck.

"What's wrong?"

Audrey closed her eyes. "Nothing. Just tired."

"We didn't have to come back here," she said. "Though I do love fucking in this room."

Audrey laughed a little. "Yeah, it has its intended effect."

"Apparently, I'm not having my intended effect," she said, settling in next to her. "At least not lately."

"I'm just tired," Audrey said, wanting another shot of something strong.

"I can tell." She reached over and touched her face. "I shouldn't have had them call us back."

She shouldn't have gone back there with her. The room felt sacred to her, like it was hers and Lillian's alone.

"I'm ready for another drink." She was ready to go look for Lillian and get the hell out of that room.

"Don't you think you'd better slow down?"

Audrey turned to face her. "No. And I don't need you saying something either."

"I'm just worried you won't be able to drive home."

"I'm fine."

She was. She was barely buzzing. In fact, she was feeling and thinking way too much.

"You've been drinking way too much lately."

"I said I'm fine." She clenched her jaw, about to lose her temper. "Are you coming or not?" She headed for the door.

"I already did," she said, walking out ahead of her.

The music slammed into Audrey as she exited the Midnight Room, causing her to stumble a little as she walked through the paneled glass walls, having to press her palms to some of them to steady herself.

"You need help?" Janis said, coming back for her.

"Nah, just the music is so loud."

"I think we'd better get you home."

"Nah. Not yet."

Janis helped her to her seat and Audrey grabbed a beer, sipped at it, and tried to casually look over at Lillian's table.

Her heart sped up and then dropped when she saw her. She was looking incredible in tight jeans and a sleeveless blouse the color of her eyes. Skin as milky pale as ever. She was laughing with her friends, arm wrapped around Carmen, who was even smiling as well.

"She looks good," Janis said, sitting on the armrest of her chair.

"Who?" Audrey asked, taking a chug from her beer and carefully looking away.

"Lillian."

"I hadn't noticed."

"Uh-huh. Why don't you go talk to her?"

"Nah."

"Why not? You obviously—"

"I said no."

"Fine."

"Why don't you go home?" she said. "I can manage."

"Because I don't want to."

"Fine."

"You want me to go?"

"I want you to leave me the hell alone."

Janis stood. "What the fuck is wrong with you?"

"Nothing. Now move." She wanted to watch Lillian, wanted to watch her from afar all night long.

"No."

"Goddammit." Audrey stood and made her way to the bar where she had a better angle. But when she arrived, she was disappointed to find Lillian already gone. "Fuck me," she said, motioning for another beer.

"No thanks, and you've had enough," the bartender said. It was the same one who was seeing Lillian.

"Not your job to look after me," Audrey said. "So fuck off."

"It is my job, and no, I will not fuck off. Why don't you fuck off and go home? There's nothing for you here. Even your girl is leaving."

Audrey turned and saw Janis weaving through the crowd, headed for the door. She shrugged. "Oh well."

"So sober up."

"No, thanks."

"Maybe you should listen to her," a voice said from right next to her. A warm hand soon followed, touching her shoulder. Audrey met Lillian's eyes and nearly melted right off the stool. She tried to play it cool, though, by glancing away and tapping at the bar as if demanding another drink.

"I got it under control," Audrey said.

"I don't think you do," Lillian said, sliding onto the stool next to her.

"I don't need you and her," Audrey said, glaring at the bartender, "telling me what to do."

"The name's Brea, and what did I tell you?" Brea asked, directing the question to Lillian. "You're best to just leave her alone."

"What gives you the right to tell anyone anything?" Audrey asked, fed up with her mouth.

"I care about her," Brea said. "Which is more than I can say for you."

"Oh, that's right," Audrey said. "You two are an item now. Well, don't let me interrupt."

Lillian gave Brea a look, and if Audrey wasn't mistaken, she would've said it was a dirty one.

"I would like to talk to her," Lillian said to Brea. "Alone."

Brea wiped down a glass and rolled her eyes. "Whatever." She turned away and headed for the other side of the bar.

"You really do need to control that hunk of meat," Audrey said. "She's dangerous."

"Funny, that's what she says about you."

"Huh. Go figure. Better watch out, then."

Lillian touched her shoulder again. "I'm not afraid."

Audrey looked at her, so drunk and so turned on at her proximity. "Are you flirting with me, Lillian? Because I'm a little fucked up."

"I noticed. And no, I'm not flirting."

"Of course not." She laughed. "That would be living a little."

"I'm going to ignore that."

"Okay," she said, not really caring. She didn't need her help or her sympathy.

"I came over here to talk to you."

"Why?"

"Because you look like you could use a friend."

"I have friends."

"You look like you could use another."

Audrey tapped the bar. "I could use another drink."

"No, I don't think so. I think I should drive you home."

"I don't need a ride."

"I'm afraid you do. Come on." She stood, leaned into her slowly, and slipped her hand into her back pocket where she deftly retrieved her keys. She was so close Audrey could smell her scent, and she briefly closed her eyes wanting to get lost in it. She swayed from her intoxication when Lillian helped her to stand.

"Yeah, I think we need to get you home."

"That was for you," Audrey said. "Because you're so close."

"Uh-huh."

"It was. I miss you," she said, having to lean on her to walk.

Lillian laughed as they wove between bodies. "I doubt that."

"I do. I miss you like crazy."

"What about your new girlfriend? She hasn't been keeping you occupied?"

"She's not you," Audrey said. "She's so not you."

"Audrey, don't." They exited the club and Audrey breathed deep, thanking the heavens she didn't feel sick.

"I think...I love you, Lillian," she slurred. "I think I do."

Lillian helped her to her car. "Audrey, you're drunk. You don't know what you're saying."

"Yes, I do."

"No, you don't. I used to tell cab drivers I loved them when I would get wasted. Cab drivers, strange women, anyone around me."

"I'm not like that," Audrey said. "Why won't you fucking listen to me? I'm telling you I love you." Her chest tightened as emotion came burning up through her.

"Because you're drunk." Lillian held Audrey's shoulders and stared into her eyes. "Tell it to me straight and then I might actually listen."

"What would you say?"

Lillian helped her duck into the car. "Say it to me straight first."

"I don't want to," Audrey confessed, knowing she'd never be able to.

"That's what I thought." Lillian started the car and they rode in silence for a while before she reached over and took Audrey's hand.

"Your girlfriend seems nice. Would you like me to call her for you?"

"She's not my girlfriend."

"Oh. I thought she was."

"You mean you're paying attention?" Her hand felt like sunshine warmth on Audrey's. It anchored her into the present, keeping her from drifting off on her small dinghy in the calm, calm sea.

"I see, yes."

"Thought you didn't care."

"I told you I cared, remember?"

"And that you wanted happiness for me."

"Yes." Lillian glanced over at her as she accelerated from a green light. "But I don't think you are happy. It's why I came to talk to you. I've been where you are, Audrey."

Audrey laughed, pulling her hand away. "So you came over to save me? Is that it?"

"I came to help."

"I don't need your help, Lillian." I *need you. I want you. Can't you see that?* She rubbed her forehead and fought against the impending headache.

"I wish you would come to a meeting with me."

"I'm not going to any fucking meeting. I'm not an alcoholic."

"No?"

"No. I can stop anytime I want."

"Then why do it at all?"

"Because I don't like to think." *Or feel. Or exist all alone.* She smacked her forehead, wishing her inner monologue would stop. She had to drown the fucker out.

"I think a meeting might help you, Audrey. You can learn how to think and feel again without needing the numbness."

"No, thanks."

Lillian sighed.

"I told you I don't need any help."

"Okay."

They pulled into the apartment complex and Lillian slowed in front of Audrey's building. She put the car in park and sat with her hands on her thighs.

"You look beautiful tonight," Audrey said softly.

"Thank you."

"You look beautiful every night."

"I do not."

"Yes, you do." Audrey looked up toward her stairs. "Would you like to come up?"

"I'll help you inside," Lillian said. "Then I really should go."

"Okay." Audrey opened the door, thrilled she was actually coming inside. She couldn't wait to hold her and touch her. Kiss her sweet-tasting lips, hear her soft moans.

They walked up the stairs and the neighbor's cat was at her door, scarfing down what appeared to be food.

Audrey's stomach sank. "Oh no."

"What?"

She found the door unlocked, Janis standing at the other end.

"I see you found a ride home," Janis said, looking to Lillian with a hand on her hip.

"What are you doing here?"

"I was worried."

"Then why did you leave the club?" Audrey wasn't buying it.

"Because you refused to let me get you home."

"Yeah, well, I'm home and I'm fine."

"I see that." She looked at Lillian again.

"I'm Janis," she said, offering her hand. "We haven't been introduced."

"Lillian."

"Yes, I know. Audrey speaks fondly of you." Audrey glared at her, daring her to say more. But it wasn't necessary. Janis took the hint. "Well, I should obviously be going."

"No, I'll go," Lillian said. "I just wanted to make sure she was okay."

"No. Don't." Janis slung her purse over her shoulder and

slipped into her shoes. She breezed past them, leaving them on the front stoop as she hurried down the stairs.

Audrey walked inside, not giving her a second look. Janis knew she shouldn't have been there. She hadn't been invited. They'd talked about this just the other week.

"I thought you said she wasn't your girlfriend," Lillian said, stepping just inside the door. She pushed it closed when the cat tried to come inside.

"She's not."

"Does she know that?"

"Yes." Audrey helped herself to a glass of water and offered some to Lillian who politely refused.

"I should be going," she said, looking uncomfortable.

Audrey set her glass down and walked toward her. "No. Stay." She reached out and touched her face. Lillian angled into it at first but then pulled away.

"I can't."

"Why?"

"We've gone over this. You know why."

"Because I scare you."

"Yes."

Audrey was a little shocked at the admission. She'd suspected as much, but hearing it was another thing altogether.

"I do?"

"Yes." Lillian fumbled with her hands.

"Why?"

"Audrey, I don't want to do this."

"I've been seeing the same woman," Audrey said. "I did that for you." She couldn't believe she was admitting it, but she was too drunk and too desperate to care.

"What?"

"I did it to show you that I could be stable."

"Audrey, that is wrong on so many levels."

"Janis knows. She just wants to have fun."

"This, what I just saw, doesn't seem like fun."

"It's fine."

"I have to go."

"Please don't."

"Audrey, I can't do this."

Audrey crossed her arms, tears brimming. "You both say you want to help me and then you both leave. How fucked up is that?"

"I am willing to help you, Audrey. But you have to want to help yourself," Lillian whispered. "I can't be a part of this." She reached in her pocket and pulled out Audrey's keys. She set them on the kitchen counter. "If you need a ride to get your Jeep tomorrow, just let me know."

"I won't. Don't worry." She'd be damned if she'd ask her. "Just go."

Lillian looked at her for a long moment. "Audrey, I do care. More than you know. And I am here for you. Just a phone call away. But you need to be there for you too. I can't help you alone. Okay?"

Audrey looked away as emotion bit her throat.

"The ball's in your court, Audrey."

Then she slowly turned and walked out the door.

Chapter Fourteen

Lillian walked quickly from her car up to the high school football field. The sun was bright and piercing, and she tugged down her visor to help shield her eyes. The day was beautiful, and she was thrilled to be a part of such a special event. She couldn't thank Rain enough for inviting her.

She hurried along quickly, paid her entrance fee, and then searched the crowded grounds for Rain. She spotted her right away and headed for her over near the vending area.

"Hey you!" Rain said as Lillian ran up. "Don't you look sporty."

"Hey yourself. You too." Rain was wearing running shorts and a Walk for Breast Cancer T-shirt. Her ball cap was pulled tightly on her head, ponytail threaded through. Totally adorable.

"Thanks so much for doing this for me," Rain said. "Usually, the schools have plenty of volunteers for these meets, but today we came up short. I think it's because of that local marathon."

"Probably. And yeah, you bet, this is no problem. I'm excited to be here. It sure beats sitting at home." That seemed to be all she'd done lately. Sit at home and stare at the phone, waiting for Audrey to call. She even stopped going to The Griffin, unable to watch Audrey drink her life away or have a wild time with the blonde. Whatever Audrey was up to, she couldn't bear to be witness to it.

She wished Audrey could see that she wanted to be in her life. Just in a healthy way.

And as for Holly, she'd been thinking a lot about her too. But not in the way she usually did. Now it was more grounded and reality based. Things hadn't been that great. There'd been problems, ones she'd chosen to ignore. Helping her patients in similar situations had helped her to see just what her problems had been and why she'd feared rocking the boat. All along, she'd feared Holly would leave her. And even though she'd tried to smooth things over and pretend, Holly had left anyway. She would've been better off facing their issues head on. At least then she could've realized just how unhappy she was, not just Holly.

She looked around and caught sight of some of the athletes, all dressed up in their running uniforms. Some were in wheelchairs, some were in leg braces, and others stood with coaches along the sidelines. All had broad smiles on their faces, and many were waving up into the stands at friends and family.

"I love doing these meets," Rain said. "These kids just don't get the chance to compete otherwise."

"And I take it they like competing?" Lillian asked with a smile.

"Oh, yes."

"Win or lose?"

"Oh, yes. And there is no win or lose. Just win. They all get medals."

"How cool."

"It is."

"So what do you need me to do?"

"We hand out the water."

"Okay."

"The water is over here, and we need to put it on ice and wheel the coolers over to the shade. The athletes stop by our tented area after the race to get their medals, T-shirts, and water."

"Sounds great."

"Yep, so let's get started. We have a lot of water to carry over."

Lillian followed her to the concession stand and picked up a case of water. Then she followed her to the tented area near the finish line on the field. The work was grueling, one case after another, but eventually they had enough to start with, and athletes lined up right away, wanting water before the race.

"It's warm today," Lillian said, wiping her brow and handing over two bottles.

"Yes, it is." Rain settled into a pocket chair next to her and began fanning herself.

"Thank you," a young boy said as he took his water with a smile.

"You're welcome," Lillian said. "Good luck." She dumped more ice into a cooler and sat down herself.

"This is so exciting. I'm excited for them."

"Just wait until the races start. You'll be cheering so hard you'll go hoarse."

Lillian laughed and removed her sunglasses. Under the tent the shade was vast, so she didn't need them. She was rubbing her eyes when she caught sight of someone. She blinked a few times and stood, needing to make sure.

"Is that?"

"Oh yeah," Rain said, standing alongside her. "I thought she might be here today."

Lillian stared in disbelief as Audrey walked with a young athlete, near the starting line, arm around his shoulder.

"You mean you knew she might be here?"

Rain sat again and looked very guilty. "She's at every meet."

"Rain! Why didn't you tell me?" Lillian put her sunglasses back on and sat, not wanting to be seen. She'd been avoiding Audrey for a reason. Seeing her was just too painful and it brought her growing feelings closer to the surface. Feelings she wasn't quite ready to admit to yet.

"I didn't think it was a big deal. And honestly, I didn't think you'd come. You've been such a homebody lately, I never know."

Lillian sighed. "Shit."

"So you're not friends anymore?"

"It's complicated." She wasn't about to tell her just how complicated.

"You care about her, don't you?" Rain asked softly.

Lillian pressed her lips together, watching Audrey as she bent to a knee with the boy, pointing down the race lane.

"Yes." More than she'd like to admit. More than she ever thought she could've.

"So what's the holdup?"

"I just don't think we can get past our differences." That was true, but there was more to it than that. She feared Audrey's way of life, yes. But more than that, she feared the strong feelings Audrey brought out in her.

"She's too wild?"

"Something like that."

"Well, how wild can she be if she's helping out here?"

Lillian looked over at her, her point hitting home. Lillian had to fight for a reason why in order to convince herself. "She's still wild, Rain. Besides, I think she has a girlfriend."

I think I love you, Lillian.

The words kept replaying in Lillian's mind over and over, oh so sweetly, like a favorite song that wouldn't leave her mind. She sipped her own bottle of water and wished she were home where she could relive the moment again and again without interruption. Where she could curl up in bed with Audrey's T-shirt and pretend the words were real, their meaning pure and deep. Oh, how she wished they were.

"You can like someone and not be able to be with them," Lillian said softly.

"Well, whatever happens, I'm glad I gave your name to the deejay that night," Rain said.

Lillian was too, although she didn't say it.

"I'm so worried about her," she confessed. "Her drinking, partying…" She purposely left out the rest.

"Did something happen?" Rain asked.

Lillian looked down at her hands, the sight of Audrey and the memory too much to handle at once. Her emotions got the better of her and her excitement grew as she relived it. She had to tell someone.

"Well, she told me that she thought she loved me."

Rain gasped. "Are you serious, Lil?"

Lillian nodded. "Yes. But she was drunk when she said it."

"Oh my God. This is huge. Lillian, she's—"

"She was drunk, Rain. I'm pretty sure she didn't mean it."

"But what if she did?"

"She didn't. She wasn't serious. I don't even know if she can be serious about anything."

Rain came back quickly. "I've seen her here countless times, and I can tell you, she's very serious. These kids count on her and she's here for them."

Lillian looked over at her again. Audrey was still talking to the boy, patting his shoulder and then running in place as if showing him what to do. Could Audrey be serious? Did she mean what she said?

"Really?" Lillian asked, hoping what Rain was saying was true.

"Yes. They love her."

Lillian looked over at Rain, knowing her very well. "You didn't ask me here by accident, did you?" She saw volunteers at every station and plenty more milling around. "Rain, damn you."

"What?" She held up her hands. "I just thought you might want to see her in a different light."

"I don't need to see her at all. It's too—"

"Much?"

Lillian closed her eyes and nodded.

"What you said about her girlfriend…they're not like that. I know Janis a little, and she's far from girlfriend material."

"So what? I should be okay with Audrey just fucking around like usual?"

"I don't know, Lil. Maybe it's not like that. Maybe Audrey's trying to prove something. Or maybe she's trying not to think about you."

Maybe she's really doing it to show you she can date one person at a time. Just like she said.

"I don't know. I don't want to think about it." Yet it was all she did.

"Okay. But you know, even Carmen's okay with you liking her."

"Oh, she is not." Lillian smiled and handed out another water bottle to a little girl in a wheelchair.

"We talked about it when you went over to help Audrey. Sure, we wish she was different and more suitable for you, but we do want you to follow your heart."

Lillian wasn't sure what to say. She just kept watching Audrey.

"We know you care about her, and that's what's important. And if she's telling you she loves you, then..."

"It's not like that."

"Yes, it is. You're just afraid of her."

"Well, don't you think I should be?"

"Based on what I see here? No. Based on what I've seen at the club in the past, yes. But not recently, Lil. Recently, she's been miserable and everyone can see that. And I think it has everything to do with you."

"She's just lost in the booze," Lillian said.

"And why do you think that is? Remember how lost you got in it over Holly?"

Lillian looked at her. "You can't be serious."

"I think she cares about you, Lil. A lot. According to Janis, you're all she talks about."

"Janis told you that?"

"Yes. She said she's so miserable she's thinking about calling it off because Audrey just isn't fun like she thought she would be."

Lillian rubbed her temple, her stomach fluttering. Audrey talked about her? Thought about her? For real?

I think I love you.

Did she really mean what she'd said?

Lillian reached for a water and took a long gulp. Was it possible? Audrey in love with her?

She flushed at the idea as her heart accelerated. Audrey.

She stared at her, taking in everything about her. She noted her toned and muscled arms glistening with sweat in the sun; her small, round breasts; her long, muscled legs, tanned from time outdoors. She longed to run her hands through her midnight hair and wondered what she smelled like right now. Sweat and cologne? Like when they'd fucked?

She clenched her legs together as she thought of it. Suddenly, she longed to be near her, to touch her, to look deep into her eyes.

"We're getting ready to start," Rain said, standing.

Lillian stood too and homed in on Audrey, who had settled her athlete at the starting line. Then she ran toward the finish line and clapped her hands, ready for the start. The starting pistol went off, causing Lillian to jerk, and the runners were off, running as hard as they could toward the finish line. The crowd went wild as the runners gave it their all, many having trouble soon after starting. Audrey jumped up and down, her athlete going slowly, struggling to stay in running form. She cheered him loudly and left her spot at the line to run along next to him on the side, in the grass. She clapped and cheered him on, encouraging him every step of the way.

Lillian held her hands at her chest and squeezed, cheering for the boy herself. Rain was next to her, yelling as loud as she could as the first of the runners finished the long sprint. Audrey hopped along the sidelines, yelling louder.

Lillian bobbed on her toes. "Come on, come on. You can do it."

Audrey's boy finished at last, coming in fourth, and Audrey went wild, hugging him right up off his feet and twirling him around.

"She's been working with him for a while," Rain said with a smile. "This is the first race he's finished."

Lillian's heart swelled as she watched them embrace again and again, the boy waving up into the stands. She didn't know whose grin was bigger, his or Audrey's.

"That was amazing," Lillian said. "Really. Very touching."

"Oh, it is. Especially if you know everyone's story."

"Audrey's amazing," Lillian whispered as she watched her wipe her eyes and wrap her arm around the boy.

"She does a great job and she cares about these kids. You can tell."

"Yes, you can."

"Here they come," Rain said, pointing to the first of the runners. She opened the cooler and began digging out the water. "We have several more races and activities before the day's over, so we have to keep everyone hydrated."

Lillian dug in with her and handed out water after water, congratulating each runner as she did so. They proudly displayed their medals and many talked furiously about the race and what they'd just done. It warmed Lillian's heart, and when she saw Audrey approach, her entire body warmed and she fought to remain still, a part of her wanting to run up and throw her arms around her.

"Lillian," Audrey said softly, seeming to be genuinely surprised. So surprised she seemed at a loss for words. She whipped off her sunglasses as if to make sure her vision wasn't playing tricks on her. Her dark eyes sought with curiosity. She wrapped her arm around the boy and elbowed Olivia, who stood next to her.

"Hi, Audrey."

Audrey blinked a few times quickly. "I'm—surprised. How long have you been here?"

"Long enough." She smiled.

"I-I don't know what to say." She looked away and blushed, and Lillian knew she remembered all the things she'd said during their last two encounters. Did this mean she'd meant them? Or that she was embarrassed by them?

"Hi, Lillian," Olivia said with a smile. It seemed to light up her entire face.

"Hi, nice to see you again."

"You too. You're all this gal talks about."

Lillian felt her eyebrow raise. "Am I?"

Audrey elbowed her again, this time not so gently.

"Uh-huh. All the time. You're a beautiful little thing," Olivia said, causing Lillian to blush. "I can see why she's crazy about you."

"Olivia," Audrey said under her breath.

"What? She is. She should know."

"Who's this?" Rain asked, obviously trying to fill the long silence that followed.

Audrey looked down at the boy under her arm and pulled him in close. "This is Kyle," she said proudly.

"Hi, Kyle," Lillian said, handing him a water. "I like your medal."

Kyle held it up for all to see, grinning from ear to car. "I ran," he said, looking up at Audrey. "Fast."

Audrey laughed. "You totally did."

"He did great," Lillian said. "You did great," she whispered to Audrey.

Audrey looked at her with burning irises. "I did?"

"Yes. I was thinking maybe, we could...you know...go for a meal sometime or something. If you're, you know...ever ready." Audrey stared at her lips for a long while. "I've been ready."

"Why haven't you called, then?"

"Because I thought that after the mountain trail..."

"I told you I care."

Olivia cleared her throat, but Audrey ignored her, holding Lillian's gaze.

"You sure?"

Lillian nodded "Very sure."

"She'd love to," Olivia said, squeezing Audrey.

Audrey smiled, staring at Lillian for a long moment. A moment that only seemed to include the two of them.

Eventually, Rain broke the silence. "I'm sorry to interrupt, but, Lil, your phone's ringing."

Lillian broke her stare and turned to grab her phone from the chair.

"I'd better go," Audrey said.

Lillian shook her head. "Do you have to?"

"Yeah, I really should. But I'll be around. You staying?"

Lillian was about to nod when she looked down at her phone and saw the caller ID.

"Who is it?" Rain asked, coming to look with her.

Lillian looked up at her and then at Audrey.

"It's Holly."

"Holly?" Audrey asked, confused.

Rain looked over at her and pressed her lips together as Lillian stepped away to take the call.

"It's her ex."

CHAPTER FIFTEEN

Audrey drove in a daze, completely turned off and shut down after the morning's happenings. The look on Lillian's face when she'd gotten the phone call had said it all. And Audrey had been so close to reaching her, she could almost reach out and touch her. But now the ex was back, and what she wanted, Audrey had no doubt. She wanted Lillian.

She looked over at Janis, who was attempting to tame her hair in the high wind, and rolled her eyes. She shouldn't even be bringing her, but Viv had said to bring a date, and Audrey didn't want to think about Lillian and what had almost been.

Why did she have to answer that call?

But it would've happened sooner rather than later. Holly would've come by or she would've kept calling. Anything to get Lillian. Just like she'd do anything to get Lillian.

She wound her way through Viv's new neighborhood and parked her Jeep a ways down the crowded road.

"Try to have fun," she said over to Janis, who seriously looked like she'd rather be somewhere else. She was in a miniskirt and a short leather jacket. Not exactly family-style attire. But Audrey didn't care. She didn't care about anything other than what Holly wanted.

"Yeah, this sounds like fun," she said sarcastically, looking around the nicely manicured front yard. "Sitting around with married folk celebrating a birthday always gets me hot."

"You didn't have to come," Audrey said.

"Yes, I did. I'm your date. You said so yourself. You have to look respectable."

"There's nothing respectable about us." She laughed a little and rang the bell again. Her palms were sweaty, and she hoped she looked presentable enough in dark jeans and a button-down shirt. She badly wanted to tear off the shirt and just sport the tight tank underneath, but she didn't think it would bode well. Not yet.

The door opened. "Well, look who it is," Viv said with a broad grin. "McCarthy, as I live and breathe." She held out her hand and then yanked her in for a hug.

"Relax. It hasn't been that long," Audrey said, secretly thrilled at the warm welcome.

"The hell it hasn't." She patted her on the back. "Come in, come in."

Audrey stepped inside and turned to introduce Janis.

"Viv, this is Janis. Janis, Viv."

"Well, hello, my dear," Viv said, kissing her hand. "Welcome to our humble abode."

"Thanks," Janis said smiling, obviously pleased with the welcome as well. "I like your yard."

Viv laughed. "We will have to let my wife know. She takes pride in all that landscaping stuff. Be careful if you get her started talking about it, though. She'll never shut up."

She led them farther inside, and Audrey noted how nice the smaller home looked with newer furniture and nice art and photographs on the walls. It smelled of new carpet and home cooking. For an instant, she was envious. It beat the hell out of Viv's old loft space and her own tiny apartment.

"The place looks great," Audrey said.

"Thanks." Viv stared her down for a long moment and then smiled. "It's good to see you."

"You too." But she was still nervous as hell.

"Everyone's going to be thrilled to see you."

She led them into a large living room where a dozen or so women mingled.

Becky caught her eye and she came over carrying a beer, arms outstretched. "Audrey, what the hell!" She enveloped her in a tight hug. "I'm surprised as hell to see you here."

"I am too," Audrey said, gathering laughs. She too was surprised she'd come. But sitting at home and wallowing in alcohol and her sorrows was getting her nowhere. Lillian had been right. And a part of her hated that. She'd opened up to her, and Lillian had turned her down, again and again, just like everyone else in her life. But she couldn't drink herself to death. It didn't solve anything. She had to pull herself up and prove that she could change. She'd been doing a good job here lately, but it took one tiny step at a time. Seeing her old friends was another tiny step in the right direction.

"And she brought a date!" Becky said to everyone. "Wow, Aud."

"This is Janis," Viv said, introducing her to the room.

"Janis!" they all piped. "Welcome."

"Wow," Janis said, "Thanks." She smiled at Audrey as if to say *maybe this isn't so bad after all*, then shifted her gaze to an attractive butch who was offering her a drink. They crossed the room and headed for the kitchen counter, where another woman Audrey didn't know was mixing drinks.

"Who are all these people?" Audrey asked, a little overwhelmed.

"Mostly Viv's and Kayla's friends. I didn't know a lot of them either until recently. They're good people, though. At least so far as I know." Becky looked to Janis. "What about your girl? Is she good people?"

Janis was flirting with the butch, sipping her beer and laughing too loudly. She sat on a tall stool and crossed her exposed legs, causing more than a few heads to turn.

"She's all right, I guess. Been seeing her for a while now."

"No kidding? Audrey McCarthy? You're seeing someone?"

"I can be normal," Audrey said, liking the way it sounded even if it was a bold-faced lie. She wasn't seeing Janis. They were fucking, and Janis was riding her last nerve. But she was tired of people predicting her behavior and assuming things about her.

"I guess you can."

"Didn't know that about me, did you?"

"To tell you the truth, no. I didn't think you had it in you."

What Audrey really wanted to say was that she didn't. At least not with Janis. Maybe she did with Lillian, if Lillian would stop running from her. But then again, that's what people seemed to do.

"You okay?"

"Yeah. Just need a cold drink."

Audrey walked with Becky to the cooler, grabbed a soda, and headed for one of the empty sofas. The party was in full force as more women arrived, and everyone was hugging, laughing, and chatting up a storm. For a moment, Audrey almost pictured Lillian walking in, holding a gift, wishing the birthday girl a happy day. She could easily see it, just as easily as she could see herself slipping up next to her and wrapping a loving arm around her, as if they were the party's most well-known couple.

But, alas, Lillian didn't walk in, and Audrey was left alone, sitting and drinking and saying hello to old friends as they came by. After about an hour, she glanced over at Janis and found a small crowd around her. Apparently, she was doing body shots off the butch.

It didn't surprise her since Janis didn't know a stranger. But still, she'd hoped she would've behaved a little more, especially since she was supposed to be her date.

"What's the story with her?" Viv asked, coming to sit down, large margarita in hand. "She always like this?"

Audrey could tell she was trying to tread lightly. She didn't want to offend Audrey, but she was concerned nevertheless.

"Pretty much."

"And you're, you know, okay with that?"

Audrey shrugged. "She likes to have fun." A part of her was embarrassed, but she wasn't about to do anything for fear of it leading to a bigger scene. She'd hoped Janis would behave herself, but how could she ask her to when they never asked anything of each other? If she had, Janis would've mistaken it for something more, and Audrey didn't want that.

"Yes, she apparently does." Viv crossed her legs and sipped

her drink. "So how have you been?" She patted Audrey's leg and smiled.

"Oh, you know. Same old me. Just working and going out."

"But you have a girlfriend now. So that's changed."

"Well, I'm trying to give it a chance. Settle down a little."

Viv looked over at Janis and clicked her teeth. "Uh-huh." She changed the subject. "So how's your mom? Did you ever go and see her?"

Audrey shifted uncomfortably on the couch. She'd hoped this wouldn't come up. "No, not yet."

Viv nodded but didn't say anything for a while. "The offer still stands, you know."

"I know."

"I'll go with you anytime."

"Thanks."

"She just looked so bad."

"She usually does." Audrey pictured her mother sitting in her trailer, smoking up a storm, sipping cheap vodka, watching soap operas, bitching about the world. She hadn't looked well in twenty years.

"She looked worse than usual. Real thin. Not good at all. And, Aud, did you know she's on oxygen?"

Audrey looked at her quickly. "No." She was too shocked to try to downplay it. Oxygen? Jesus, maybe things were bad.

"I'm telling you, it's not good. And she's got a really bad cough."

Audrey had known the coughing would get worse; it had only been a matter of time. She imagined her mother on oxygen sitting in that trailer, coughing her lungs out, and suddenly, she longed to see her.

"And she asked about me?"

Viv nodded once again. "Yes. She sounded sincere, Aud. Not the same old cynical Ima Jean. She wanted to know how you were and what you were up to. She sounded hurt that she didn't know those things."

Audrey scoffed. "She always does that. Tries to lay on the

guilt." It was her mother's pattern. Bitch about her, tell her she's no good and that's why her father left, then lay on the guilt for Audrey never coming around. Audrey had been through it so many times she'd finally stopped seeing her. There was only so much a person could take.

"I don't know. It sounded different this time. I know how she was, Aud. She was awful to you. And I wouldn't wish that on anyone. But what if she really has changed?"

"What if?" Audrey didn't quite buy into it, but still, she was concerned enough to go and see her.

"Don't you think it would be worth it to go and find out? To see if things maybe can get better? For healing's sake?"

"I don't need healing."

Viv smiled softly. "Audrey, yes, you do."

"I'm so tired of people saying that to me."

Viv grabbed her hand and squeezed. "Maybe it's time to listen."

Audrey sighed and gulped at her drink. It was a mistake to come. Janis was acting out, now kissing the butch for all to see.

"And another thing," Viv said. "I don't know what you're trying to pull with her, but it's not working."

"She's fun," she said, even though it hadn't been fun in a long while.

"Can I be honest with you, Aud? She's not the one for you."

"Like I said, she's fun."

"You're not serious, though? Please tell me you aren't. We can all tell you're not."

"Why does it matter?"

"Because I care about you, Aud. You can do better than that." She glanced over at her as she continued to flirt with the butch. "So much better."

"What if I can't?" She'd tried. Lillian didn't want her. She was damaged goods. And now her ex was back to swoop in and kill any chance of anything.

"Trust me. You can. But you have to want it. Do you want it? I mean really want it?"

"What? Love?"

"Yeah. No bullshit."

Did she? "I don't know. I—" She considered telling her about Lillian but then changed her mind, not liking what she'd no doubt hear.

"Let me tell you something." Viv looked over to her wife. "When you find it, you'll know, and you will do anything to get it."

"Really?"

"Yes. You won't be able to do anything but think about her, and you'll go through heaven and earth to be with her. No matter what that means. Some people lose themselves, which isn't good, but with some people, they find themselves. And that, my friend, is worth so much more than this." She jerked her thumb back toward Janis.

"I'm sorry. I didn't think she'd act like this."

"Don't worry about it. At least she's keeping Kip entertained. She's usually bored spitless at these parties."

"Thought you didn't have friends like that anymore."

Viv laughed and sipped her margarita. "We're married, not dead. We'll always have single friends, I imagine." She elbowed her. "Which is why I've been trying to get you to come over."

"I just thought it would be all kids and bouncy houses and stuff."

"Sometimes there is. But sometimes we have parties just for the adults. We need breaks too, you know."

"I bet you do."

"Oh, trust me, we do. All of us. So how 'bout you? You taken any breaks lately?"

"What do you mean?"

"I mean," she sighed, "I mean you look like hell, Audrey. I'm worried."

"Oh Jesus, I'm fine."

"You sure don't look it."

"I've just been working out a lot more."

"You're supposed to work out to be healthy. Not look like death warmed over. So don't give me that crap. It's not just working out. It's more."

Audrey finished her soda, ready to leave. "I should go."

"No, wait."

"Yeah, I should go. Janis is out of control and I feel like shit anyway."

"I'm just worried about you, Aud. We all are."

Audrey looked around the room. Most of her friends were talking with others, but they still glanced over at her and smiled softly every now and then. They were worried smiles, not well disguised at all.

"I'm fine. Really."

"You'll get well?"

Viv knew Audrey knew how to make herself well. Get better sleep, eat better, chill with workouts. Audrey had gone through times like these before, usually after a rough patch with a lover. But that had been years ago. Back when she gave a shit.

"Yeah."

"You swear it?"

"I swear it." It was time, and as she caught Janis sneaking another kiss with Kip, she knew it was time for a lot of things.

"And do yourself a favor," Viv said. "Lose the chick."

Audrey stood. "I'll see ya, Viv." She headed over to Janis and interrupted her conversation. One that was filled with mindless giggles and nuh-uhs.

"I'm leaving," Audrey said.

Janis's eye widened as she caught sight of her. "Oh, okay."

"You coming?"

"Do you think Kip could give me a ride?"

Audrey trashed her soda can and headed for the door. "Yeah, Kip can give you a ride."

"Really?" She rose, and they all three headed for the door. "Thanks, Aud."

"In fact," Audrey said as they stepped through the front door, "Kip can give you a ride from here on out."

Janis looked pouty. "Oh, no. Aud."

"We both know it's for the best."

"I know, but…well, it hasn't been fun lately, has it?"

Audrey shook her head as Kip watched with eager interest.

"No, it hasn't."

"Okay, well, give me a hug."

Audrey allowed Janis to embrace her. Then she turned and left them.

❖

Audrey left the party and climbed back into her Jeep. She drove away loudly, tires smoking and spinning. She pounded the steering wheel as she thought about Lillian and all the things her friends had said.

We miss you.

So good to see you.

Where you been?

She thought especially hard about Viv. *When you find someone, you'll know, because you'll do anything to be with them.*

Anything.

Audrey looked in her rearview mirror and she didn't like what she saw. A woman out of control, living life by way of the wind, needing a damn drink to get through it all, no matter how small. She drove aimlessly for a while, thinking about everything, thinking about nothing. The sun set behind her and evening settled in around her. She continued to drive even when the air chilled her skin and her body and eyes protested.

She drove on.

Eventually, when she next focused, she'd slowed her Jeep in front of her mother's house. The trailer sat snug in a row of others, lined up like matchsticks in a mobile home park. Audrey could remember riding her bike in and out of the row of trailers, timing herself to see how long it would take her to get to the end. She never could beat the kid next door, no matter how hard she tried.

After staring at the trailer for a long while, she finally climbed down out of her Jeep and crossed the gravel lot for the front door.

The same old welcome sign still hung next to it, long ago rusted, rust running down the side paneling of the trailer. She touched it carefully, unable to remember when her mother had first hung it.

The trailer still smelled the same. She could tell just by standing on the stoop. The smell of cigarettes, along with home cooking and old furniture. The scent reminded her of childhood and times she both liked and dreaded recalling at the same time. She knocked on the screen door before she changed her mind and walked away.

She cleared her throat and strengthened herself as she heard her mother cough and start moving around. When the door opened, Audrey had to blink to focus. Her mother stood looking hunched and frail, pale and wrinkly.

"Hi, Mom."

"Audrey?" She pushed open the screen. "It must be a miracle."

"Hi." Audrey stepped inside and gave her a quick hug, fighting back tears. She looked so different, so beaten and helpless. Her mother held her longer, though, tighter. She felt like a sack of bones in her arms.

"What brings you around?"

"I was out driving around."

"Thought you'd stop by?"

"Yeah."

They pulled apart and Audrey hurriedly wiped away a tear and moved to sit on the tiny green couch.

"Well, it's good to see you." She sat in her recliner, fit right in the old groove of it, and adjusted her oxygen in her nose.

"This is new," Audrey said, pointing to the oxygen, heart racing. Viv had tried to prepare her. She realized that now.

"This old thing?"

"It's oxygen, isn't it?"

"Yeah. They gave it to me a few weeks back. Said I have emphysema and something called COPD."

"What's that?"

"Chronic obstructive pulmonary disease."

Audrey rubbed her chin, trying to remain calm. She'd heard of it before, and she knew it wasn't good.

"Means I can't breathe."

Audrey sat back and took a deep breath as her mother coughed some more.

"Are you okay?"

She waved her off. "Happens all the time."

"Are you...going to be okay?"

She wiped her nose with a tissue and studied Audrey with her steely eyes. "I'm fine."

Audrey laughed a little, knowing she must always sound just like her. "I understand. I meant are you going to be okay?"

"You want to know if I'm dying?"

Audrey looked away and focused instead on her childhood pictures that hung on one far wall. From first grade all the way up.

"That why you came? That friend of yours tell you I was dying?"

"No, Mom," Audrey said carefully. "I told you I was just out driving around."

"You're still full of shit, aren't you, kid?" She laughed and coughed again.

Audrey couldn't help but smile. She never could pull one over on her mother. "I guess I am."

"You get it honest. Your father was always full of shit too."

Audrey met her gaze. "I know, Mom. You've told me that a hundred times."

"He was handsom,e though. Like you. Real dark. Real looker. Had me hook, line, and sinker, he did."

"Are you going to be okay, Mom?" She had to know.

She waved her off again. "I'm fine. Don't have lung cancer or anything like that. I just can't breathe."

"That sounds pretty bad."

"It's not fun."

"You on oxygen all the time?"

"Yes. Even have to sleep with it. I don't wear it when I eat, though. Can't stand that." She looked away this time and they sat in silence for a while, the television softly playing a popular rerun.

"Do you need anything?" Audrey finally asked.

"You asking because you feel sorry for me?"

"Mom, no. Come on."

"Well, you don't ever call or come around. Now all of a sudden you're here and offering to help. What am I supposed to think?"

Audrey dropped her head into her hands. She'd hoped it wouldn't turn out like this, but it always seemed to. She looked at her mother sitting there all alone. So bitter and frail and all alone. She'd been by herself ever since her father had gone, bitching about everyone and everything, pushing people away. Audrey looked in her eyes and saw herself in forty years. Alone, bitter, with no friends and nothing to do but watch reruns and drink herself to death in her run-down apartment. But something inside her was different tonight. Something snapped and broke loose and she couldn't hold back. She wouldn't end up like this. She would do whatever it took to change, starting with confronting her mother.

"You don't ever call either, Mom. It goes two ways."

Her mother blinked, obviously surprised at the remark. "You're just like your father."

"Am I? Because I haven't heard that one either. Tell me how much I'm like him, Mom."

Her mother eagerly took the bait. "You are. You're just like him. You abandon me just like he did. He left me with you all alone—"

"I know. He was a bad man, Mom. A bad man. He shouldn't have left you."

Her mother clamped her mouth shut, obviously unsure what to say.

"Yeah, he was wrong," she finally said.

"He was, Mom. He was wrong. But that has nothing to do with me."

She stopped rocking in her recliner.

"Stop blaming me for everything. I'm not him. I never was. I was just a kid."

Her mother didn't say anything, just stared straight ahead.

"I was just a kid, Mom. Mom, do you hear me?"

"Yes, I hear you."

"Stop blaming me for his shit. Stop telling me I'm no good and that's why he ran off. Stop saying this shit to me."

Her mother chewed on her lower lip and looked at her. "But you left me and you never come around."

"Because I get this! I've been getting this since I was five. I'm not good enough, smart enough, girlie enough. I'm just like him. A little him. He left. He was no good. He didn't care. He didn't love me. He left because of me. Come on, Mom. I was a kid. I didn't deserve that and I don't deserve that now."

Audrey stood, her emotions getting the better of her. "I'm me, damn it." She headed for the door, the tears too close. She should've never come. She should've known better.

She reached out for the door.

"Wait."

It was said so softly Audrey almost didn't hear it. She didn't turn until she heard it again.

"Wait."

She turned slowly and found her mother struggling to get up. "Mom, don't."

"Aw, shut up, I'm fine." She walked up to her and touched her face. "That's why you don't come around? Because of me?"

Audrey hesitated.

"Tell me."

"Yeah."

Her mother looked down, and when she looked back up, she had tears in her eyes. "I didn't know."

"I know."

"Why haven't you said something?"

"What was I supposed to do? If it's one thing you taught me, it's to respect you. So I have. But you haven't respected me."

She held her face tighter with cool, soft hands. "Your father didn't want another child," she said softly. "We were too old, he said. So when you came along, and he eventually left, I guess I blamed you."

She began to tremble and Audrey held her hands.

"You don't have to do this, Mom."

"Yes, I do. You need to hear that I loved you from day one. Day one. And I've never stopped. I just was so hurt when he left. And you, you looked so much like him and acted so much like him, it was like salt in the wound. But…you didn't know. You were just a kid. And you're still a kid. A kid to me. And I hurt you."

"Mom—"

"I'm sorry, Audrey. I'm sorry."

She hugged her tightly and shook with sobs.

Audrey hugged her back, wiping her own tears on the back of her hand. "All this time I've felt so unlovable, like no one would ever think I'm good enough."

"You have?"

"Yes."

"Oh, Audrey. I'm so sorry. What have I done?"

They held one another and cried for a long time. Audrey for herself, for the wounded child inside her and for her mother who had obviously had her own wounds to deal with.

"You are worthy of love," her mother said when they pulled apart. She wiped Audrey's cheeks and held her face. "You hear me?"

"Yes."

"Do you believe me?"

Audrey thought of the look on Lillian's face at the track meet. Warm, inviting, full of caring and passion. How could she deny that for herself?

She couldn't. Not any longer.

"Yes."

"Good."

They embraced again and Audrey felt the pain and anguish she'd always carried with her begin to lift away. Like a rising mist it came off her, leaving her feeling light and almost weightless.

"Tell me you'll come around more?" her mother asked.

Audrey was honest with her. She had so much to do, so much to live for. "I'll try."

Her mother smiled. "I suppose I can't ask for any more than that. I'll try too. I promise."

Audrey nodded. "I promise too."

CHAPTER SIXTEEN

H i, baby."
    Lillian halted on her front walkway. Holly was standing by the door, grinning. Wearing loose faded jeans and a tight white tee. She looked every bit the same, just like Lillian remembered. Her heart rate accelerated, and she thought briefly about fleeing. Instead, she asked a very important question.

"What are you doing here?" Lillian had just pulled in from work and she was exhausted, having had little sleep since Holly's phone call.

"I told you I wanted to see you." She tried to hug Lillian as she walked up, but Lillian pulled away.

"What's wrong?" Holly looked concerned, so concerned she helped Lillian by unlocking the door.

"You still have your keys?" Lillian wasn't sure how she felt about that. At the moment, she was annoyed and her insides started twisting into knots.

"You said to keep them. In case I ever wanted to come back." She smiled, showing off her beautiful teeth. She'd had a haircut recently. Lillian could tell by the tan line along the edge of her short, dirty blond cut. She wondered if she did it for her. To try to impress her somehow.

"That was a long time ago, Holly."

Lillian entered the house and so did Holly, right behind her. Lillian sighed and set down her satchel, wanting nothing more than to stretch out on the couch with some iced tea. But relaxing, she feared, would be long in coming.

"So you meant it, right?"

"When I said it."

She didn't know how to feel with Holly being back in her house. She'd wanted nothing more for so long, but now she felt ambivalent.

"So you don't mean it now?"

Lillian thought for a moment. "No."

Holly pocketed her keys and walked around the living room. She caught sight of a lamp and went to unplug it, intent on moving it. She'd always preferred it by the window.

"What are you doing?"

She stopped. "Moving the lamp."

"Leave it."

She rose slowly and moved along nonchalantly, eyeing the walls. "You left all our pictures up," she said, touching a few.

"Yes."

"Why?" She smiled over at her again and Lillian had to look away, the memories too much.

"I was stupid."

Holly came toward her. "Come on, Lil. Don't be like this. I'm here now."

"Yeah, you're here now. Why?"

She held out her arms. Lillian noticed a tan line on her ring finger. "Because I'm back."

"You're back?"

"Yes."

"Just like that?"

"If you want me. And I know you do."

She enveloped her into a tight hug and Lillian caught her woodsy scent. It sent her mind flying and her heart into her toes and back up again. Oh, how she had missed her, missed this. And yet she just couldn't bring herself to return the hug.

"This'll change your mind," Holly whispered, capturing her lips in a kiss.

Lillian made a small noise of surprise, and Holly mistook it for passion and deepened the kiss, darting with her tongue.

Lillian's bones seemed to go out of her, and she hung in her arms, allowing the kiss to continue. Holly was back. Holly wanted her. Was she dreaming?

"There," Holly said. "That's my girl."

"You're back," Lillian said, still in a dreamlike state. "Why?"

Holly looked into her face, obviously surprised by the question. "Because I want to be."

Lillian regained her focus and grabbed her hand. She pointed to the ring mark. "You mean you recently broke up with someone and that's why?"

Holly turned from her and walked away. "Don't do this, Lil."

"Do what? I just want the truth. Did you even miss me at all?"

"Of course I did." She palmed the back of her neck.

"Really? Because you never called."

"I couldn't."

"Why?"

"Because—"

"Because there was someone else."

Holly dropped her hand and Lillian felt sick. She'd always secretly suspected, but finally hearing it and admitting it to herself was so much harder to take than she ever could've imagined. She had to ease herself down onto the sofa and force herself to breathe. How could she have been so purposely blind? What had been the point? To avoid the hurt? To avoid the painful reality?

Yes, that was exactly what it had been. Because the reality was too much to bear. The reality was too hard to face. Right now, she just wanted to curl up in the pain and cry.

"You knew why I left," Holly said, crossing her arms.

Lillian didn't speak; she couldn't.

"I told you a thousand times I was unhappy. A thousand times. But you didn't want to listen. You just wanted to live in your own little world where everything was peachy keen and pretend like nothing was wrong. The perfect little therapist life."

"Me? You're the one who had to have everything perfect.

Nothing was good enough for you. Not the house, not the furniture, not me. Tell me, Holly, because I'm beginning to realize, what exactly was good about our relationship?"

Holly looked at her and her face flushed with emotion. "I—we—" But she dropped her hands and turned away again.

"You were miserable, and I ignored it, I'll give you that. But I was unhappy too." Her voice cracked on the words because she'd never admitted that to herself before. "I just took all that you dealt and forced it down, pretending like it was all okay because I didn't want anything to change. And I didn't want to face the pain of something being wrong."

"So what are you saying, Lil?"

"I'm saying I was unhappy too. I'm saying that for many different reasons, we didn't end up good. I'm saying…that I want you to leave."

Holly stood very still. She didn't even blink. "Oh?"

"Yes, I think I'd like to be alone."

"I thought you wanted me back."

"I thought so too." But she thought of Audrey and her kisses and the way she was with that boy at the track meet. She thought of her deep eyes, of her thick lips, of the way her dark hair always fell across her forehead. She thought of the way she'd said "I think I love you,. Lillian" and how upset she'd become when Lillian blew it off.

She thought of all these things and knew in her heart that she definitely did not want Holly.

"I'll leave you alone, then," Holly said as she walked toward the door. It was a pivotal moment, one where Lillian used to say "Wait" and then apologize for whatever she'd said.

But this time, she let her go.

CHAPTER SEVENTEEN

Audrey walked into The Griffin and headed straight for the bar. The music was loud and the dance floor crowded, but the place seemed a little sparse for a Wednesday night. She sat on a stool and squared off with Brea, who sauntered over with attitude.

"Beer?" she asked with a pleasured smirk.

"Water," Audrey said, holding her gaze.

Brea scoffed. "Since when?"

"Since none of your business."

"Going the fuck-off route, are we?"

"Yes."

She held up her hands. "Whatever, woman." She slid over a bottle of water and pushed Audrey's money away. "On the house."

"No, thanks." Audrey shoved the money back toward her.

"Seriously. It's on the house. I hear you've been laying off the beer. Good for you."

"I don't need your approval," Audrey said and then regretted it, knowing she sounded like her mother. Fucking genetics. Too proud for their own good, she and her mother were.

"Whatever. Take it or leave it," Brea said.

Audrey unscrewed the lid and took a sip. "Keep it for my next bottle."

Brea nodded and took the money. "Okay."

Audrey looked toward Lillian's table. She was nowhere to be seen, but Audrey wasn't surprised. She hadn't been at the club since the day of the track meet. She was no doubt in the arms of her ex, happy as a little lark.

"I hear she's all torn up," Brea said catching her line of sight.

Audrey said nothing, surprised at the information.

"Her ex came back," Brea said, as if Audrey didn't know.

Audrey sipped her water. "Yeah, I know."

Brea leaned on the bar. "I guess she wants Lillian back."

"I'm not surprised." Who wouldn't want Lillian?

"I was."

"I wouldn't have left her in the first place," Audrey said, watching Lillian's table closely.

Brea pulled back with surprise. "What?"

"You heard me."

"You really like her?"

"I love her," Audrey said, never feeling more clearheaded in her life. And she didn't mind saying it aloud either. She'd say it to anyone willing to listen.

Brea shook her head. "Shut up."

"I'm serious." She held her gaze, daring her to protest.

"You better be. I don't want to see her get hurt."

"I would never hurt her, and she doesn't need your protection. She's a big girl, and your attitude is probably loathed more than it's appreciated."

Brea wiped the bar and shifted her gaze away. "Yeah, well, I care."

"A lot of people care, and they don't act like a maniac."

Audrey left her water and wandered through the dance floor. She declined a dance and made her way to her favorite chair. She smiled when she saw Viv already there, beer in hand.

"Here comes the devil," she said, rising to hug her.

"Not anymore," Audrey said, sitting alongside her in another chair. "Thanks for coming."

"You bet." She crossed her leg over her knee and sighed, looking around. "God, it's been years since I've been here."

"Yep."

"Place hasn't changed much."

"Nope. Just the Midnight Room."

Viv turned around to stare at the glass panels. "Might have to bring the missus here to give that a go."

Audrey laughed. "Maybe."

"So what's up, woman? You look better than the last time I saw you."

"That's good." She smiled. "Not much, I've just changed a few things, and I wanted to share them with my longtime friend."

"You laying off the booze?"

"Yeah."

"Good, good."

"I can't drink my life away."

"No, you definitely can't. And there's no reason to."

"I realized I didn't want to end up like my mom."

Viv looked over at her. "You saw her?"

Audrey nodded. "Right after the party. You were right. She looks pretty damn bad."

"I was surprised to see her out and about," Viv said. "She looked so frail at the grocery store."

"She is frail. Though she tells me she's fine. Says she just can't breathe."

Viv chuckled. "That sounds like Ima Jean."

"So anyway, we sort of made peace."

"You're kidding?"

"No, I finally stood up to her and told her how I felt."

"Audrey." She shifted in her chair. "I can't believe it."

"Me neither."

"How'd she take it?"

"Pretty well. She even apologized."

"Wow. This is great news. I'm glad to hear it. And I'm happy for you."

"It helped me a lot," she said. "Made me take a hard look at my life and at hers. I just couldn't live with the verbal attacks anymore. She and I both deserve better."

"Yes, you do."

They sat in silence for a while, both of them watching the dance floor, amused at some of the women. Viv eventually started talking about her kids and how wonderful they were and how she'd like for Audrey to come around more to get to know them. Audrey agreed, thrilled at the chance.

"So let me ask you something," Viv said, finishing her beer. "What are you still doing here at The Griffin? I mean, you sound really good, look better, and you seem to have changed a lot in a short span of time. So what gives? What's the appeal?"

Audrey thought for a moment. "I need to be here," she said. "To prove that I can do this, to be social, to move on with my life."

"This doesn't have anything to do with Janis, does it?"

Audrey laughed. "God, no."

"Good, she was nothing to be upset about. So I guess the real question is, who do you need to prove something to?"

Audrey thought about saying Lillian, but it went deeper than that. "Myself."

Viv seemed pleased. "Good answer."

"I can be here and not behave like an ass. I can visit with friends, watch the women, and maybe even share a dance or two."

"But you're not looking for love?"

Audrey looked over at her. "I've found love."

Viv scooted to the edge of her seat. "Excuse me?"

Audrey smiled. "I have. And she's wonderful."

She looked over at Lillian's table and her stomach flipped when she saw her arriving to sit down. She had on khakis and a light colored blouse, probably just arriving from church. The sight made Audrey's heart swell.

Viv followed her line of sight. "That her?"

"Yes."

"She's beautiful."

"Yes, she is."

"Her friends seem to really love her to, the way they are hugging on her."

Audrey scanned the table and the surrounding crowd quickly, looking for anyone who lingered, looking for Lillian's ex. To her relief, Lillian seemed to have arrived alone.

Audrey watched her closely, able to tell right away that a lot had transpired since she'd last seen her. She looked pale, thinner, and she seemed distant. Like her eyes weren't focusing on her surroundings. She was sitting quietly staring off into space. Her friends were all around her, touching her shoulders, trying to talk to her. But Lillian didn't seem to be responding.

"Why don't you go say hi?" Viv asked.

"It's complicated."

"How so?"

"Her ex came back."

"Ohhh. So is she back together with her?"

Audrey shrugged. "I don't know."

"So go say hello."

"I'm not sure she feels the same way about me as I do her."

"Even more reason to try."

"I don't know. She has a lot on her plate right now."

Viv stood and stretched, smiling down at her. "Now, this is a woman I'd like to see at our next get-together. No more Janises."

Audrey laughed softly. "No more Janises."

"Remember what I said about love. About being willing to do anything to get it and keep it. I think you've already taken some of that to heart."

Audrey smiled up at her. "I have."

"Keep going, woman. It'll be worth it. I promise."

Audrey stood and gave her a long hug. "I'll keep you posted."

"You better." Viv looked around and gave her a wink. "Next time I think I will bring the missus."

Audrey patted her back. "Definitely." She watched her head toward the exit. A feeling of contentment washed over her just then. She was healthy and happy, and she'd managed to mend her friendships as well as start anew with her mother. Life was pretty darn good. Only one thing was missing.

"Hey," a voice said from behind her.

Audrey turned to find Carmen, who surprisingly came up to stand next to her with a smile.

"Fancy meeting you here," Audrey said with a deep laugh.

"Yeah."

"Mind if I sit?" Carmen motioned to Viv's empty chair.

"No." Audrey watched her with wide eyes, wondering what this was all about.

"Aren't you on the wrong side of the dance floor?" Audrey raised an eyebrow.

Carmen started to smile but then stopped. "Yeah, I guess I am. Truth is, I need to talk to you."

"About Lillian?"

Carmen nodded.

"I was afraid of that."

"She's all to pieces."

"About her ex?"

"Yes. Holly. And about you."

"Me?"

"Surprised?"

"A little."

"I just need to know one thing. Do you really love her?"

"Is this where you lecture me about treating her right or else?"

"I don't think I need to do that, do I?"

"No."

"Then answer the question."

Audrey looked over at Lillian who had her head in her hands. "Yes, I do love her."

"Will you continue to see other women?"

"No. I'm not interested. Even if Lillian doesn't want me. I'm changing my life."

Carmen studied her long and hard. "I can see that."

"You've been keeping tabs on me?"

"Absolutely."

"Why?"

"Because I think Lillian belongs with you."

Audrey looked back to Lillian, who still looked all to pieces. She rose, ready to call it a night. "That's great, Carmen, and I appreciate the support."

"But?"

"But it looks like Lillian still needs to come to that conclusion herself."

CHAPTER EIGHTEEN

Lillian walked up to the front door of The Griffin, pulling her raincoat on tight. The night was cool with gusts of blowing rain, a small April shower blowing through Phoenix. She bypassed several women huddled near the entrance and recognized one as the woman who was on the phone the very first night she'd met Audrey.

"Excuse me," Lillian said as she approached her. The woman looked surprised but friendly.

"Yes."

"I know this may sound strange, but a while back you were on the phone out here. I overheard your conversation and you said something that stuck with me."

"Really?"

"Yes, you said there are some that come broken, but they're repairable."

The woman thought for a moment and then nodded. "Oh, I was talking about pocket watches. I collect them."

"Watches?"

"Yeah, you know, as in time."

Lillian laughed. "I wasn't expecting that."

"Not what you thought?"

"No. Not at all. But I suppose it does make sense. Time can repair almost anything, can't it?"

The woman seemed a little lost and Lillian shook her head.

"Never mind. I just—thank you for your time." She gave her arm a gentle squeeze and then walked inside.

The place thumped loudly with music, and bodies swarmed toward the bar and dance floor. Lillian weaved through the women and found her way to her table where Rain and Carmen sat. They stood when she approached and greeted her with big hugs.

"How are you, Lil? Long time no see."

"I know, it has been a while."

"She's happy at home," Rain said. "Making her blankets and relaxing."

Lillian sat with a sigh. "I have been pretty relaxed, but I wouldn't say I've been happy."

"You mean telling Holly to take a hike for the fifth and final time didn't do it for you?" Carmen asked.

"Surprisingly, no. And damn it, that woman is stubborn. She's made my life a living hell lately."

"I just can't believe the truth came out," Rain said. "That she had left you for someone else."

"I know. I was so blind. So caught up in her."

Carmen gripped her hand. "You did the right thing, sweetie. You deserve better."

Lillian felt the words sink in, and she looked up across the dance floor, searching for Audrey.

"She's not here," Rain said. "Not tonight."

"I wonder why," Lillian said, hoping to see her, to catch a glimpse of her raw beauty and captivating smile. She'd missed her lately, missed her a lot. And she couldn't stop thinking about that day at the track meet and the look she'd seen in her eyes. Damn it, why did Holly have to interrupt?

"She hasn't been here since I had a talk with her," Carmen said.

"You had a talk with her? About what?"

"About you," Rain said.

"Me?" Her heart rate accelerated a bit and she searched both of their faces.

Carmen sighed and squeezed her hand. "She loves you, Lil."

Lillian blinked. "She—"

"She really does."

"And she changed her life," Rain said. "She ended things with Janis, she hasn't been drinking here at the club, and she seems to have sworn off women."

"She told me she's not interested in other women," Carmen said. "Even if you don't want her."

"I don't understand," Lillian said, trying hard to catch up. "She told you all this?"

"Most of it we've seen firsthand," Rain said. "But she did tell Carmen she loved you."

"I think you should follow your heart, Lil. And I'm sorry I implied otherwise. I was wrong about her. Obviously, people can change."

"We just, we wanted to be sure before we said anything," Rain said. "I've always had good feelings about Audrey based on what I've seen at the track meets, but you're my best friend, and well, I feel so responsible for this whole mess. At the very least, I can tell you my true feelings in regard to Audrey. I think she's okay."

"I don't know what to say."

"Well, how do you feel?" Carmen asked.

"I feel like...I feel like hell when I don't see her. All I do is think about her. Right from the start. I feel like she's got so much love to give if given the chance. That maybe she hasn't had a lot of love in her life. I feel..."

"Yes?" they said in unison, leaning forward.

"Like maybe I need to find her."

CHAPTER NINETEEN

For the first time ever, Audrey entered The Griffin with her nerves on edge. She headed for the bar and squeezed herself onto a stool where she could get a good shot of Lillian's table. A quick glance told her Lillian wasn't there. She breathed deeply and ordered a water, hoping it would calm her racing nerves.

She'd arrived a little later than usual, hoping to be able to walk in, see Lillian right away, and ask her to talk. But it seemed she'd have to wait it out some; more time for her nerves to play on edge.

"Hi, Audrey," Rain said as she scooted in next to her.

"Hi."

"I just wanted to let you know that I filled out that form you e-mailed me about my goals and everything."

"Oh, great."

"So we can get started again?"

"Sure, give me a call tomorrow and we'll schedule a time."

"Um, tomorrow may not be good." She looked incredibly guilty. "For you, I mean."

"Huh?"

"Never mind. I'll call you on Sunday."

Audrey watched her walk away. She was completely confused and she searched once again for Lillian to no avail. Carmen saw her and gave her a quick wave. Audrey waved back, still a little unnerved by Carmen's approval. She sipped her water and tapped her fingers along the bar. Where was Lillian? The whole thing would be so much easier if she had her damn phone number. Of course, she could find it, just like she'd found her address, but she didn't want to risk calling that way. At least with the flowers she'd been anonymous.

"Audrey McCarthy?" a bartender asked, coming to stand before her.

"Yeah?"

Audrey saw Brea in the near distance, watching. She gave Brea a nod and she pulled out a bouquet of white roses and laid them on the bar.

"These are for you."

Audrey thought she was seeing things. She delicately touched the roses and found a card tucked away inside. She smiled before she opened it, knowing what it would say. She slipped it out and read it. It said simply, *More*.

Just then, the deejay quieted the crowd and "Let's Get It On" started up. The strobe lights started and the crowd went wild. Audrey flushed, suddenly understanding. The deejay called out, "Ladies, it's that time again. Time for two lucky ladies to take a trip to the Midnight Room."

More cheering, and Audrey's heart felt like it was going to jump right out of her chest. She searched the crowd desperately but still couldn't see her. Her name was called and the spotlight found her, blinding her. There were more cheers and even pats to the back.

"And our other lucky lady is Lillian Gray."

The crowd went wild again, as if they had known all along. Audrey shielded her eyes, trying to find Lillian. And suddenly, the crowd parted and out she walked. Audrey felt herself heat as their eyes locked. Lillian was wearing a black leather skirt and a tight black top. Her legs looked long and lean in black stilettos. She moved seductively, confidently, her hair slicked back in a tight ponytail. And when she reached Audrey, she smiled just a little coyly.

Without saying a word, she leaned in, grabbed a single rose, and ran the tip along Audrey's jaw.

"More," she whispered, kissing Audrey's ear.

Audrey trembled, swallowing hard. She looked deep into her clear blue eyes. "Okay."

Lillian smiled and took her hand, this time leading the way and causing the crowd to part. She even pushed out her arm, keeping a few people at bay. The music continued, the crowd nearly hushed. Lillian tugged her along gently, running her free hand across the glass panes of the partitions as if lightly stroking the shadowed women behind them.

Audrey watched her move, captivated by the sway of her hips, the strong movement of her legs. She held her head high and every so often glanced over her shoulder with a seductive smile.

"Here we are," she said as they reached the tasseled door.

"Where's Beastly?" Audrey asked, surprised not to see her.

"She took a break. A long break."

"Oh."

Lillian grinned. "Come on." She tugged her inside, and Audrey saw that the entire room was lit in candlelight. The red velvet walls seemed to breathe on their own, pulsing with seductive softness.

"Lillian—" Audrey started, truly moved.

"Shh. You're not to say a word." She pulled her over to the couch where she forced her to sit. Then she straddled her leg and pressed a finger to her lips. "These are the rules."

"Rules?" Audrey grinned.

"Shh. Yes, the rules. You're not to speak. And you're not to touch me unless I say so. Understand?"

Audrey nodded.

"Good." She leaned in and planted a hot but soft kiss on her lips. One after the other, just enough to tease. "I have something I need to tell you," she said, looking into her eyes. "It was very hard for me to come to terms with it because I fought it so hard. And for a while, you scared the shit out of me."

Audrey tried to speak, but Lillian shushed her again with her finger. "You still scare me but for totally different reasons. Now I'm just afraid of losing you without getting the chance to tell you that I've fallen madly in love with you."

Audrey searched her face, felt her tremble. She reached up and stroked her jaw, but Lillian caught her hand.

"Do you love me, Audrey?"

"Yes," she whispered.

Lillian kissed her fingertips. "I thought so. I'm sorry for not taking you seriously. I was just so scared."

"I know," Audrey whispered again. "I know."

"Sweet, sweet Audrey," Lillian said, touching her face. "My gorgeous, beautiful woman. What am I to do with you now?"

Audrey watched her. She desperately wanted to kiss her, and Lillian seemed to know, because she leaned in and teased her again with her lips.

"Admitting to myself that I love you has done things to me, Audrey. Crazy things, wild things. I've done nothing but dream about you for so long. It's nearly driven me mad." She nibbled on her neck. "And your scent, God, your scent. I've slept with your T-shirt, inhaling that scent for nights on end. I even put it in my purse to inhale at church." She laughed. "I've gone insane for you, Audrey.

"So insane, I..." She leaned back and hitched up her skirt. "Here," she said breathlessly. "Feel me." She took Audrey's hand and placed it between her legs.

Audrey felt her hot slickness at once and she gasped, completely turned on.

"You feel me?" Lillian asked.

Audrey nodded.

"I'm so hot for you," she said. "So hot." She moved a little, bearing down on Audrey's hand. "Let me show you, baby. Go inside me."

Audrey slid her fingers up inside her, causing her to call out. She felt slick and wonderfully tight.

"Oh, God," she said. "Oh, Audrey. Fuck me, baby. Fuck me." She began to move against Audrey's fingers, riding her back and forth.

"Yes, yes!" Lillian gripped Audrey's shoulders and pumped her hips, harder and faster. She moved her hips around and around, bearing down on Audrey's fingers. Then she lifted her shirt up and off and tossed it to the side. "Touch me here," she demanded, grabbing Audrey's hand. She brought it to her breast and said, "Pinch me. Pinch my nipples."

Audrey did so, softly at first and then with more vigor. She watched her closely, mesmerized at the sight of her.

"Do you like what you see, Audrey?"

Audrey nodded.

"Tell me."

"Very much so."

"You like me like this?"

"Yes."

"I feel free now," she said, breathless. "Like I can do exactly what I want to. How I need to. Without fear of needing to run from you."

She bucked again wildly as Audrey tugged on her. "I want you, Audrey. In every way. And I want you to have me in every way too. Okay?"

"Yes," Audrey said, shoving her fingers deeper inside her.

"Oh God, oh God, Audrey. I'm coming. I'm coming."

She moved like a madwoman, like someone possessed as she climaxed all over Audrey's hand, calling out into the Midnight Room, calling out to the moon. Her muscles strained, and her voice caved, and she eventually collapsed into Audrey, nibbling on her neck as she giggled.

"You bring out the wild woman in me," she said, still breathing hard.

Audrey felt her heat, felt the moist skin of her chest and neck. She slowly removed her fingers and stroked her back.

"I like that I do."

"Mmm," Lillian purred, "me too."

"I'm able to talk now?"

Lillian perked up. "You're not supposed to."

"Why not?"

"Because I want to have my way with you."

"You just did."

"Oh no, I didn't."

"Come on. Let's go home and go to bed." Audrey wanted nothing more than to ravish her completely and fully in the privacy of her own home.

Lillian pushed herself upright and tugged Audrey up along with her.

"You want to go home?"

Audrey nodded, noting the change in her once again. Lillian licked her lips and moved her back toward the wall, breasts moving slightly as she did so.

"Wild Audrey wants to go home?"

Audrey stumbled backward. "I'm not wild Audrey anymore."

"Not wild Audrey? Well, that's a shame." Lillian shoved her backward into the wall. "Because I'm looking for wild Audrey right now."

Audrey swallowed and fought for breath. Lillian took advantage and yanked up her shirt to squeeze her nipples, bringing Audrey to her tiptoes.

"Yes, I like this Audrey. Can she come out to play?"

Audrey steeled her jaw, the sensation too much. "Are you sure?" she asked.

"Oh, yes."

She gripped Lillian's wrists and turned her in one powerful move. She pinned her against the wall and dropped to her knees before Lillian had the chance to protest. She kissed up Lillian's thighs as she hurriedly inched up her skirt, and she found her flesh with her mouth just as Lillian was about to say *wait*.

Audrey groaned and feasted on her, fast and furiously, sinking Lillian's ass back against the wall. Lillian moaned and tugged at her hair, but Audrey wouldn't stop. It was a battle of wills, a cat-and-mouse game, and Lillian had awakened the sleeping giant. Audrey wasn't going to stop until she came in her mouth.

"Audrey," she panted. "Oh my God, Audrey."

"Mmm," Audrey groaned, loving the feel of her slickness against her chin. She swirled her tongue around and around, smothering and then teasing her clit. She did it harder and faster until Lillian was pulling on her hair and slamming her head back against the wall in ecstasy.

"Audrey, I-I-I'm coming."

And she came all over Audrey's face, pumping herself into her, holding Audrey's head fast against her. And just as she was about to come down, Audrey reached up and slid her fingers deep inside, sending her over the edge again, this time causing her legs to give out.

Audrey caught her by the waist, wrapping one hand around her while she gently pulled her fingers out of her. Lillian buckled to the floor, half-lying in Audrey's lap. She laughed throatily as she stroked Audrey's face.

"You're insatiable," Lillian said, kissing her lightly along the jaw. "And so damned gorgeous." She looked into her eyes and then softly kissed her lips. "I love you."

Audrey held her tighter and stared into her eyes for a long while, loving the warmth and acceptance she saw inside them. "I love you too."

They kissed again and Audrey felt her heart flutter as Lillian slipped her tongue inside her mouth.

"Can we please go home now?" Audrey said. "Before I have you all over this room?"

"You still want more?" Lillian asked, grinning.

"You have no idea."

"I think I really like wild Audrey."

Audrey laughed as Lillian stood. "Then you'd better run, because wild Audrey intends to have you." She rose and pinched her ass, sending Lillian on the run for her clothes.

"No more Midnight Room?" Lillian asked, rounding the couch to slip on her shirt.

Audrey playfully chased her, catching her in a firm embrace. She inhaled her hair, her neck, her pale skin. She kissed the jumping pulse in her neck.

"Not tonight," Audrey said. "But who knows? Maybe we'll be back tomorrow."

Lillian smiled up at her devilishly. "I like the sound of that."

About the Author

Ronica Black spends her free time writing works that move her, with the hope that they will move others as well. She is a firm believer in "that which does not kill you makes you stronger." She keeps stepping, keeps writing, and keeps believing that women are far stronger than they think they are. She's an award-winning author with nine books currently published by Bold Strokes Books.

Books Available From Bold Strokes Books

Silver Collar by Gill McKnight. Werewolf Luc Garoul is outlawed and out of control, but can her family track her down before a sinister predator gets there first? Fourth in the Garoul series. (978-1-60282-764-6)

The Dragon Tree Legacy by Ali Vali. For Aubrey Tarver time hasn't dulled the pain of losing her first love Wiley Gremillion, but she has to set that aside when her choices put her life and her family's lives in real danger. (978-1-60282-765-3)

The Midnight Room by Ronica Black. After a chance encounter with the mysterious and brooding Lillian Gray in the "midnight room" of The Griffin, a local lesbian bar, confident and gorgeous Audrey McCarthy learns that her bad-girl behavior isn't bulletproof. (978-1-60282-766-0)

Dirty Sex by Ashley Bartlett. Vivian Cooper and twins Reese and Ryan DiGiovanni stole a lot of money and the guy they took it from wants it back. Like now. (978-1-60282-767-7)

Raising Hell: Demonic Gay Erotica, edited by Todd Gregory. Hot stories of gay erotica featuring demons. (978-1-60282-768-4)

Pursued by Joel Gomez-Dossi. Openly gay college student Jamie Bradford becomes romantically involved with two men at the same time, and his hell begins when one of his boyfriends becomes intent on killing him. (978-1-60282-769-1)

The Storm by Shelley Thrasher. Rural East Texas. 1918. War-weary Jaq Bergeron and marriage-scarred musician Molly Russell try to salvage love from the devastation of the war abroad and natural disasters at home. (978-1-60282-780-6)

Crossroads by Radclyffe. Dr. Hollis Monroe specializes in short-term relationships but when she meets pregnant mother-to-be Annie Colfax, fate brings them together at a crossroads that will change their lives forever. (978-1-60282-756-1)

Beyond Innocence by Carsen Taite. When a life is on the line, love has to wait. Doesn't it? (978-1-60282-757-8)

Heart Block by Melissa Brayden. Socialite Emory Owen and struggling single mom Sarah Matamoros are perfectly suited for each other but face a difficult time when trying to merge their contrasting worlds and the people in them. If love truly exists, can it find a way? (978-1-60282-758-5)

Pride and Joy by M.L. Rice. Perfect Bryce Montgomery is her parents' pride and joy, but when they discover that their daughter is a lesbian, her world changes forever. (978-1-60282-759-2)

Timothy by Greg Herren. Timothy is a romantic suspense thriller from award-winning mystery writer Greg Herren set in the fabulous Hamptons. (978-1-60282-760-8)

In Stone by Jeremy Jordan King. A young New Yorker is rescued from a hate crime by a mysterious someone who turns out to be more of a something. (978-1-60282-761-5)

The Jesus Injection by Eric Andrews-Katz. Murderous statues, demented drag queens, political bombings, ex-gay ministries, espionage, and romance are all in a day's work for a top secret agent. But the gloves are off when Agent Buck 98 comes up against the Jesus Injection. (978-1-60282-762-2)

Combustion by Daniel W. Kelly. Bearish detective Deck Waxer comes to the city of Kremfort Cove to investigate why the hottest men in town are bursting into flames in broad daylight. (978-1-60282-763-9)

Ladyfish by Andrea Bramhill. Finn's escape to the Florida Keys leads her straight into the arms of scuba diving instructor Oz as she fights for her freedom, their blossoming love…and her life! (978-1-60282-747-9)

Spanish Heart by Rachel Spangler. While on a mission to find herself in Spain, Ren Molson runs the risk of losing her heart to her tour guide, Lina Montero. (978-1-60282-748-6)